Learning to love . . .

Emily rose up on her toes, until her shoulder just fit under his arm, and nestled her head near his chin. She would have desired to stay just so forever.

Nor did Daniel Lennox seem to desire otherwise, for he wrapped his arms tightly around her. Through the bandages, Emily felt his heart racing like a runner's and prayed he would not rip through his stitches altogether.

"I must confess," he said, and she heard not only gratification, but also humor in his voice, "I thought you had promise when you first arrived in Glenfell, Miss Clarkson. But it appears your abilities exceed even my fondest expectations."

"I believe you are insulting me, sir," Emily said slowly, trying to match her tone to his. "For a lady would never own to such skills as those to which I believe you refer. But I learn very quickly, you see, and just wanted for an excellent teacher."

Miss Clarkson's Classmate

Sharon Sobel

A SIGNET BOOK

SIGNET
Published by New American Library, a division of
Penguin Group (USA) Inc., 375 Hudson Street,
New York, New York 10014, USA
Penguin Group (Canada), 90 Eglinton Avenue East, Suite 700, Toronto,
Ontario M4P 2Y3, Canada (a division of Pearson Penguin Canada Inc.)
Penguin Books Ltd., 80 Strand, London WC2R 0RL, England
Penguin Ireland, 25 St. Stephen's Green, Dublin 2,
Ireland (a division of Penguin Books Ltd.)
Penguin Group (Australia), 250 Camberwell Road, Camberwell, Victoria 3124,
Australia (a division of Pearson Australia Group Pty. Ltd.)
Penguin Books India Pvt. Ltd., 11 Community Centre, Panchsheel Park,
New Delhi - 110 017, India
Penguin Group (NZ), cnr Airborne and Rosedale Roads, Albany,
Auckland 1310, New Zealand (a division of Pearson New Zealand Ltd.)
Penguin Books (South Africa) (Pty.) Ltd., 24 Sturdee Avenue,
Rosebank, Johannesburg 2196, South Africa

Penguin Books Ltd., Registered Offices:
80 Strand, London WC2R 0RL, England

First published by Signet, an imprint of New American Library,
a division of Penguin Group (USA) Inc.

First Printing, December 2005
10 9 8 7 6 5 4 3 2 1

PUBLISHER'S NOTE
This is a work of fiction. Names, characters, places, and incidents either are the
product of the author's imagination or are used fictitiously, and any resemblance
to actual persons, living or dead, business establishments, events, or locales is
entirely coincidental.

The publisher does not have any control over and does not assume any responsibility for author or third-party Web sites or their content.

In memory of my parents,
Beverly and Irving Kolodny,
Who would have enjoyed a story about a working
man and a teacher of disadvantaged children,
And who inspired a love of reading in the many
lives they touched and influenced.

Chapter One

*T*he absurd and completely inappropriate pleasure Miss Emily Clarkson felt upon watching her mother disappear into a throng of passengers on board a departing ship turned to horror when Mrs. Evangeline Clarkson turned on her heel and made haste for the gangplank.

"Oh, good heavens! She is coming back!" Emily clutched her aunt's arm with one hand, and her thudding heart with the other.

"Impossible!" snorted Constance Clarkson, shaking her off. "I never saw a woman so determined on her course as your mother. She has spoken of this wretched mission of hers since before your father died, and is not likely to be deterred by any interference. Nor the sight of her only child crying at the docks."

"I have not shed a tear," Emily said under her breath. "But Mother is most certainly returning. Perhaps she forgot something."

"A sense of duty to her daughter, perhaps? Financial obligations to your father's hospital?"

"Dear Aunt, you must forgive her. I did years ago. Her calling is not to motherhood. Nor to domestic concerns." Emily watched as Mrs. Clarkson pushed aside an elderly woman carrying an oversized bundle and argued briefly with a man in uniform. "Nor to delicacy of manners," she added.

Aunt Constance laughed. "I can forgive her anything for having given me the care of you so many years ago. She gave up a most precious gift."

The tears Emily could not shed for her departing mother now blurred her vision. Not sufficiently, however, to miss her mother climbing over a bulky trunk and its straining owner.

"And yet she seems to be making her way back to us," Constance continued, slowly and with a touch of annoyance.

"Dear child!" Mrs. Clarkson waved her hands wildly, slapping an elderly woman in the face. "I have almost forgotten!"

"Go to her," Constance said calmly. "See what this is about, and let there be an end to it."

Emily said nothing, but continued to watch in dismay as her determined mother cut a wide path through the crowd of boarding passengers. Heads turned in anger, and one or two gentlemen attempted to restrain her, but Mrs. Clarkson was not one to be deterred from a goal, no matter how unreasonable it might appear. So it had been her whole life, from the time she jilted a wealthy earl to marry a struggling medical doctor, through all her humane missions to the needy in Ireland and Wales, and to her present objective to establish a school for freed slaves in America. Mrs. Clarkson was an admirable woman, if an indifferent mother.

"Go to her," Constance repeated, and pushed Emily forward.

"I almost fear her words."

Constance laughed again, though Emily saw nothing in the least amusing about her mother's apparent change of heart. Life in Mrs. Clarkson's circle was always confusing, spontaneous, entirely disorganized, and sometimes dangerous. Plans were made to be broken. Social obligations were forgotten and ignored. Conventions were turned on their backsides.

Life proved perpetually eventful.

The problem was that Emily was not an eventful sort of girl. Like her calm and sensible aunt, she longed for normality, for quiet, for introspective afternoons spent in the parlor reading instructive essays or creating exceedingly fine needlework designs. Her friends and beaux were from respectable families and she always met with them in the company of Aunt Constance.

Suddenly, and quite unexpectedly, as she looked up to answer her mother's desperate cries, she felt quite alone.

"I have almost forgotten!" Mrs. Clarkson shouted again.

"Your ticket, Mother? Your books? Your sturdy boots?" Emily asked helplessly. What good could a reminder now serve, with the ship's crew preparing for departure?

"Silly child, of course not! I am well prepared for my journey; you oversaw the packing yourself."

"Then what is it, Mother?"

"A little obligation. I quite forgot a tiny promise I made to Lady Gray. You do remember her? She is one of the patronesses of your poor father's hospital."

"Of course. We dined at her town house on more than one occasion. Have you a message for her? A small gift perhaps?"

"Not quite." Mrs. Clarkson looked vaguely uncomfortable, which was sufficient to make her daughter extremely uneasy. "Something I forgot to tell her."

"Mother?" Emily hoped her stern tone was distinguishable above the roar of the crowd.

"I forgot to tell her I am on my way to America. I am sure it would not matter so very much to her but I promised I would take on the post of schoolmistress at her brother's new mill school."

Emily blinked several times, not sure she comprehended the point of her mother's pronouncement.

"Lady Gray's brother? He is patron of a mill school?"

"Darling, it is even better than that. He owns the mill."

"And there is a school for the children who work there?"

Mrs. Clarkson clapped her hands in delight. "He is an enlightened man. He will not have five-year-olds running the machinery nor tolerate any similar abuses. Instead, he wishes to educate the children of his adult employees. Hence, the school."

Emily waited patiently for her mother to continue, though fully aware they were running out of time.

"I am sure he is an admirable old gentleman, if I may use that title to describe a man who owns a mill. And I am sure he will be terribly disappointed you will not be able to fulfill your obligation to him. I suppose it is why you have trampled over your fellow passengers? Do you wish for me to write him of your defection?" Emily asked.

Mrs. Clarkson looked horrified. "You must not do that; he will be inconsolable. In fact, there is no hope for it, my dear. You shall have to go yourself."

"I?" Emily's cry most certainly was heard above the thrum of the crowd. "It is impossible!"

"Why so? If not I, why not my daughter? You have far more patience, and are even more learned. Besides, you have absolutely nothing to gain by spending every minute with your aunt."

"I like to spend time with my aunt."

"And you should like this more. It will give purpose to your life, my dear."

"And my most immediate purpose shall be to inform Lady Gray's mill-owning brother that there will be no teacher named Clarkson to run his fledgling school. If you prefer, I shall deliver the message myself."

"Excellent, my dear." Mrs. Clarkson started to back away. "As the mill is up north in Glenfell, your resistance might be softened by the time you get there."

"Glenfell? Where on earth is . . ."

But Emily's words were cut short by the interference of two bulky crewmen, who started to slip the gangplank from its supports. Her mother momentarily disappeared from view. Her voice, however, was indomitable.

"Excellent! You shall love it there. Take your aunt, if you will. She might be able to help with the little ones. And do give my regrets to Lady Gray's brother. I am sure he will not be disappointed in you."

And, so timing her exit, Evangeline Clarkson scampered up the tilting walkway.

"Mother!" Emily cried into the wind, as desperate as any abandoned child.

"Console yourself, my dear," came Aunt Constance's voice at her shoulder. "An hour ago, you were pleased your mother was leaving you."

"I have had a sudden change of heart, Aunt. Now I find I want nothing so much but that she stay."

On the day after Evangeline Clarkson's triumphant departure for the American wilderness, her daughter sought refuge in the parlor she shared with her aunt. Comforted by its sensible orderliness, Emily knew she could gather her thoughts there so that she might compose a tactful letter of refusal to Laura, Lady Gray. And yet it was not as easy as she had supposed.

She could not doubt Lady Gray understood something of her mother's character, for Mrs. Clarkson was ever known as an independent thinker. But she was also reputed to be a woman who remained devoted to her causes, and Lady Gray would have supposed the education of poor children to be one of them.

In addition, Emily must convey that she, herself, did not share her mother's passions. She did not wish to leave her comfortable home, her gentle aunt, her kind friends. She liked her life just as it was.

Emily finally put her pen to the paper, and broke the point.

She examined the offending object as if it were a personal affront, and then calmly reminded herself that this whole business proved nothing more than a minor irritant. Why did she care what Lady Gray's brother did, or what promises her own mother made?

She was not her mother, nor did she care to be. She had spent most of her life distancing herself from that erratic lady, who demonstrated her affection only in rare shows of attentiveness or interest. For Evangeline Clarkson, a daughter was simply not compelling enough to borrow time away from urgent causes; a grown daughter so unlike herself was an embarrassment.

Emily was only left to wonder why her mother thought her worthy enough to take on such a project.

Perhaps her mother valued her more than she had ever imagined. Her thoughts had just begun to turn onto this hitherto unexplored avenue when she heard Aunt Constance clear her throat.

"Dear aunt! I did not hear you enter." Emily pushed back her chair and turned in her seat.

"You seemed very preoccupied. I would not disturb you, but for some urgent business. Mr. Tilden is arrived and wishes to speak to you."

"Mr. Tilden?" Emily frowned. She, of course, immediately recognized the name of her late father's solicitor, but had always before been summoned to his office on matters of business. What compelled him to call upon her now? Unless . . .

"Aunt Constance? Do you and Mr. Tilden have something to announce to me?" she asked mischievously. She had always wondered about the relationship between her father's younger sister and his oldest friend. Neither had ever married, and they certainly seemed to regard each other with affection.

Constance looked blankly at her niece and then blushed with dawning realization.

"Do not be impertinent, child. Mr. Tilden appears agitated."

"So he should be," Emily teased. "But I suppose I must see him, though surely his excuse for coming must have been yourself."

"Do not imagine it," Constance said under her breath, and let her niece pass before her. "He is in the library."

Emily was at last persuaded of the proof of Aunt Constance's denial, for no man would attempt to do any romancing in the dark, stagnant air of Dr. Clarkson's abandoned library. Though her father had moved from his childhood home more than twenty-five years before, he had never found a convenient time to transport his collection of medical tomes to his own town house or hospital. His younger sister was left to the care of it and, several years later, to the care of his only child. Dr. Clarkson had treated the library and Emily with equal affection, noting from time to time that the dust settled on neither.

Constance always treated her brother's possessions with care; after his death three years ago, that care had become reverential.

Emily reflected only briefly on these matters as she crossed the hall and pushed open the heavy oak door. Edward Tilden stood with his back to her, examining a book.

"Mr. Tilden? What a pleasant surprise!" Emily said clearly.

The man turned quickly, almost dropping the book, and stared at her for a few moments.

"Miss Emily. I am not yet accustomed to seeing you as an adult, looking the very image of your mother."

Emily knew it was a compliment, for her father had often told her how he dared to court the most beautiful woman of the season of 1790, and how no one was more surprised than he when she accepted him over her more impressive suitors. She also knew her mother's dark beauty had been exotic in her time, but was decidedly less desirable in 1819.

"I believe that is a compliment, sir. And yet there are few who would actually mistake me for my mother. Some say I seem years older than she."

"In matters of responsibility, dear, certainly not in appearance," Aunt Constance said reprovingly, behind her.

Something in their words seemed to affect Mr. Tilden most deeply, for he cleared his throat and loosened his cravat.

"Shall we move to the parlor?" Emily asked, wondering at this display.

"I am afraid . . . I am not here on a social call, Miss Emily. I have matters of an urgent—and unpleasant—nature to discuss."

"Dear God, it is not my mother? Her ship?" Emily asked, and blindly felt her way to a chair.

"It is about your mother, but as far as I know, her ship remains seaworthy," he said, and pulled some papers out of a case. "I will get to the matter at once."

"Please do, Edward," Constance advised. "You have near caused Emily to faint."

"What I am about to say will not make her better, Connie."

Emily only vaguely noticed the familiarity. "I am prepared for it," she said.

Mr. Tilden looked doubtful, but went on. "I hope I am not presumptuous to guess Mrs. Clarkson did not discuss any recent financial arrangements with the two of you. It was not in her nature to bother with such things, and she readily dismissed me when I suggested we involve you in her plans. Therefore I felt it prudent to wait until she left for America to come. We could not meet in my office, because what I am about to do is highly unprofessional. My only excuse is that I consider myself a friend."

"Of course, Mr. Tilden. Be assured we appreciate your efforts on our behalf."

"I hope you know you may always count on me."

"Edward, you are baiting us most unkindly. Please get to the point," said Constance.

"Well, then. The point is that Mrs. Clarkson has diverted whatever monies remain from her husband's investments and her own portion into the Free Home School in America. The house in which we are standing remains her property, and home to the two of you for as long as you wish, but I must tell you there has been no allowance made for its care. Nor, I believe, for any additional expenses the two of you may have."

"Edward . . ." Constance began.

"Connie, I should like to discuss a solution with you."

"This is neither the time nor the place, Edward," Constance said firmly.

Emily looked from one to the other, wondering how she could have trivialized what so clearly rested uneasily between them. That her aunt should have denied a lover for so many years was neither coquettish nor a game; the sudden insight did not make Emily feel any easier about the present circumstance.

"I shall leave the two of you alone for a few moments," Emily said uncomfortably, and rose quickly.

"Do sit down," Constance said without looking at her. "I have my own portion, left to me by my father. We can manage very well without my brother's allowance."

"Do not let your pride blind you to certain necessities, Connie. I know what it costs to maintain this house. I also know what is needed to keep two ladies in fashionable respectability."

"Emily and I will work out a budget for ourselves. We are accustomed to some measure of thrift, in any case."

"You are sensible women who have had to compensate for the impulsiveness of a dear relation in the past. But these current problems may prove insurmountable. Will you allow me to help?"

No more words were exchanged, but the tension in the room was palpable. Emily held her breath, looking at her pale aunt and at the flushed lawyer. Her presence was barely noticed.

"I will await your message, then," Mr. Tilden said stiffly, and shuffled his papers back into the case. That he had never needed to refer to the legal documents suggested how very clear was the financial situation. The other, more emotional, situation was made clear by his parting words. "I am well accustomed to doing so."

"How long has he wished to marry you, Aunt?"

Constance remained as she was, staring out upon the rainy London street, standing in the shadowy warmth of the arras at the window. "I suppose you mean Edward." It was not a question. "We knew each other when we were quite young. Your father always brought him home, so he could scarcely escape the acquaintance."

"Indeed. But acquaintance is very different from love. I am sure he loves you."

"How would you know?"

Emily was taken back. Indeed, how would she? She had never recognized it in any of the men of whom she was fond, nor was she certain it had defined her own parents' relationship. Theirs was a partnership of another sort, she imagined, devoted to good causes and human rights, and solidified with a fierce sense of independence. She loved her aunt, for certain. But when she looked at her, she did not see what Edward Tilden saw.

"I need not have been to heaven to know what it would be like, Aunt."

"That is no answer."

"Nor have you given me one. Why have you never married? I presume he asked you, probably more than once. And you need not pretend; I know precisely where his thoughts were leading."

"Impudent girl! People will say I have not done a good job of raising you."

Emily smiled. "They will say you have raised me all too well." She sat silently for a moment, and then a thought suddenly occurred to her. "Oh no! That surely is not the reason for it!"

Constance finally turned away from the window, grinning a little sheepishly.

"You, of all people, can hardly fault me for it. Your mother and father loved you, but had no interest in the care of a small child. They would have left you to the care of governesses, or indifferent tutors, only occasionally checking your progress. Of course I had to take you in, and raise you as a stranger could not. Edward told me he would accept you into his household, but I felt you should live in the Clarkson home."

"But you could have had children of your own. They would have been like brothers and sisters to me," Emily protested.

"Perhaps." Constance did not sound as if she had any

regrets. "But I am not so very old, and could still be a mother."

"I beg you, then! Accept Mr. Tilden's offer! Now that I finally understand your situation, I want it above anything."

"You are speaking from a misguided sense of guilt, my dear. In any case, to accept Edward now would be almost vulgar. It should seem as if I were doing it for the money."

Emily said nothing, wondering how much her own enthusiasm for the plan was motivated by that very thought. Indeed, one of them should "do something for the money," and the answer was now clear.

"I shall go to Glenfell and take Mother's place at the school," she said firmly.

"It is a ridiculous plan," Constance said, dismissively.

"It is a perfect plan. I shall earn enough money to support the house, even while fulfilling a family obligation. You, at the same time, will be free of me at last and . . ."

"Emily! What an unkind thing to say!"

"I meant it in the most generous sense. You will finally be relieved of your family obligation, and can make Mr. Tilden a happy man."

"But I will not be a happy woman until you are wed."

"I may never be wed," Emily said firmly. "You have given me an excellent model of how little deprived I may be as a result."

"And I cannot allow you to travel to Glenfell alone. It is not at all proper."

"I am not traveling as a lady, Aunt. I am traveling as a paid employee of Lady Gray's brother. It will be for his wife, if he has one, to worry about the proprieties."

"I believe him near in age to his sister."

"Better and better. I shall have a youthful mentor in his wife. As the wife of a mill owner, she may be wealthier than me, but she may not feel herself above speaking to a schoolteacher."

"You are not a lowly teacher. You will always be a lady."

"And my mother? And father? One a reformer and the other a caregiver in a sour-smelling hospital? Both out to cure all the ills of the world? What did they think of proper ladies and gentlemen?"

"They thought enough to be determined to make you one."

"And so I shall be, then," Emily sighed, finally relenting. "I shall earn a weekly wage until our circumstances change and then leave it all behind me. I do not believe I can make poor children learn anything of which they are not capable, nor do I think Lady Gray's brother will succeed in his efforts. I expect I shall be the one to tell him so, for my mother would never have admitted it."

"There is no need for you to go to Glenfell, my dear," Constance said, though Emily noticed she did not forbid it.

"No, there is not. But as my other options could only involve marriage, I consider it a worthy bargain. There is nothing but your company to tempt me here, Aunt. Yet you must not fear: I doubt if there will be anything at all to tempt me there either."

Daniel Lennox caught hold of a twisted rope and lowered himself into the bowels of the machinery in the dyeing plant. Beneath him, the swift waters of the river washed away the poisons that whitened the massive bolts of cotton fabric that would soon be stitched into sails for British naval vessels. And to the right and left of him, those bolts hung suspended like snow-shrouded limbs of a tree, waiting for their baptism in the Fell.

Someone shouted from above, and he squinted up into the large white cavern through which he descended.

Noland Haines, his American foreman, seemed concerned about something. As usual.

Daniel smiled and tormented his friend by shaking his lifeline up a bit. No doubt Noland had just learned that the owner of the GlenLennox Mill was himself seeing to the snag in the workings of the machinery and had come immediately to warn his reckless employer of the grave consequences to his health and safety. The speech was one Daniel heard fairly often, one in which Noland reminded him of his many responsibilities and of the many people whose welfare relied upon Daniel Lennox's well-being.

Daniel, if not straining his arm muscles holding on for his life, would broadly shrug and continue whatever it was that had caused Noland so much distress in the first place.

For he, of all people, understood his place in Glenfell society, where tradition ran as strong as the river on whose banks the great mill was constructed. His own grandfather,

William Lennox, had built the first buildings in the complex with his own hands and with nothing more than a vague promise of backing from the Duke of Glendennon, whose estate rose high on the palisade on the opposite bank. Cleverness and hard work—and a reasonable measure of luck—contributed to the success of the venture, and William Lennox never asked the duke for any favors.

That is, only once. And Daniel, smiling again, decided to erase that thought from his mind.

He twisted his large body onto a small ledge and almost immediately discovered the cause of their present difficulty. A crease in the thick canvas, indistinguishable from above, jammed the works; it was a trifling that set his schedule back more than an hour. Bracing himself against the massive cogwheel, Daniel yanked at the cloth with all his strength, and finally set it free. In doing so, he managed to smack his head with his own hand, and cursed himself for his carelessness.

Perhaps he ought to pay more heed to Noland Haines.

He paused awhile, reveling in the reawakening of his heart's lifeblood. Indeed, the mill was his great love, and owned the advantage of being more steadfast and sturdy than any woman. It comforted him when he was in pain, and repaid his vigilance with more than a very generous income. And he knew he did not stand alone in his affection for the place; over two generations, it had stood at the very center of the thriving community that had grown up around it on the west bank of the river.

"Dan!" Noland's voice, deep and sonorous, managed to make itself heard over the groaning machinery.

"I am done here, Nolly," Daniel called up, and tested the rope before he made his ascent. "Fear not; all is well."

He climbed up through the works of the dyeing plant, stopping only once to unravel an errant piece of cloth from a screw. He knew his foreman had him plainly in sight and could have no current cause for worry.

But when, at last, he hefted himself up the last four feet of open space, Noland did not look particularly relieved.

"There is blood on your hand," he said. "And on your head."

"Nothing to fear," Daniel said jauntily and intentionally

jarred Noland's sensibilities by running the white sleeve of his shirt over his forehead.

"And you have gotten chemicals on your trousers," Noland continued critically. "There are spots upon them."

Daniel finally grew impatient. He was weary after his recent exercise and his eyes burned from the chemical wash that infused every wooden beam in the dyeing plant.

"To what do these criticisms pertain?" he asked a little roughly. "I have satisfied your concerns by emerging from my mill alive. Do you expect more of me?"

"I know you too well to expect more of you. But there is someone just arrived who is likely to be disappointed."

Daniel stopped tugging at his clothes and looked questioningly at Noland. "The lady teacher? Mrs. Clarkson? Damn! Was she not expected last week?"

"You may recall a message you received from your sister alerting you to a delay."

"Hmm. I believe there was something. Did the old biddy lose her copy of Fordyce's *Sermons*? Did she need it to fortify herself against the rigors of the North Country?" Daniel unsuccessfully tried to brush some grime from his white shirt and then gave it up entirely. He was the mill owner and the lady's employer, after all. What did it matter what she thought of him?

"I believe she will not be the one to require sobering sermons, Dan."

"A battle-axe, then? Where does Laura find these women?"

"Come see for yourself. But I think you ought to reserve judgment until you meet the lady."

"She is likely to stifle my excuses with a glance, is she?" Daniel asked laughingly, and shrugged himself into his jacket. He started to walk up the hill toward the courtyard of the mill complex, knowing Noland would be sure to follow.

"Oh, of that I am certain," said the voice behind him, sounding far too cheerful.

Chapter Two

*E*mily stepped out of the darkness of the carriage . . . into the darkness of the mid-autumn day. Her nostrils itched from the immediate assault of soot-laden air. But she was too much a lady to scratch or sneeze into her lace while she knew interested faces gazed out upon her from every window facing the little courtyard in which she now stood. The desire to return to the carriage felt overwhelming, the last chance to escape from her odious obligation very tempting.

"This is GlenLennox, miss," said the coachman, struggling with her trunk full of books. "You are certain it is here you want to be and not across the river at Gleneyrie?"

He made a jerky movement with his head, and Emily's eyes followed the general direction he indicated. She saw the river valley just beyond, and heard the rush of the water that supplied energy to the industrial works. A great wilderness rose up on the opposite bank, intersected by a jagged line formed by a road. Her eyes vaguely followed its route until, at the crest of the hill, she discerned the gray stone turrets of a castle, proud against the sky.

No, she thought unhappily. I would indeed prefer to be at Gleneyrie, a place solitary and still. I would sooner climb yonder hill with my trunks on my back and do battle against an ogre than remain in this dismal lowland.

"Who is the owner of Gleneyrie?" she asked hopefully. She had never heard of the estate but perhaps she knew the family and could take refuge while she revisited her uncertain future.

"The Duke of Glendennon, miss. A bit of a recluse he

is, but the duchess is young and the duke's grandson lives with them. They occasionally entertain the quality."

Miss Emily Clarkson was quality. Or had been, until she was reduced to earning a wage to support herself. The coterie about the duke's place would not be likely to welcome the mill's schoolmistress to its lofty sanctuary.

"They are not expecting me at Gleneyrie," she admitted, much to the relief of the man, who waited upon her word to put down his heavy burden. "Indeed, I am uncertain of my welcome even here."

Emily's gaze returned to her more immediate surroundings. In their own way, she supposed, they were impressive as well. A cluster of buildings, spewing out smoke, made up the walls of the courtyard, and beyond it stood row after row of similar structures. A small stone house, of greater age than the others, might well have been the original mill, but it appeared to have another purpose in its present life. Two men, dressed respectably enough, stood in the doorway, watching her intently.

Emily turned away, but only to see two other men approach from the river road.

They were not merely curious, but seemed purposeful in their stride and manner. Well, so would she.

She lifted her chin, stifled a second sneeze and started toward them, knowing the formal rules of societal behavior no longer applied in her wretched circumstances. She would announce her identity to them, and ask to be taken at once to Mr. Lennox.

"I am Miss Clarkson, the new schoolmistress here," she called to them. The larger man missed a step, but caught up to his partner in a moment.

Perhaps because he had thus caught her attention, she studied him first, and with greater scrutiny as they drew closer.

He seemed vaguely familiar, yet she could not recall a man whose features were marked with such contrasts of light and darkness. His hair, a little longer than was fashionable, was as black as her own but for the small flecks of gray in its midst. When he stood not ten feet away, she realized it was dust in his hair, and not evidence of aging. In fact, he did not look many years older than herself.

His eyes were light, so pale their blueness might have been called "icy" if she could have but discerned any coldness in them. Instead, they were lively and curious, and fringed by the longest lashes she had ever seen on a man.

He stopped suddenly, and his partner walked into him.

"I am sorry we were not available to meet you at once," the shorter man said. At least, that is what Emily thought he said, for his accent was inscrutable. His manners were infinitely better, for he removed his hat as he said: "My name is Noland Haines, and I am the foreman of the Glen-Lennox Mill."

"And you are also American, I believe." Emily smiled a little uncertainly. "My mother was so drawn to your native shores, she sent me here in her stead."

"We are delighted to have you with us, Miss Clarkson." He glanced up at his frowning partner. "You are as welcome as your mother would have been."

The cheerful greeting dropped between them in silence, since it was painfully apparent that the next words ought to come from the tall, dark man. Emily looked at him, expecting him to be avoiding her gaze, but was surprised to realize his light eyes were directly upon her. His expression was even more inscrutable than his friend's accent.

"My mother is better trained as a teacher," Emily said artlessly, regretting her candor almost instantly. As much as she resented her obligatory employment here, and her very real need for wages, reason insisted this could be the very best opportunity she would ever be offered.

The tall man cleared his throat. "It is not the only asset needed for employment here," he said in a strained voice.

Impatient with his demeanor, Emily opened her mouth to demonstrate some of the wit for which she was renowned in her circles in London. But she bit off her words when he raised a hand to his forehead.

"Goodness, you are hurt!" she cried.

He seemed startled, as surprised by it as she, and looked down at the crusts of dried blood between his fingers.

"It is nothing," he said a little sheepishly. "I injured myself while fixing the works in the dyeing plant, just yonder."

"May I help you? I know something of doctoring. My father . . ." Emily stopped when the man thrust his hand behind his back. The edges of his unbuttoned jacket pulled apart, and Emily saw blood and dirt on his white shirt.

Her impatience grew, scarcely tempered by sympathy for this difficult man.

"Mr. Haines," she began, though she continued to meet the light eyes of her reluctant patient, "surely my welcome might have been delayed so this man could receive medical attention. Mr. Lennox would not want to lose the services of one of his workers."

"I am Mr. Lennox," the man said, and smiled an unholy grin.

Emily caught her breath, humiliated and angry. Why had she imagined her employer to be a man of a certain age? And why did she think, because of his illustrious relations, that something of the veneer of civility would have rubbed off upon him? To be standing thus, and allow others to do his speaking, was beyond rudeness.

Indeed, it was beyond endurance. She was a desperate fool to come to this place; every moment would be a punishment. Lady Gray, of placid disposition and gentle humor, surely must have escaped it at her first opportunity. And she, Emily Clarkson, would seize the next.

She turned on her heel and walked past her trunks to the still-open door of the carriage.

"I believe I have come to the wrong place after all," she said to the startled driver, as she stepped up into the vehicle. "Please return me to London."

"Miss Clarkson!" She recognized the voice, and resented the humor she heard in it. "Miss Clarkson!"

Mr. Lennox came to the door, blocking out the bleak sunshine. When he stepped up onto the board, the balance of the vehicle shifted precariously to one side. And yet Emily did not fear an accident as much as she feared something else she could not name.

"Have you forgotten something?" he asked with an innocence she presumed false. "I rather doubt it. Considering your pile of trunks, I would say you have depleted the storehouses of London."

She studied him as he stood half in shadow, half in light, and thought his features even more dramatic than when he stood in the sunshine. A small scar revealed itself on his chin; his nose, cast into shadow, looked as if it had once been broken. She tugged her shawl across her breast.

"You believe yourself very amusing, Mr. Lennox, and yet I can assure you that humor at another's expense is rarely funny. And never appreciated. Indeed, it seems I have forgotten something. I have forgotten how much I enjoy my life as it is, in London. I realize, even after just a few minutes of time at your mill, there is nothing that can persuade me to remain here."

She had wished to insult him, and yet when she saw by his expression how well she had succeeded, she felt a pang of regret. She did not like him at all, but it was not in her nature to give pain to anyone. Even to an insensitive, rude brute.

"I see. Is there a gentleman, then? Does your commitment to me separate you from one you love?"

"I do not see how . . ." Emily began, and then thought of Aunt Constance sobbing her farewell in the door of their unaffordable town house. "Yes, it does separate me from one I love."

"An unhappy circumstance, and one I did not imagine when I offered your mother a place to live and work. I cannot help that my property is here, but I hope you may find some pleasure in our landscapes. And perhaps I can offer you some compensation to make you forget your current estrangement."

"This is insufferable, sir. It cannot matter to you whom I love, or if I require some compensation for an unhappy separation. It is not your business."

"Of course it is my business. I am not engaging in a flirtation with you, I am endeavoring to hire you to do a job for me. But it is not any job, and such things matter to me."

Emily distrusted him on her instincts, particularly because those instincts were aroused in wholly unexpected ways. She did not trust his words, which sounded altogether too gentle and sincere, nor his manners, which seemed like the preliminaries to a seduction. She did not trust herself, so uncustomarily confused about what she ought to do.

"You shall have to find another lady to take my place."

One dark eyebrow rose quizzically, and in the semidarkness, Emily discerned the glimmering of a smile upon his face. She had the uncomfortable feeling he interpreted her words in a way she did not intend and she suspected it was a familiar habit of his. It did not make her feel any better about her present situation.

Or give her any hope for the future.

"But I want you. My dear Miss Clarkson, you need not look so fearful. For I also have another love. She is somewhat cumbersome and demanding, but rewards my efforts on her behalf with much gratitude. Ours is a happy partnership."

Emily felt an unbidden jolt of disappointment. It was absurd she should feel thus, when this man could only prove the very last she might ever consider as one dear to her heart, but she could not escape it. Mr. Lennox proved a very intriguing, engaging man, no matter his rough manners and life.

"Your love surely would not be pleased to hear you call her demanding and cumbersome, sir."

He laughed then, a great swelling sound that started deep in his throat. Emily felt the compulsion to laugh along with him, even though she did not doubt it would be at her expense.

"You are not the first woman to suggest such a thing to me; my sisters remind me of it often enough. But come along, Miss Clarkson, I should like for you to meet my children."

His children! Emily now knew herself for a wretch, thinking entirely inappropriate thoughts about a husband and father. But she did not think any more generously of him, for he knew very well the things he had suggested to her, and how wrong he had been for speaking thus.

"Oh, do come, Miss Clarkson," he added impatiently. "You have already made your unhappiness clear to all of us, and I doubt there is anything I can say to make you feel otherwise. But you have traveled long and hard to reach our humble enterprise, and must feel some weariness. My housekeeper will expect you for dinner, and last week the maids made up your bed in the schoolmistress suite of the dormitory. You must satisfy them for this one night, at least. The coach will pass through tomorrow, and I shall put you on it myself if you do not wish to stay."

"I know already I do not wish to say," Emily said firmly.

"And you are a woman of strong conviction."

"Indeed, I am, sir. I do not profess the same lofty idealism as my mother, but my beliefs are clear and unambivalent."

She felt a surge of energy having uttered such words, knowing they sounded a good deal more convincing than she sometimes felt. And so, asserting some modicum of superiority, she nevertheless allowed Mr. Lennox to take her gloved hand, and pull her gently from the safety of the coach.

"I am in your debt, Miss Clarkson," Mr. Lennox said in her ear. He then turned away to call out orders for her trunks to be removed from the coach and carried away, tipping the perplexed coachman. Mr. Haines nodded with undisguised pleasure and walked away to take up some business on the other side of the courtyard. Soon the coach departed in a cloud of dust and rain of gravel.

"I owe you a great deal, Miss Clarkson."

She looked at Mr. Lennox, confused. "Do you mean my wages?"

He laughed again, and Emily realized she liked the sound enough to endeavor to cause him to do it more often.

"That is a matter you must take up with Noland, for he made the arrangements with your mother." He gestured for her to walk next to him, and they started toward the river. "No, indeed. I was thinking of my debt to you for allowing me to preserve certain illusions."

She was not sure she had heard him correctly.

"I hold a great deal of authority here, Miss Clarkson. It would not do my reputation any good if my employees were to witness my being bested by a woman. If you had taken off in your coach, the damage to my reputation would have been irreparable."

"I do not believe you for a moment, sir. A man possessing all I see here need not fear the rebuke of a lady, no matter the difference in their stations."

He laughed to himself, but this time, Emily did not feel the same uplift of joy.

"You think us very different in our stations, do you?"

"How can it be otherwise? I am sorry it is so, but the truth is unavoidable. My father was the younger son of an earl. And my mother the granddaughter of a duke. You are a mill owner."

"I see. Does it not signify that one of my sisters is Lady Gray and another engaged to Lord Eastbourne? Or that your mother is a schoolteacher and your father a doctor? Or that you yourself are prepared to teach in my school? Does it not make me somewhat more elevated than yourself?"

"You are insulting, Mr. Lennox."

"No more than you to me, Miss Clarkson."

"You can scarcely be a gentleman if you make a point of it."

"I see," he said slowly. Emily suspected he knew precisely where he was going, and carefully timed himself along the route. "Then the rules of polite behavior dictate you may abuse me, but I am unable to return the parry? It seems most unfair."

"Life is unfair," Emily responded quickly, swallowing the bitter taste of the words. "It is a simple truth."

"And as a schoolmistress, you must be devoted to the truth."

"I am ever honest," Emily said, not entirely honestly.

He glanced down at her, and Emily thought he saw altogether too much for comfort.

They walked along in silence, which gave Emily the illusion of victory. Indeed, she was not very sure what she had won, but felt satisfied in any case. There was something inherently rewarding about besting a man who held too high an opinion of himself.

But perhaps he had received much encouragement from others. They passed buildings clicking with energy, in which the steady hum of machinery and conversation could be heard, and in and out of which moved a steady supply of raw materials and finished cottons. Carts lined up at each yawning doorway and were unloaded according to their burden. Men and a few women looked up as Mr. Lennox walked past them, and greeted him cheerfully. He appeared to be a very popular employer.

Without stopping, Mr. Lennox led her around a corner, and the scenery changed so abruptly that Emily gasped. When she looked up at him, he did no more than nod his head, but she understood it was an invitation to survey the scene of destruction before them.

And yet destruction seemed too rough a word to describe

the damage a recent fire had wrought upon the landscape. Each blackened tree seemed to have been picked delicately apart and the ground looked as smooth as velvet. A large stone building stood solidly against the backdrop of the river, the sun streaming through its open windows and roofless exterior. The pungent scent of ash lingered in the still air.

"How very dreadful," Emily said. "The loss of this building must have been very unfortunate for your operation."

"My loss was nothing compared to that of others," Mr. Lennox said tersely. "But come along; I did not bring you here to dwell on recent tragedy."

"And yet you wished for me to see this," Emily said.

"I will not deny it. It has some connection to your responsibilities here."

"You forget, sir, I have not accepted any responsibilities here. I am merely grateful for a respite after a long journey."

He said nothing, walking along in silence until they reached a narrow path by the river. It looked loosely graveled and not the sort of place Emily would wish to travel with a strange man. But when he reached for her hand to assist her down the crude stone steps, she accepted him.

"It is a very attractive prospect," Emily said conversationally, trying to dispel the awkwardness she felt. "The only river I know is the Thames, and it is a wretched sewer."

"And yet London would not have grown to its proportions without it," he said knowingly. "And Glenfell would be nothing without the Fell."

Emily would have liked to retort that Glenfell did not look like very much as it was, but the sound of children's voices stopped her abruptly.

"Your children, sir? It sounds as if there are a great many of them. Your wife must be a very busy woman."

Unexpectedly, Daniel Lennox laughed. "I expect they would keep any woman very busy. An ordinary woman might hesitate to own them, which is why I was determined to find myself the most worthy."

Poor Mrs. Lennox, Emily thought. To be selected in such a contest as this. And yet it was possible to see how a young artless thing might have been drawn to good looks and imposing stature, and the promise of comfort a mill like this would bring.

Emily wondered how many of the children resembled their father.

As he helped her up a rise in the path, she knew she would have her answer soon enough. At least a dozen children, dressed alike and of all proportions, raced across the wide lawn to them as soon as Mr. Lennox came into view.

Mr. Lennox held up a hand to stave off a flood of questions and excitement, but did not back away from the close circle of the children. "Here is Miss Clarkson, who was so anxious to meet you, she has not yet unpacked her trunks." He looked at Emily, daring her to defy him.

She said nothing as she smiled a little tentatively, and looked down at the children.

They ranged in age from approximately two years to twelve. Mr. Lennox must have married at a very early age, but perhaps that was the fashion in the northern towns. And yet, when she looked at the children more closely she saw blonds, brunettes, and redheads among them, and a similar variety of eye colors. None had their father's lashes, nor his remarkable eyes.

Those eyes were upon her now.

"You have played a joke upon me, Mr. Lennox. You will not have me believe these children are your own," she said.

"I have not misled you in the least, Miss Clarkson. These children lost their parents in the fire that destroyed the building you espied a few moments ago. They are the orphans of the mill. And since I am the mill, they are now mine."

Emily felt herself go light-headed, and thought she would be ill. But too many eyes were upon her, and there was too much hope within them, for her to make a public display of her feelings. She understood why Mr. Lennox had delayed her departure for a day, why he had brought her past the scene of the fire, and why he had felt she ought to meet his "children."

He hoped to seduce her. He played upon her sympathies, her compassion, and her sense of obligation to attempt to get precisely what he wanted.

And looking at him just now, with his hands calmly resting on the heads of two of the boys and the others crowding into his protective shadow, Emily thought him a man who always got precisely what he wanted.

Chapter Three

*E*mily pushed back the heavy draperies, and looked out upon the landscape painting that was her view from the window of her bedchamber. Sir Joshua Reynolds would find great sustenance here, and Thomas Gainsborough would give up his country portraits of homely gentry altogether if he could but paint this prospect forevermore. Heavy moss hung from ancient trees nourished by the spilling river that ran between their roots. A grassy knoll, untrodden and lush, invited a dozen birds to feed upon it. And beyond, the dense wilderness rose on the other side of the Fell, casting the area into darkness though the sky was light.

Turning from the window, Emily thought the view within equally splendid. Mauve bed linens and a green woolen rug brought rich color to the schoolmistress' chamber and were much grander than those with which she was familiar in London. The mahogany furniture was polished to a warm glow and was very elegant. It felt a place one could enjoy forever, yet Emily would sample its delights for just one night. Her only obligation was to have dinner with its owner and his wife.

And to persuade herself that she might walk away from the mill and its orphaned children without feeling the slightest degree of guilt.

"Miss Clarkson?" A gentle voice interrupted Emily's disquieting reverie.

"Mrs. Bernays?" Emily already recognized the voice of the housekeeper of the dormitory. In the few moments they had already shared, witnessed by a silent Mr. Lennox, she found Mrs. Bernays to be a well-mannered, affectionate sort of woman, who could scarcely control her tears when describing the plight of the young children in her care. "Do come in."

The plump woman came through the door with surprising grace and stared appraisingly at Emily.

"I doubt Mr. Lennox might have found a teacher to rival you, Miss Clarkson," she said. "I must say, the green of your gown suits you admirably."

"I would hope to be known for my teaching abilities, rather than my appearance," she began, before catching herself. "But of course, as you know, I shall not remain here long enough to consider my reputation. I shall leave tomorrow."

Mrs. Bernays smiled knowingly, leaving Emily somewhat disconcerted. "Mr. Lennox's carriage is here just now, to take you to Shearings. That is Mr. Lennox's home, and very grand."

"Is it very distant, Mrs. Bernays?" Emily asked, momentarily confused. "I understood he lived on the property of the mill."

"Oh, very close, indeed. Shearings is just downriver, south of the mill buildings. Mr. Lennox's father built it in such style, to provide Mrs. Lennox with the comforts to which she was accustomed. And to thumb his nose in the face of the Duke of Glendennon."

"The gentleman who lives on top the hill opposite? Is there rivalry between them, then?" Emily was raised knowing she ought not gossip with servants, but instantly forgave herself since she was now one herself. Or would be, if she stayed in Glenfell.

Which of course she would not.

"I cannot speak of it, Miss Clarkson," Mrs. Bernays said with a sniff, putting Emily in her place. "Mr. Lennox forbids it."

"Oh dear, he sounds like a very strict sort of employer," Emily said airily, pulling her pride snugly around her.

Mrs. Bernays looked at her in surprise, and then smiled a little sheepishly. "You must not judge him so hastily. He has his reasons for behaving thus."

Emily sighed. "Indeed, I believe he has his reasons for acting however he pleases."

"That he does." Mrs. Bernays smiled broadly, as if Emily

had just uttered the highest praise. "And so he sent his carriage for you, though you can easily walk the distance."

Emily's thoughts returned to the immediate present.

"To Shearings," she said. "Of course. I must make myself ready."

"I believe you will do as you are, Miss Clarkson," said Mrs. Bernays, and bowed her head deferentially as she opened the door into the corridor.

Daniel looked anxiously out the window and wondered if his new driver had managed to lose himself between the dormitory and Shearings. Blast the man! He should have stayed with the bale carts, rather than be trusted with such precious cargo as this.

For if he, Daniel, did not sufficiently impress the fickle Miss Clarkson this evening, he would lose her to London. And he knew not where he might turn for another schoolmistress suitable for his experimental undertaking.

Back in London, his sister Laura had already plowed the fertile field of the civic reformers and avid philanthropists. Harriet Martineau was too volatile, too fiery a speaker to ease the damaged spirits of the children. Fanny Wright was already in America, and soon would be joined by Mrs. Evangeline Clarkson. Letitia Mulgrave forever railed against the injustices of the class system, but preferred not to dirty her hands by coming close to those she sought to champion.

For it was not enough to find a person capable of teaching reading and arithmetic to the children of the mill; Daniel was in need of a woman who thought such children were worthy to be educated. To be sure, he knew little of Miss Clarkson's opinions on that matter, but her family credentials were impeccable. Her parents must have bequeathed something to their only child.

And yet she seemed as elitist and lofty as those he would have rejected out of hand. Her chin, pert and lovely as it was, pointed toward higher expectations and her eyes looked critically on everything around her. Particularly on Daniel Lennox.

He would have to prove his worth if he would convince her to stay at GlenLennox Mills. She had too easily seen through his ploy to garner her sympathy by bringing her to the children, and he now must convince her of his own honest intentions and merits. Dignity prevented him from being entirely candid, but there was no hope for it. She would have to take him as he was.

He glanced down at his dark jacket and carefully tied cravat and wondered what was the current fashion in London. He had not seen his sisters in months and regretted it all the more now, for they would have set him straight in that regard. And yet, he thought he appeared respectable enough, and dared to believe he would make a good impression. His dear sisters grudgingly admitted he could devastate an unsuspecting young female.

Unfortunately, the divine Miss Clarkson was already too suspecting.

And she was already too near at hand for him to do anything to change his strategy. Daniel heard the clatter of horses in his drive and a glance out the window confirmed her arrival.

He walked toward the glowing fireplace and endeavored to position himself casually, his elbow on the mantel, as if he had not been watching for her arrival for the past twenty anxious minutes. But soon he heard the bell announcing her arrival, the hushed words in the foyer, and the small footsteps across the marble floor to the drawing room where he awaited her.

"Sir, Miss Emily Clarkson is here to see you."

"Of course, Winters. Please show Miss Clarkson in. And have Mrs. Winters bring us some . . . refreshment."

Daniel lost his thread of speech as a vision in green crossed the threshold and poised herself not ten feet from him. Miss Emily Clarkson lifted her stubborn chin as her hands smoothed down the bodice of her emerald gown and revealed enough of her anatomy to convince Daniel that she had charms even surpassing that little chin. She looked nothing like a schoolmistress ought to look, and would drive some of the older boys into blissful distraction.

As she was now doing to someone too old to be a boy, and too determined to be distracted.

"Mr. Lennox? You seem remarkably quiet this evening," she said, and turned her head toward the portraits on the wall. Small pearl earrings danced at her ears, and contrasted with the dark curls of her hair. "Did you not promise me an evening to relieve the monotony of travel?"

"I did," he said, knowing full well she understood the real reason why he had her here. However, anyone witnessing their conversation might have thought she had come with the intention of seducing him, rather than the opposite. "I am only surprised at the formality of your dress. We are not so grand in Glenfell."

He saw his mistake at once. He knew he must not allude to the simpler life in the north, for Miss Clarkson would not be impressed. He now expected her to put him in his humble place.

"Did you not invite me to dine with you and your wife tonight? Mrs. Lennox would think me a poor thing if I did not dress well enough to show my gratitude for the kindness." She looked from one side of the room to the other, avoiding his eyes. "Will Mrs. Lennox be joining us shortly?"

Daniel sucked in his breath, regretting that this moment came as soon as it did. He knew he would be made accountable for his implied untruth earlier in the day, but had hoped he might convince Miss Clarkson to stay before he confessed. Delaying now would only make his punishment worse.

"There is no Mrs. Lennox, Miss Clarkson," he said.

Her eyes narrowed as a flush spread across her features.

"Then you have purposely misled me, sir. I would not have arrived unchaperoned if I had known there was no mistress within."

Daniel waved his hand dismissively. "Oh, we have chaperones enough. Everyone wishes to take a look at the new schoolmistress. But I think you misjudge me, for surely you misled yourself."

"I recall every word we spoke, sir."

"Then you will remember I spoke only of my love, and how steady she was," he said. "It is the mill, of course. She is the great lady who gives me continual joy."

Miss Clarkson bit down on her lip, fighting to control her anger. She succeeded in not saying anything, but her thoughts were readily revealed in every other part of her shaking body.

"Do you doubt me?" Daniel taunted her, perversely desiring an unfettered response.

"Sadly, I do not, sir," she said at last. "But I believe you have lived too long in these parts. Preferring a mill to a woman suggests a deranged intellect. I am sorry to say this, but I will speak of this conversation to Lady Gray when I return to London. Perhaps she will know what to do to help."

"You are a quiz, Miss Clarkson! Do you not think my dear sister has already done her part in providing a cure?" Daniel said recklessly, letting her think what she may. "And I never recall saying I preferred my mill to a woman."

Mrs. Winters entered at that unfortunate moment, bearing a large tray of delicacies, or whatever it was his sisters called those tiny portions of meat and bread covered in sweet sauce. They were hardly sufficient to satisfy a real hunger.

He glanced up at Miss Clarkson's beautiful face, and realized he had a hunger of a different sort.

"Thank you, Mrs. Winters. Allow me to introduce Miss Emily Clarkson, who would have been our new schoolmistress but for the fact that she has some compelling reasons to return to London."

Dear Mrs. Winters' wrinkled face glowed with pleasure. She carefully placed the tray on the table by the fire, and grinned pointedly at Daniel as she rubbed her hands together.

What Emily Clarkson was making of this show, he could not imagine.

"It is a pleasure to meet you, Mrs. Winters. Mrs. Bernays has been most complimentary when she has spoken of you, and assured me I would be well taken care of when visiting Shearings."

"But it is to be short-lived, of course, since you are to depart on the morrow," Daniel interrupted. "I do not recall what you said, however. Something in Glenfell did not suit you sufficiently?"

"Oh, miss. If there is anything you desire, you need only speak to myself or Mrs. Bernays. We wish you to stay so much. And so do the children. We try our best to mother them, but they need someone like yourself to teach them and guide them."

Miss Clarkson opened her mouth but no words came out. She glanced accusingly at him, but Daniel only shrugged a

little helplessly, letting her believe Mrs. Winters entirely
spontaneous.

Indeed, she was, but how admirably did she advance his
own cause. Why, he might absent himself from this conversation altogether, and leave Miss Clarkson in the company
of his two housekeepers, and get his way with the greatest expediency.

He was tempted to do it, but then Mrs. Winters ex-
empted herself as she bustled happily out of the room.

"You do see how very much your presence is desired in
our humble neighborhood, Miss Clarkson. Might you not
think upon it in the same spirit as that which drove your
saintly mother to America? Would it not be a noble mission? A challenge?"

"Perhaps. But not compelling enough to keep me."

"Ah yes, of course. I have forgotten you have a lover in
London. Or have you misled me about him as I mayhap
did you?"

"You need not insult me, sir. I have not misled you at
all. Your sister will tell you I have received three offers of
marriage this year. And one of my suitors writes me very
pretty poetry."

"Poetry?" Daniel asked, making it sound like a foreign
tongue. He noticed she did not say she had accepted any
of those offers. "I fear you are correct in your assessment
of Glenfell's limitations, Miss Clarkson. I do not know of
a single gentleman in these parts who ever wrote a word
of poetry. I am sure I am incapable of it myself."

Emily Clarkson studied him for a few moments, her body
trembling slightly. Dear God, what had he said to anger
her now?

Then suddenly, unexpectedly, she broke out in laughter,
a sound so sweet he thought music played in the room.

"It is just as well, Mr. Lennox. A poet must be very sure
of himself before he dares to address his words to a lady.
A poorly played poem might have the effect of offending
the object of its affections." She nodded thoughtfully, as if
she knew much of this. "But you surprise me, Mr. Lennox."

"How so, Miss Clarkson?" he asked, though he thought
he did not really wish to hear her answer.

"Why, you seem so very sure of yourself in all things.

Have you never addressed a poem to a lady? Or to a cotton mill?"

He saw the source of her good humor now; he was the object of her sarcasm. Well, he had endured worse in his life, and for less gain than procuring a schoolmistress for his restless orphans.

"I believe I once penned a few lines to a wheelcart, but it came to nought."

She laughed again.

"Do have some of these little meaty things, Miss Clarkson. Mrs. Winters will be offended if you do not partake and then praise her heartily for her efforts. But perhaps I am mistaken, for I believe you have already made a conquest. Yes, I am sure of it. Mrs. Winters, bless her traitorous heart, is now in your camp. You might murder me here and leave bloodstains on the priceless carpet, and be praised for your delicacy."

She smiled and turned a shoulder as she reached for one of the delicacies. He wanted nothing so much as to kiss her in the soft shadow of her collarbone, and therefore waited until she finished before he took a step forward to serve himself.

"Mr. Lennox, you are trying to tempt me to do something I do not wish to do."

Indeed he was.

"But I doubt I can be persuaded to remain here."

"I can think of nothing more I can do to change your mind," he said as he offered his elbow to escort her to the dining room, "except to entice you with Mrs. Winters' excellent cooking."

Mrs. Winters' cooking was indeed excellent, Emily thought. She, who rarely paid much attention to the meals prepared for her in London, fancied there was something fresher about the taste of the vegetables and the flavor of the trout here in Glenfell. The harvest surely was a local one.

"I caught the trout myself," Mr. Lennox said idly, as if reading her thoughts.

She looked across the great table at him, disconcerted by how familiar it felt to be doing so. She had known the man a few hours, and yet was perfectly at ease dining tête-à-tête in his home.

"You appear to be a man of many talents, Mr. Lennox. Did the poor fish put up a great battle when you hooked him? Did he bloody your hand this afternoon?"

Daniel Lennox held up a hand, and Emily noticed it was bandaged.

"I suppose it would have made a very good story, but I regret to say the cause of my injury was not anywhere as dramatic as you suppose. A bolt of cotton canvas jammed the works at the dyeing plant, and I went in to wrench it free."

"The dyeing plant?" Emily uttered in disbelief.

He studied her for several moments, while the candle-light danced across his features. Suddenly a light came into his eyes, and it had nothing to do with the candles.

"One does not die in a dyeing plant, Miss Clarkson. It is an inoffensive building, wherein the bolts of natural fabrics are bleached bright. The Royal Navy seems to prefer it for the sails of its ships. I am sorry to disappoint you, but you are unlikely to find anything ominous at GlenLennox Mills."

"And yet people have died here, tragically and recently."

"Yes, they have," he admitted. She could see the subject pained him.

"Do you know the cause of the fire?"

"I have my suspicions," he said sharply.

"That in itself sounds ominous."

"But you need not fear," he said firmly. "It is my problem."

"Your responsibilities seem considerable, Mr. Lennox. You must repair your mill, tend to orphan children, and even catch your own dinner," Emily said lightly.

"Do you not think it gives me some merit, Miss Clarkson? I may not be as grand as the gentlemen of your acquaintance, but I may deserve some measure of credit. And, as I do not write poetry, I surely should be additionally elevated in your estimation."

Emily laughed, finding pleasure in his self-effacing wit.

"It is no wonder you do not write poetry, sir. I cannot imagine where you would find the time."

"And that is the very issue at hand!"

"I beg your pardon?"

"If I could find one worthy person to take on the care of the children, I might have time to pen pretty phrases."

As an argument, it was ridiculous, and unanswerable. Still, Emily could not help but be caught up in the gaiety of the moment.

"If you promise, sir, to never write a single verse, I might be persuaded to assume a position in your classroom." She laughed.

But when she looked across at him, she saw he was not laughing.

Emily sat on her bed, too tired to fall asleep and too confused to seek refuge in a book.

She was certain she had not had too much to drink at table, and had no evidence she had been drugged. She certainly had not been blackmailed or coerced into saying something she did not wish, nor passionately seduced into doing something she did not desire. Indeed, she had held her own in the battle of wit and persuasion just a few hours before.

And yet, she had struck a bargain to do the very thing she had said she would not be persuaded to do. She had agreed to remain in Glenfell, and be schoolmistress at the mill school, until a suitable substitute could be found.

She ought to have felt deflated, depressed, in vehement denial.

But a little sprite danced in the corner of her imagination, tantalizing her into believing she had got precisely what she refused to believe she wanted. To have given in was, oddly, to have triumphed.

She knew Daniel Lennox to be cunning and deceitful, and rough around his very good-looking edges. She knew he tried to impress her only to get her to work for him. And she knew that a mill owner, a man of business, was not at all a desirable companion for a young lady of a certain class and expectations.

And yet, for all this, she could not help but believe the win was all hers. She would remain in Glenfell.

Chapter Four

*E*mily had scarcely closed her eyes before she woke to the hum of voices and gentle tapping at her chamber door. She emerged from beneath her cocoon of warm blankets to face the pale pink light of the dawn and the realization that Glenfell was already alive with industry.

"Children! What on earth on you doing here?" came a sharp voice from the hallway. "Away with you to the classroom. You may start on your letters until Miss Clarkson and I join you shortly. Margaret, I expect you to be in charge of the younger ones. Daniel? You will listen to what Margaret has to say."

Emily reached for her dressing gown, and ran barefooted to the door. She opened it to a smiling young woman who stood with her hand poised to knock.

"Good morning, Miss Clarkson," she said. "I could not be sure Mr. Lennox told you at what time classes begin and doubted you are accustomed to keeping country hours. It is a new day."

"Indeed, it is," Emily said, stifling a yawn. "I suppose it is not possible for the schoolmistress to appear in her nightclothes?"

The woman turned her bright eyes on Emily and giggled. "You would be a bonny sight, I daresay. Half the mill would empty out as the workers would desire a formal education, of a sudden. And then where would that put Mr. Lennox?"

"I could think of a few places to put your Mr. Lennox, and none of them pleasant," Emily ventured, stepping back.

The woman laughed out loud as she entered the room.

"Oh, Noland warned me you were about to give Daniel a run for it, and make no mistake about it," she said cheerfully. "He may yet find something to distract him from his wheels and pulleys and the price of cotton in America."

Emily solemnly digested this disquieting statement, and decided to pursue the safest tidbit. "Noland?"

The woman looked at her in surprise. "Noland Haines, Mr. Lennox's office manager of the mill."

"Ah, yes. We met briefly yesterday."

"It appears as if you made a much stronger impression on him than he did on you, Miss Clarkson. Daniel and Noland have scarce spoken of anything else since your arrival yesterday."

Emily decided to let that pass, for now.

"You seem to be on familiar terms with them both. But you have not even made me free with your name."

The woman owned the grace to look sheepish. "I am so sorry, Miss Clarkson. I am Ellen Worthington. And if I seem familiar with the two gentlemen, my excuse must be that I am to marry Noland Haines and he is Daniel Lennox's excellent friend."

"He is American."

Ellen Worthington gave a little shrug. "We cannot help it. I have managed to overlook his painful accent and now consider him the finest of men."

"And yet he is Mr. Lennox's friend," Emily said thoughtfully.

"Miss Clarkson, you sorely misjudge Daniel. You cannot yet know how much good he has done, how very noble he is."

"Noble?" Emily assumed her London air. "Surely even a man who deems the education of mill children to be necessary cannot be elevated quite so high as that."

Miss Worthington looked as if she was about to say something, and then abruptly changed her mind.

"And all I yet know of him is that he somehow tricked me into remaining here at GlenLennox," Emily rushed on, "and has prevailed upon my sympathies. I fear the children are his pawns, and I will not sit quietly by while he uses them for his purposes."

Miss Worthington leaned forward, and raised a slim brow. "And what are his purposes, do you suppose?"

The schoolmistress was momentarily silenced. Indeed, what could Mr. Lennox be thinking in educating a poor group of orphans, claimed by no one but himself, and whose expectations could not extend very far past the confines of his mill?

"To be better served by educated workers in the future?" Emily guessed. Indeed, she could not think of a better answer, nor one to truly prove Mr. Lennox's selfish motives. She thought of her mother's purpose in going to America, propelled by the idealistic notion that education might free people from slavery. And suddenly understood that the children educated at GlenLennox today would not be bound to remain at GlenLennox forever.

Miss Worthington's bright eyes watched her closely and seemed to know what she was thinking.

"And yet I will not believe so much good of him," Emily insisted stubbornly. What did she know of Mr. Lennox, after all?

"Then will you suspend judgment for the sake of the children? You rightly proclaim them innocents. They would have been, but for the losses they endured. They need you, Miss Clarkson: I cannot say it plainer."

"You are a very wise woman, Miss Worthington. I wish I could have your assistance in the company of my students."

Miss Worthington was visibly surprised. "But you do, Miss Clarkson. Did Mr. Lennox not tell you? No, I see he did not. I have been keeping the children occupied for all these weeks, and will work with you in the classroom."

"Indeed?" Emily could scarcely contain her relief. "But why are you not the schoolmistress? Surely Mr. Lennox did not have to look so far as London."

"Oh, I have not the education required to be a teacher to others. Nor am I a lady like yourself," Miss Worthington answered, though she seemed as genteel as anyone Emily knew in London. "And, of course, I am soon to be married. Noland would not permit me to work, and I should be busy with other things. You know."

Emily was not certain she did, for she knew too many married women with little to occupy them but gossiping and planning tedious dinner parties.

"And that is why Daniel so specially wanted a teacher unencumbered by marriage and likely to remain so. He seeks constancy in the lives of the children and, in my present situation, I am not the one to provide it."

"And I suppose I meet his requirements?" Emily said tartly.

Ellen Worthington stood and studied Emily, surely assessing her matted hair, rumpled nightdress, and reddened eyes.

"I am almost certain you do, Miss Clarkson. Though I doubt if either of you yet realizes it." She looked as if she would explain herself, but went on to other matters. "We have a long day ahead of us, and it appears it started for you a good deal earlier than you hoped. Why don't I join the children in the classroom, and we will wait upon your arrival?"

"I should appreciate it above all things, Miss Worthington," Emily sighed.

Though embarrassingly tardy in reporting for her first day in the classroom, Emily was not overly hasty in making her way down the broad stairs of the dormitory to the classroom below. She had washed and dressed carefully, and wore a neat tailored gown that had scarcely wrinkled in her packed wardrobe. As she caught her reflection in the glass of the wide window in the hall, she thought it suited her present occupation even as it flattered her slender figure. In London she might have worn it to a Ladies' Society meeting and attracted little attention.

The dormitory Mr. Lennox had built was apparently not entirely complete, for workmen still labored on the roof and outside walls. But within, all was fresh and clean, and furnished tastefully. Emily thought herself the only occupant of the uppermost floor. As she descended, she heard the sounds of the house, and realized the floors below hers belonged to the children and to the maids who cared for them when they were not in the classroom. And finally, the noises on the ground floor left her in little doubt that her charges were to be educated in a large airy room she had glimpsed the night before, one that opened onto a garden. A wide central foyer separated the classroom from a dining hall, and Emily wondered if she was expected to eat with the children.

Now that she had committed to some length of time at

Glenfell, she did not expect an invitation to Shearings would be made to her again.

Thus resolved and resigned, she caught her breath and opened the door to the classroom.

Twenty heads looked up in unison and gave a collective sigh. Emily imagined she read depths of understanding on their childish features and guessed they had believed she would not come. Feeling oddly humbled and guilty at the same time, she walked toward the large desk in front of the room, wondering if she should smile or look severe.

It proved the lengthiest ten feet she had ever trod. She reached the desk, and grasped the knobs atop the chair, and noticed several piles of papers and books waiting as if she herself had left them there the day before. In the center of the desk was a small collection of odd offerings: an apple, a teacup, a string of wooden beads, some pebbles, and a swatch of blue silk.

And when Emily looked up, she smiled.

The natural wisdom of that decision was clear at once: she was answered in kind by the smiles of the children.

Miss Worthington broke the spell, only to prolong the pleasure.

"Allow me to introduce Miss Clarkson, children. Some of you met yesterday. But here, in this classroom, is where we will meet and work together for some time to come."

The conclusion to this pretty little speech made Emily conclude Miss Worthington had, perhaps, some help in composing it. If Mr. Lennox intended to seek her favor by embarking on a campaign of persuasion, he undoubtedly would enlist many minions. The future wife of his manager was a very likely candidate.

"And have we anything to say to our new schoolmistress?" Miss Worthington asked expectantly.

Apparently they did not, though one boy dropped a book on another's foot.

"Did we not practice something very special?" There was a note of desperation in Miss Worthington's voice.

Several children glanced out the window at a passing oxcart, which Emily did not think was special at all.

"I would very much like to hear it," Emily said softly, and was instantly rewarded by a chorus of young voices. The poem they memorized might have been composed by

Thomas Gray, but was so garbled in the cacophony of voices she could not be certain. From smallest to oldest, they all seemed intent on purpose and effort, and looked uncommonly pleased with themselves. So, for that matter, did Miss Worthington.

Emily would not spoil their pleasure.

"Oh, very well done! I had no idea there was so much talent here and such interest in poetry. Why, I believe we shall have to learn a great many works by the famous poets!"

Several of the boys groaned and seemed to be looking about for the means of escape. The smallest girl squirmed in her seat, and Miss Worthington sighed a little too dramatically.

"You will not find it an easy task," she whispered.

"I do not doubt it," Emily answered, but heard, felt, the challenge in her own words. Absurdly, the most severe of her concerns were already evaporating, though she knew she had scarcely begun to earn her salary.

She was no more prepared, nor educated, nor talented than she had been the day her mother thrust this burden upon her. And yet, some part of her now seemed determined to prove her worth.

Daniel Lennox would have found the present circumstances humorous if he had not believed his relationship with Miss Clarkson so uncompromising. That is, though he had spent much of his childhood trying to devise means by which he might surreptitiously escape the prison of the classroom, he now wondered how he might endeavor to make his way in.

It was absurd, even humbling. That the master of the GlenLennox Mill, a man of great influence and power in the neighborhood, should be sneaking about under the windows of a schoolhouse trying to hear what was being said within, was the stuff of farce. That the schoolhouse should belong to him, and its two teachers be his employees, went beyond any sense of reality. But there it was.

Daniel stood in the shadow of the beams that would eventually frame a second classroom and realized he had a fair view of the children in their seats through a makeshift window. They were writing on their slates, bent over their desks like little clerks slaving away for a wealthy merchant. He watched as Timothy leaned over to study what his sister Margaret had already written and as Daniel Whitlow made little stick-figure illustrations. He saw the twins Charlotte and Lydia tease each other with a pheasant feather and Little Dan slip his shoes off and rub his stockinged feet against the polished surface of the floor.

The children were very much as they always were. But what of their reluctant schoolmistress?

Daniel edged closer to the window and knocked over a bucket filled with . . . well, he was not sure what it was, but was careful not to get it on his shoes. He leaned against the pane, grateful he did not fall into a well, or crash through the glass. Miss Clarkson seemed to have a peculiar effect on him; but when he looked through the window, he saw he was not the only one so intoxicated by her presence.

She sat at the large desk he had brought over from Shearings, though she looked a fairer sight at it than he ever had. Her hair, as dark as the slate behind her, was twisted into some top-braided thing like what his sisters preferred, but wisps of hair framed her face and made her look far more delicate than a woman in her position ought to be. She wore a high-necked gown that paled against the flush of her skin, and it was so fitted on her that Daniel was sure he now had a flush on his.

She looked very intent on correcting the work of one of the older boys, Daniel Crimshaw. And Daniel Crimshaw's gaze was equally intent on her breasts. Whatever learning was going on in the boy's mind was not at all the sort of thing Daniel had intended.

Feeling a surge of some indefinable energy, he walked around the side of the building and slipped through the door. There were an abundance of empty seats in the back of Miss Clarkson's classroom, and he settled himself into one of them, folding his long legs into a position that was tolerable, if not comfortable.

Nell Worthington saw him at once and waved a little book at him. She was working with one of the girls and glanced toward Miss Clarkson, who seemed oblivious to everything but the words on young Crimshaw's page. He wondered how long he could remain here and not attract her notice. He also wondered what she would do when she discovered him.

But then, he thought being punished by Miss Clarkson might offer some remarkable possibilities. He would wait his turn.

Miss Clarkson looked uncommonly pleased with herself when she looked up at Daniel Crimshaw. She smiled at him as she spoke and pointed to his slate with just the sort of enthusiasm Daniel Lennox had hoped his new schoolmistress might achieve. But young Crimshaw, the little badger, never let his gaze wander from her breasts. When Miss Clarkson lifted the slate and held it just under her neck to block his impertinent staring, Daniel could not help but laugh out loud.

Now he certainly was in for it. Miss Clarkson turned her wide dark gaze on him and her splendid smile disappeared. She said something quickly to Crimshaw, who scuttled back to one of the front desks. But while Daniel was half out of his cramped seat, expecting a confrontation, the schoolmistress exacted the worst sort of punishment on him.

She ignored him.

Gently, firmly, she asked her students to put down their slates and close their books. She whispered something to Nell, who nodded and quietly left the classroom. And then she picked up one of Walter Scott's most recent adventure novels, and started to read aloud.

Daniel settled back in his chair, hardly noticing how uncomfortable it was. Instead he watched her graceful form move up and down the aisles, speaking in the voices of the myriad characters as if she already knew the parts and how it would end. Her words were notes of music: distinct, eloquent, a siren's song.

And she had the same effect on the children. They sat as if in a dream, watching her, hearing her, straining forward if she turned in the far direction. So uncommon was their behavior, Daniel would have called the doctor if he had not exhibited the same symptoms himself.

How long they continued in their trance he could not say, but he sensed their disappointment was as keen as his own when Miss Clarkson gently closed her copy of *Rob Roy*.

"I think we are all in need of some air and sunshine," she said as she walked to the door. "Miss Worthington tells me there is an excellent collection of hoops and balls for our use and I believe I see her just yonder. Shall we rest from our studies?"

Miss Clarkson did not have to repeat herself. The bubble of enchantment burst almost immediately, and there was a mad scramble to form the lines to pass through the door. Daniel watched as each of his children paused briefly as he or she met the schoolmistress at the door, and she rewarded each with a pat on the head and a sugar drop. He saw no reason why he should not expect the same—or better—so he waited until there remained only Timothy and Margaret, and joined the line himself.

When Miss Clarkson saw him she put her hand behind her back.

"Mr. Lennox!" she said in a falsely gay voice. "I did not expect you to be a student in my school. Is your education so poorly lacking you must apply for help with the children?"

"I daresay I learned enough to get by in life. But one never knows what one has missed. I have not yet read Mr. Scott's newest volume. I hope it surpasses *Old Mortality*."

He saw he surprised her, which had been his intent. It was not the time to disavow her of her prejudices, but he was tiring of her belief that he was the village idiot. He met her gaze and saw amber sparks in the deep brown of her eyes.

"I think you may enjoy *Rob Roy,* for it is one of his best. I have already read my own copy at least three times, so you may borrow mine when I am through with it here."

"I believe my own awaits my attention in my library. I have a fair collection and you may avail yourself of it at any time."

"Thank you," she said, and moved to pass him and go through into the garden. He did not budge and saw, to his pleasure, that it bothered her.

"Did you learn something this morning?" she asked a little breathlessly.

"Indeed, I did. I learned these chairs are capable of exquisite torture. I shall have to call upon my carpenters to construct something more comfortable if you expect to get through all of your precious book. I will not allow my children to be keen of mind and sore of backside." He waited for her to laugh, as nine out of ten women of his acquaintance surely would have done. But she did not. She looked expectant, waiting, her lips open as if she would speak but had not the words.

"But then, they might not even notice," he continued. "You seem to have enchanted them, Miss Clarkson. It is an unexpected quality in a schoolmistress and one for which I dared not hope. Now I suspect the little rogues will do whatever you desire." He paused, and realized he had managed to say the one thing to give her pleasure. Surely it could not be so easy. "It is a valuable stock in trade. Perhaps you will use it on my workmen someday."

Whatever brief advantage he had gained was now gone. Miss Clarkson frowned and backed away. "I do not wish to participate in the activities of your mill, Mr. Lennox. For the children, I make a special case. I will stay with them until a replacement can be found, as I have already said. But I will not be here long enough to educate the mill workers."

"I did not ask you to educate them. Only to get them to do what I desire."

"As to that, I would think you an expert yourself."

"My dear lady, I could not even get your own mother to take my school over the wilderness of America!"

"And yet you must have some ability, Mr. Lennox. I cannot imagine why else there are four Daniels in my little class. Perhaps you were closer to the truth than you dared admit when you said you feel responsible for the children of the mill."

"Miss Clarkson, you are ever honest and therefore I am sorry to disappoint you. In truth, those little boys bear my name out of simple respect. It is a custom in the country, you know. Children are named for the local gentry, perhaps with some expectation that they might find favor later in life. In this case, unfortunately, that favor has come many years too early."

"Their parents would have advanced their sons further if they had named them for the Duke of Glendennon. He surely is the loftiest person in these parts."

"I will not dispute it," Daniel said a little sulkily.

"And are there many boys bearing his name?"

"None that matter. The duke is yet to father a son."

"Well then! All the more reason to seek his favor, I would think. It might not do you any harm either."

"To father a son?" Daniel asked, wondering why this topic, of all things, should be interesting to her.

Miss Clarkson blushed. "To seek his favor, Mr. Lennox. Surely it would be advantageous for you to have a noble patron."

"I manage well without, Miss Clarkson."

"Is there nothing you desire, Mr. Lennox?" she asked, and lifted her face towards his. He was right about her talent for seduction, though he could not believe her thoughts were running in the same direction as his.

"I prefer to believe that what I desire will not be gained through noble influence, Miss Clarkson," Daniel said and, as if someone had nudged him from behind, started to lean toward her. Her lips parted slightly and her eyes remained fixed on his cravat.

"Dan! How unaccustomed a place to find you! In the classroom?" A voice Daniel knew too well, and would prefer to never hear again, came up behind him. He turned around to face his cousin, Peter Havers.

"Aha! Now I see what tempts you. It is no simple arithmetic or geography, but the lady I assume is your new schoolmistress." Peter bowed deeply from the waist and his pale blond hair swept forward like a drapery. "Welcome to Glenfell, dear lady. I would not have thought my cousin to have such excellent taste."

Daniel did not like the way Miss Clarkson's dark eyes glowed at Peter's stupid compliment.

"And yet we share some of that taste, do we not? Or do you merely admire Jane from afar?" Daniel asked pointedly. "But allow me to introduce Miss Clarkson to you. I am in her debt since she came in her mother's stead."

"We are all in Miss Clarkson's debt," Peter said in an accent he had affected after a trip to London two years before. He was capable of turning it on and off like a spigot. "For we have never been graced with such beauty and delicacy in Glenfell before."

"You are very kind, sir," said Miss Clarkson in a voice she never used with Daniel. "I can see you are a gentleman."

Was there a nerve in his whole body that would not be stripped raw by this woman? Who had sent her to him? Was she in collusion with his damned cousin?

"I am, dear lady, though it is a distinction often overlooked in Glenfell," Peter said as if he lived down by the river with the water rats. "We are a small society, and mingle regardless of rank. I daresay you will soon meet Mrs. Carroll, who is Glenfell's most popular hostess and plans most of the social events on our calendar."

"I would be delighted, sir. But I am surprised the duchess is not the mistress of Glenfell society. Is it not her privilege?"

"My grandmama?" Peter said, and Daniel said something rude. "It would give her pleasure, I am sure, but the duke is rather frail and does not go out in society much. However, I come with news of the duchess."

"I thought there must be a reason for you to make such a degrading descent," Daniel said uncharitably.

"There is," Peter answered, abandoning the London accent. "I thought you would like to hear it from me, particularly. The duchess is expectant of an heir."

"And why would I wish to hear it from you?" Daniel asked, aware of Miss Clarkson's wide-eyed curiosity. "It is usually the father's place to make such an announcement. Rarely have I heard such unbounded optimism in one only remotely connected to the business. But how are you certain it is a boy?"

Peter laughed as if Daniel were a simpleton, and looked to Miss Clarkson to share his amusement. The lady looked confused.

"It is past time the duke had a son and Jane thinks the odds are in her favor. She dreamt last night of little boy toys."

"An excellent forecaster, very reliable. I suppose she would not wish to know that even though my sisters often played with my toys in the nursery, they were not heirs to any great estates."

"Your sisters have nothing to do with this."

"Nor do you," Daniel answered tersely, fully aware Miss Clarkson's eyes were trained on him. "But I thank you for your information. If I dream of little lace dresses or embroidery hoops, I shall send word at once to Gleneyrie."

"You had best stay away, Cousin."

"I intend to," Daniel returned, "Cousin."

Peter turned to the schoolmistress and reached for her hand, kissing it as he bowed. Miss Clarkson did not look particularly impressed, but, all the same, it bothered Daniel that his interloping cousin should manage to kiss her before he did. He crossed his arms over his chest and waited for Peter to leave.

When he did, Miss Clarkson spoke first.

"Your cousin offers a pleasant diversion, but I am much belated in returning to the children. Is there anything else I might do for you, Mr. Lennox?"

Indeed, there is, he thought. But, instead, he looked over her shoulder to the large desk.

"I wonder at the collection of small items on your desk."

"Of course. They are gifts to me from the children. Some may be a good deal more useful than others."

"I see. Well, one never knows when there will be a shortage of rocks; you will be quite prepared," Daniel said, and was absurdly pleased to hear her laugh. "But I also see a swatch of blue fabric. Might it be silk?"

"It might, sir. I suspect one of the girls brought it."

"Do you mind very much if I abscond with it?"

"With my silk? I would not think it suited you, sir."

"You may yet find me full of surprises."

"I have already. Indeed, it is yours if you should wish it."

"I do," he said, and walked past her to retrieve it from the desk. It was a much damaged piece but useful enough for his purposes. "Thank you, Miss Clarkson. It has already proved helpful."

"Already, Mr. Lennox? And how is that possible?"

"Why, now I understand that if I wish to come to your classroom in the future, I shall have to bring an offering."

"If you behave yourself and do not interrupt my lessons, I may let you come just as you are."

"That, I believe, is a big concession on your part. Dare I imagine your first impression of me has been amended?" Daniel reached for her hand and was surprised to find it cold even when her cheeks looked flushed.

"Not at all, sir. It is just there are so many Daniels in my class, I will scarce notice you sitting there."

He looked at her hand, which he thought to kiss as Peter

had done just moments before. He changed his mind and released her.

"Then I shall have to prove myself, Miss Clarkson," he said, and walked with her out into the garden of waiting children.

Although Mr. Lennox had tantalized her with his promises of offerings and of proving himself, Emily scarcely glimpsed him over the course of the next week. She settled into a very predictable routine of work and leisure and felt the bonds of friendship forming very quickly with Ellen—now Nell—Worthington and Mrs. Bernays. The children soon distinguished themselves into individual characters and came to expect certain things of her in the classroom. Emily, in turn, came to expect things of them.

She gave up, however, on the notion of expecting things from her employer. She was not invited again to Shearings, either for dinner or for a tour of his library, and wondered why his apparent rejection of her should pain her quite as much as it did.

It was a theme upon which she dwelled far too often, as when she arose in the morning, paused in the classroom, or lay awake in her large and lonely bed. She took to walking about the fields and gardens in the late afternoon wondering where he was and if it was at all likely their paths might intersect.

They never did.

But on a misty afternoon when the morning's rain glistened in the tall grasses, Emily met up with other young men and with happier results.

As was her custom, she walked a route very similar to that by which Mr. Lennox had first brought her on her first outing at GlenLennox. She circled a large mill building, and set out through the burned-out field where so many people had lost their lives. On this day, the dampness aroused the scents of the fire and smoke, and Emily thought she would be ill from it.

But as she hurried through the rubble, she spied some movement at the far end of the field and paused, hoping it was not the children who came here.

It was not. The deep voices of two men echoed over the foundation stones of the ruins and they seemed engaged in some argument. One of them pulled off a cap as she approached and she recognized Mr. Havers' flaxen hair. The other man, very dark and stern, was not at all familiar to her.

"Miss Clarkson!" Mr. Havers called out. "What on earth are you doing here? It is a very dangerous place."

Emily came closer. "I have been walking here for over a week and have not found it so, Mr. Havers. Do you or your friend mean to tell me otherwise?"

Peter Havers looked at his companion as if he had forgotten he was there. "Forgive me. Allow me to introduce Captain Milrose, who delivers GlenLennox cotton to America. This is Miss Clarkson."

"It is a pleasure to meet you, sir. My mother is presently in America, where she is a teacher."

"I wish her well," the captain answered. "It could not have been an easy journey."

"I have not yet heard from her, so I do not know. But perhaps there will be a letter when I return to London."

"Do you not intend to stay long with us, Miss Clarkson?" Mr. Havers broke in. "I am sorry to hear it."

Emily looked at him in surprise, for he did not sound merely polite. "I never intended to stay, sir. But why does it matter?"

Mr. Havers glanced at his companion, and then toed the damp earth with his well-polished boot.

"There is a dinner party soon at Mrs. Carroll's home. Do you recall we spoke of her? I should like it very much if you would attend with me."

Emily felt both flattered and bothered by the invitation. Was it not Mr. Lennox's business to invite her? Or did he not wish to attend social occasions with one of his employees? And yet, she was not beneath the notice of the duke's grandson. In truth, she hardly knew him, but as he was Mr. Lennox's cousin, surely it was acceptable behavior to agree to be escorted by him.

"But I do not know Mrs. Carroll," she remembered belatedly. "I have not been invited."

"I assure you, Miss Clarkson, Mrs. Carroll does not issue particular invitations. We are not so formal here. And it will allow you the opportunity to meet everyone in the neighborhood."

"Will Mr. Lennox be attending?"

"Has he not mentioned it? No, I see he has not. Well, he can have no objections to what you do out of the classroom, can he? I am sure you will see him there, in any case."

Peter Havers' words had the effect of strengthening Emily's resolve at once. Indeed, what did it matter what Mr. Lennox felt or did? He had more or less abandoned her to her own resources.

"I would like very much to attend with you, Mr. Havers. Will you also be at the dinner, Captain Milrose?"

"I cannot say. You are likely to meet my sister, however."

"She is Daniel's particular favorite," Mr. Havers added.

"Then I should like to meet her as well," Emily said sweetly. When neither man said anything, she went on. "I shall see you soon, then, Mr. Havers. Good day to you both."

Both men bowed but neither extended a protest nor an offer of accompanying her. Emily looked from one to the other and turned onto the path that led to the river. As she walked away, she remained very conscious of the two men watching her, and soon heard them resume their heated discussion.

Chapter Five

Though Daniel Lennox had the means to conduct his business in surroundings of extreme luxury—or not conduct any business at all, if he should choose—he loved his cramped and somewhat mildewed office in the old mill. Built stone upon stone by his father's father, and much improved upon by the next two generations, it brought Daniel both tactile pleasures and spiritual comforts. With

Nolly at his side, a dozen men interrupting the affairs of his day, and the steady thrum of industry ever present in the workings around him, it was also a place of great companionship and joy.

He had once thought to manage his operations from the huge library at Shearings, where he was tutored in such matters by his ailing father. But as the older man grew weaker and more despondent, Daniel sought strength from the very source of their family's wealth and power. He gradually shifted his papers to a large room on the ground floor of the mill, where he could look out onto the workings of the great wheels and the large central yard where most of his people passed each day.

More importantly, the people who worked for him could see him among them, no complacent rich man, but as industrious as they.

"We shall have to have a talk with Alsop Parker, Nolly," Daniel remarked one afternoon, while otherwise enjoying such a view. He stood and stretched his back, stiff after hours at his desk. "This week he has thrice missed days in the office."

"So he has, Dan," Nolly answered, without looking up from his ledger. "If you wish to dismiss him, I would be happy to do your dirty work. In fact, it would give me great pleasure to see the old warthog leave for good. I neither trust him nor like him, and have never understood why you do."

"I do not. But there's no harm in him. Do not forget . . ."

"You need not remind me. Your grandfather and father trusted him, so you must do the same. In all other things, you are an original, but in this matter feel compelled to honor a tired legacy. I suppose it is not altogether a bad thing. Someday, when I am old and doddering, I shall have to rely on the goodness of your son and grandson to provide me with respectable labor."

"If you would like to begin collecting a pension this very day, and retire with Nell Worthington, you have my blessing."

"Your blessing you could keep. 'Tis your money I want."

"And much good may it do you. It does not seem to have worked very well for me," Daniel said, unreasonably.

"Because a lady of unstable temperament and little self-regard chose to scorn your attentions?" Nolly spoke with the confidence of a man who knew he was getting his own heart's desire. "Jane was not good enough for you, my friend."

"She was good enough for a duke."

"I daresay it depends upon the duke," Nolly said lightly.

Daniel turned away from his friend to find solace elsewhere, but it seemed even his mill yard would provide no comfort for him just now. Walking across the brick path, pausing here and there to greet men and women whom she seemed to know well, was Miss Clarkson. She wore a short red jacket which could not possibly have provided adequate protection from the cool air, but which, as it nevertheless emphasized her narrow waist and rounded hips, warmed Daniel Lennox to discomfort. Her dark bonnet, crowned with some sort of red feathery thing that danced in the breeze, was set back from her face so that one could admire her pert nose and high cheekbones. As she came closer, Daniel could see her dark eyes dancing as she took in the whole energetic scene around her, until they finally settled on the very window at which he stood.

Daniel ducked behind the screen. "We have a visitor, Nolly."

"Our good friend Alsop? Excellent."

"Nay, nothing so simple. It is a woman who seems to have befriended each person at GlenLennox, and has probably already convinced even you to side with her in every argument she might have with me," Daniel said ungenerously.

"A lady both brave and beautiful," murmured Nolly.

Daniel made a gesture of impatience. "I am not speaking of Nell, though you are lucky to have won her."

"I am lucky, but neither am I speaking of Nell. I refer to Miss Clarkson."

Daniel said nothing, knowing that to reveal something of the acutely uncomfortable stirrings he felt for the lady would make him the object of good-natured ribbing, even from his best friend. Worse, he would be pitied. Men in love seemed to pity anyone who did not share their happiness.

Surely Nolly would soon enough be disenchanted with the admirable Emily Clarkson. She undoubtedly came now to accost her employer in his own sanctuary and to make some demands on his resources. Or on his sanity. Perhaps in her idle time she had come up with ten reasons why he was not a gentleman, or why the children should be put to work in the mill. In any case, her manner might provide the perfect antidote to Nolly's unmerited praise.

On the other hand, he had been neglecting her of late. He had not returned to the school, nor spoken to her. But both Nell and Mrs. Bernays gave him daily reports on her progress and the children spoke of little else. Truly, he saw no occasion to speak to Miss Clarkson in person.

There was an upcoming occasion, however, and it did require his special attention. He might have already sought out his schoolmistress to discuss it, but hesitated to ask yet another favor of her. He also did not wish to appear too anxious, for he would not want her to believe he felt anything other than merely obliged to help her settle into society in Glenfell. It was a matter of some delicacy.

As Miss Clarkson approached the door, she slowed her step and raised a gloved hand to her brow. She brushed a few wisps of straying dark hair under her bonnet, and ran her fine teeth over her lips. Daniel knew women well enough to understand the purpose of that little gesture, and felt pleased by the compliment. Someday, perhaps, she would allow him to return the compliment and let him tell her her lips did not need to be enhanced with artifice.

Of course, he doubted such a day would ever come.

"Shall I let the lady in, or do you propose to leave her outside until she gives up her knocking?" Nolly asked, still looking down at his ledger.

Daniel snapped to attention, and glanced at his own reflection in the window to make sure his cravat was well tied. "I was merely meditating about . . . the next delivery of cotton. David will need be quick with it. And yes, I will let the lady in. She thinks me no better than a servant, in any case."

When he opened the door, Miss Clarkson swept into the room on a breeze of cold, fresh autumn air, and nodded briefly to the two occupants of the room. "I am grateful you decided to let me in, Mr. Lennox. It is unseasonably chill this morning. But did you forget how to use the latch, sir? I saw you contemplating it for an uncommon length of time."

It would not be wise to tell her he had contemplated only her, and would not mind doing so for another uncommon length of time.

"My tutor instructed me in its use, as in all things, Miss Clarkson," Daniel said, though he lied. The elderly crank who had once given him the rudiments of a gentlemanly education had told him nothing about handling vexatious ladies. "I consider myself fairly proficient at it. But I hesitated because I could not be sure you truly wished to enter such an odious place as my mill office."

Miss Clarkson stood silently, and seemed to be studying the buttons on his jacket. Looking down on her thus, he could see how her long lashes made delicate shadows on her cheekbones. They fluttered once, and then again.

"You seem to think me the worst sort of prig, Mr. Lennox. We may all confront situations unpleasant or odious, and would rather be elsewhere. But circumstances conspire against each of us, and force people to accept the consequences of the decisions we—and those close to us—make. I would rather be in London. My mother would rather be in America. My aunt would, I believe, rather be married to a certain patient gentleman than have the care of me." Her lashes seemed to be dotted with tiny drops of moisture. She looked up then, and the small smile on her lips belied her tears. "And you, sir, would clearly rather be holed up in this small tomb of an office than visit the schoolhouse and observe the progress of your children. How will you know if I succeed with them?"

Daniel shifted uncomfortably and took a step backward. She was right, of course. He, who prided himself on direct involvement in all aspects of his business, had not returned to her classroom. "I need not witness the lessons, only the results. And that will take years to achieve. As you have already assured me that your tenure is to be a short one, my time is better spent seeking a new schoolmistress than observing my present one."

As soon as the words were out, Daniel regretted them. He saw the sudden look of pain in her dark brown eyes, but could not account for it. She despised this place, did she not? And she made it very clear she considered him a poor, low thing. Why should it matter to Miss Clarkson whether he graced her classroom or not?

She stiffened and raised her arrogant little chin. "You are quite right, sir. What I can do in a short span of weeks will not engender immediate results and is therefore not worth your precious while. The ability to read does not come so easily as the construction of a building or the paving of a road. One needs to position one brick at a time and, in some cases, the foundation is very shaky."

"Can it not be rebuilt?" he asked. "Is it not my greatest hope that you will lay down those stones for my children and build sturdily upon it?"

"I am not convinced that anything so poorly conceived can ever be made right," Emily Clarkson said slowly, and Daniel would have wagered his mill they were no longer talking about the classroom. Behind him, Nolly cleared his throat a bit too loudly. Before him, his defiant schoolmistress looked thoughtful.

He leaned across his cluttered desk and his fingers closed on his hat. "Miss Clarkson, would you care to walk with me a while? I feel the need for a respite." He held out his elbow, hoping to secure her arm, but she held back.

"You take pleasure in putting me in my place, sir, but I have never before been called a 'respite.' "

"But I am every bit as rude as you prefer to believe, Miss Clarkson. There is my only excuse."

"Would that you applied your energies to some of the finer things in life. You might elevate yourself," she said, but finally relented and give him her hand. He felt his body respond to her casual touch and wondered why this difficult woman had such an effect on him. It was boyish, even absurd. Her choice of words had a meaning she could not possibly guess at.

"Mr. Haines, will you be able to manage here without me?" Daniel asked, his voice hoarse.

"Almost certainly, Mr. Lennox," Nolly said in mock deference. As Daniel followed Miss Clarkson out the door, his friend added: "And if you have not returned in an hour, shall I come to rescue you?"

Daniel turned sharply and shook his head. If he managed

to secure a full hour of Miss Clarkson's company, he did not think he would wish to be rescued.

Emily felt Mr. Lennox tug on her arm as he turned back to answer something Mr. Haines asked. She walked on, feeling somewhat defeated, understanding how very reluctantly the mill owner deigned to accompany her. Why had she even imagined that a man in his position, responsible for so much, could care about the work she did and the children's progress? After all, she had already made it quite clear she did not intend to fulfill the terms of her mother's employment.

And yet, in only a few days, Emily had discovered talents she had never known existed. She took heart and comfort from the voices of the children, and courage from their efforts. She relished their small triumphs and felt satisfaction in knowing they owed some small part of their success to her. She enjoyed the honest, open friendship of Nell Worthington, and enjoyed playing the part of mistress in a home she did not own, but nevertheless ruled. Even when she tumbled into bed, exhausted and drained, her thoughts lingered on what she had accomplished that day, and how she might begin the next.

For the first time in her life she understood something of her mother's relentless passion, of how a generous, adventurous spirit could find satisfaction in some great pursuit. Mrs. Clarkson, unable to share her husband's noble work, sought her own outlets, her own triumphs. It was not in her nature to be a society matron, nor in her inclination to be a mother.

Emily was not certain she possessed that adventurous spirit; neither was she ready to abstain from those pleasures her genteel life allowed her to expect to be her rewards. But she thought she might find momentary happiness situated as she was in Mr. Lennox's noisy, invigorating empire. If only he would let her stay.

"Miss Clarkson, I expect you have sought me out for some purpose," Mr. Lennox said, and drew her down a path sloping toward the river. "I know you would rather be anywhere but in my company, so I am certain you have something to say that is sure to vex or confound me. Come, out with it. My curiosity will kill me, which, now I think on it, might be exactly your objective."

Emily glanced up at him, hoping to see his teasing smile and his eyes bright with amusement. But instead he looked very businesslike, almost grave. It was too late, she realized; whatever glimmerings of interest she had sensed when first they met surely were dead by now. She was a fool not to have recognized that one could not persist in insulting a man and expect him to continue to find pleasure in one's company.

"I am to be tortured, then," he sighed. "Come, watch your footing here. The path needs improvement."

Indeed, she did need to watch her footing when she was with Mr. Lennox.

"I came to your . . . I sought you out, as you say, to let you . . . to announce a change in my plans," she stumbled, artlessly.

"I see," he said, and jumped off a small ledge. He turned and, as if it were the most natural thing in the world, reached up and caught her by the waist as she followed him down. He held her a moment too long, and Emily dared not look up into his face. "Will you be leaving us sooner than expected, Miss Clarkson?"

Emily thought he sounded pleased by the prospect. "No," she said slowly. "It is quite the opposite. I expect I might stay on in Glenfell longer than I anticipated. My obligations in London have been somewhat alleviated, and it is possible for me to remain."

He shot her a look, utterly unreadable, and then turned toward the churning river. She studied his set jaw, and noticed he had missed a spot while shaving. A few weeks ago, she would have taken pleasure in noting that if he were a gentleman, he would have a valet who would take care in such things. But now, she only imagined Mr. Lennox was preoccupied with too much else to have it matter.

Indeed, it did not matter. The only thing that did matter was his answer.

"And your gentleman friend?" he asked.

"My gentleman friend?" she answered in confusion. Too late, Emily realized she had fallen into a trap of her own making.

"Yes, your gentleman friend," he repeated, as if he spoke

to an idiot. "Did you not tell me I was depriving you of your lover by demanding you come to work at my school? Has the gentleman relented? Or has he agreed to follow you here?"

For the first time in weeks Emily thought about several men who had occupied her time in London, but who had rarely occupied her thoughts then or now.

"I suppose you would like to meet him," Emily retaliated, though she thought of no one in particular. "But you need not fear another guest imposing on your hospitality. I have broken it off." And then, because she could not resist, "The gentleman is heartbroken, you understand. I think it better if I stay away for a while, to allow the rumors to die down."

"I see. And why did you break it off? Were you being noble, by not allowing him to marry a woman tainted by employment?"

"What I do in my private life can be of no concern to you, Mr. Lennox," Emily said and started to walk away.

He grabbed her arm a little roughly. "If you walk that way, you will wind up in the river. And I am not in the mood to jump in after you." He loosened his grip, but urged a new direction.

Emily shook off his hand. "I am sure I would not need saving, Mr. Lennox. Especially from you. I have been to Brighton and can hold my head above water with reasonable competence."

Mr. Lennox gave a low whistle. "Can you indeed? And do you think being attached to a dipper whose bathing machine is not five feet away is comparable to keeping yourself alive in this roaring swell? I know you regard yourself very highly, but I must tell you that men, strong men who have lived along the Fell all their lives, have perished in those waters." He kicked a rock off the path, and it tumbled down the embankment. "My father among them."

"Your father?" Emily gasped. "What a tragic accident!"

"It was not an accident."

Emily sucked in her breath and the air was icy in her lungs. "Murder?" she whispered in disbelief.

Mr. Lennox took a step backward and ran his long fingers through his hair, adding to the havoc already worked by the wind.

"What have you been reading, my dear Miss Clarkson? We have no murder here in Glenfell. Ours is a small, peaceful community. Babies are born, children attend school, lovers marry, people work, men and women die in old age."

"Workers are burned to death in a mill fire, children are orphaned, the two most powerful men in town despise each other, cousins are at odds," Emily countered. "Really, Mr. Lennox, you must think me a simpleton. There is more drama here in Glenfell than I ever knew in London."

"Is that why you wish to remain?"

"Oh no, Mr. Lennox. You read me wrong. I am not the sort of person who yearns for adventure or who wishes to have her life the material for a novel. I might observe the drama around me without having any desire to have a part in it. The schoolroom is the perfect diversion for me, I believe. I do some good there, and am content. Is that not enough reason to remain a bit longer?"

Daniel Lennox did not answer, and Emily wondered if he thought her explanation insufficient. But what else did he want of her?

"Shall we walk to the old water mill, Miss Clarkson?" he asked unexpectedly, avoiding the subject she suddenly realized she did not necessarily want addressed. "It is particularly picturesque, and the subject of several landscape paintings. Reynolds himself came here to paint it, and accomplished it nobly. You may have seen the painting in my dining room at Shearings. It includes the only portrait of my estimable grandfather."

"Your father's father?" she asked casually.

"Yes. He is the only grandfather I knew. But he more than compensated for the lack of relations on the other branches of the family tree."

"But your own branch seems reasonably full. I confess, I envy it a bit. You have sisters, whereas I was my parents' only child. And you have a cousin, at least, and I have none. Other than my parents, my Aunt Constance is my only relative," Emily said.

But Mr. Lennox seemed to be brooding over his own concerns. "You have a habit of willfully misunderstanding me, Miss Clarkson, so I will warn you not to mistake what I am about to say. I do love my sisters, and enjoy the good company of their husbands and children. But families are not always congenial and some relations are capable of giving more pain than pleasure."

Emily knew at once she had opened a raw wound, though she could not account for it in anything she knew of Mr. Lennox's history. It could only be Peter Havers of whom he spoke, and she wondered anew how much a man who labored for his living must naturally envy a man who enjoyed the patronage of a duke. She guessed Mr. Lennox had not been pleased to learn she intended to go to Mrs. Carroll's dinner party with Peter Havers and therefore avoided her company.

"Here is the old mill, Miss Clarkson," he said before she could respond. "It was the first such structure along the length of this fair river, but in recent years it has been joined by more modern machinery. There are those who are experimenting with other sources of power, but I doubt if water-driven wheels will ever become obsolete. Do I bore you with this talk, Miss Clarkson?"

Emily watched the splendid antique wheel, thick with moss, catch the water and toss it downriver. Above the great arc, a rainbow bridged the Fell.

"Not at all, Mr. Lennox," Emily said, "though I am as surprised as anyone to hear myself say it. I have never given a thought to such matters, but now find myself quite curious."

"Well, then," Mr. Lennox said, looking pleased. He put his hands in his pockets and rocked gently on his heels, very much in the manner of a man who has a business proposition to discuss. "If my conversation is not entirely odious to you, perhaps you would grant me your company Tuesday night, at a dinner party given by my old friend, Mrs. Carroll. You should be introduced to many people in the neighborhood, and will begin to feel a part of us."

Emily looked up at him in dismay.

"I would enjoy a continuation of this conversation, sir. But I cannot accept your offer. Your cousin already invited me to attend the dinner as his escort, and I agreed to go with him."

"You . . . already accepted him? Without consulting me?"

"Consulting you, sir?" Emily asked in disbelief. Really,

why had she imagined him suddenly approachable? Mr. Lennox once again proved himself a disagreeable oaf. "Have I not already said you cannot dictate my personal affairs, Mr. Lennox? Your cousin asked me some days ago, at a time when you were scarcely civil to me."

"And he was scarcely known to you!" Mr. Lennox shot back.

"No more or less than you, sir. Indeed, you had already provided the introduction. Why should I not accept the invitation of the cousin of my employer?"

"Because he is not a man of honor. His aim is to bother and insult me, and to provoke me in any way possible."

"But now it is you who are insulting, Mr. Lennox."

He turned on her then, and Emily, for the first time, saw something dangerous in him. "Why is that so?" he asked.

"Because you imply Mr. Havers only asked me so he might insult you. Is it not possible he may wish to be with me?"

"It is very possible, Miss Clarkson. And I do not intend to pry into your personal affairs," Mr. Lennox ground out slowly. "But as you are my responsibility, it is necessarily of some concern where you go, and with whom."

"I am sure my Aunt Constance did not expect you to play the role of a society matron, Mr. Lennox. Neither would she think you an appropriate chaperone, though I could do much to assure her of your disinterest in me," Emily said, and realized how much pleasure it gave her to try to provoke him. "But have you any specific objection to Peter Havers? Other than he stands in favor with the Duke of Glendennon?"

"I do not trust him," Mr. Lennox said.

"Well, Mr. Lennox," Emily said slowly, observing his arrogant stance and angry eyes. "You shall have to do better than that. As an argument, it scarcely owns merit, for, you see, I do not trust you either."

Trustworthy or not, Peter Havers appeared at the doorway on Tuesday next, where Mrs. Bernays greeted him cordially, if not with her customary enthusiasm.

"Ah! Two beautiful ladies!" he said cheerfully, overlooking the housekeeper's solemn mien, and Emily's quiet greeting.

Emily glanced at Mrs. Bernays, who sniffed disdainfully,

and said, "I thank you for your compliment, sir. I am sure there are ladies who consider me quite impertinent for having accepted your invitation, as I am sure you are much in favor."

Rather than modestly demur, as would have come naturally to most gentlemen, Peter Havers preened before them. Indeed, he looked very admirable, with his bright head of hair and tall lean figure. Seeing him now in a close-fitting jacket, Emily appreciated how much he lacked Mr. Lennox's muscular strength, but looked more the gentleman in consequence.

Mrs. Bernays seemed not the least bit impressed, and Mr. Havers turned his back on her as he leaned close to Emily. "They shall have to be content with Mr. Lennox, then, to whom I usually bequeath my leavings."

It seemed such a profoundly ungenerous thing to say, Emily herself now stood unimpressed. Mr. Havers suddenly looked neither handsome nor cheerful, and certainly not nearly so gracious as his rude cousin.

"I can only hope to be a worthy partner to one so lovely as yourself, Miss Clarkson," he continued, undoubtedly for Mrs. Bernays' benefit. "And I am certain the gentlemen in London already told you how superbly your gown compliments your hair."

Indeed, the gentlemen in London told her a good many things, but she did not believe any of it.

"Her hair will turn gray waiting for you to take her to the party, Peter," Mrs. Bernays said abruptly. "Are you going or not?"

"Of course, Mrs. Bernays," Mr. Havers answered as if the housekeeper had not been ruder than a London fish-monger. "But we will certainly not be the last to arrive. I noticed Mr. Lennox's coach in the drive when I arrived."

"Mr. Lennox may come and go as he pleases, Mr. Havers," Mrs. Bernays sniffed.

"And so shall we. It pleases me to go just now, in fact."

Emily smiled because his comment seemed to require it, though his wit strained at the seams. She sent an apologetic look to Mrs. Bernays, who looked as if she would like to murder them both.

"You expect Mr. Lennox to attend, Mr. Havers?" Emily asked when they were finally out the door.

"Oh, I do not doubt it. There is a certain lady he will be most anxious to see," Mr. Havers said, and smiled too brightly.

More than a hour later, falsely buoyed by eloquent flattery, Emily finally confirmed that Mr. Lennox's purpose in coming to Mrs. Carroll's party had nothing to do with herself.

Mrs. Carroll proved an amiable hostess, and greeted Emily like a friend, confiding an interest in her work at the school.

"I wonder if I may come to visit you some day, and observe your noble endeavor, Miss Clarkson," she said. "I myself am a supporter of many of Daniel's ideas. I believe he is in correspondence with Harriet Martineau herself."

"Miss Martineau is also in correspondence with my mother, Mrs. Carroll. In fact, I believe it was she who convinced my estimable relation to venture into the American wilderness. I am here in her stead, you realize."

"Daniel must be pleased."

"I should think not, Mrs. Carroll. I do not hold with most of Miss Martineau's and my mother's ideas."

"And Daniel's?"

"I have been at his mill nearly a month and I believe I can safely say we agree on almost nothing."

"I . . . see," Mrs. Carroll said thoughtfully. "Is that why you are here with Peter? Because you and Daniel cannot agree on anything? Or is it, Miss Clarkson, because you simply prefer a gentleman from Gleneyrie to a mill owner?"

"You must think me the worst sort of snob, Mrs. Carroll," Emily said defensively, knowing Mrs. Carroll spoke the truth. "I accepted Mr. Havers' invitation for the very best of reasons. He asked me first. Belatedly, Daniel Lennox requested my company for this evening, and I cannot believe he really meant to have it."

"Of course he did, dear. Daniel always means what he says. It may be his mind was preoccupied with other things."

"I am sure of it, Mary." Mr. Havers interrupted by coming between them. "After all, he will have the opportunity to see Jane this night. I may take her company for granted, but Daniel certainly does not."

Mary Carroll looked at Mr. Havers coldly.

"She must be the very best of women," Emily said agreeably, not understanding the tension Jane provoked.

"She who was once Jane Weldon may not be so very good as some would believe. Indeed, it was once my intent to convince a certain gentleman of her obvious shortcomings. But I am cryptic, Miss Clarkson, and it is most unfair." Mrs. Carroll glanced back at Mr. Havers, who appeared distracted by a lady in white. "Jane Weldon is now a duchess, and we must respect her."

"I have heard Mr. Lennox once loved her," Emily said quietly, with certainty.

"Some believe he loves her still. Poor Miss Milrose pines for his attention, and there are others who visit him at his office on some flimsy excuse. I believe if his search for a young schoolmistress had been known, a dozen ladies would have waited in line for an interview. But he made it quite clear he sought a mature woman." Mrs. Carroll looked at Emily expectantly.

"He hired my mother for the position," Emily reminded her. "He did not anticipate the substitution. Nor desire it."

"I daresay he did not," Mrs. Carroll responded too quickly. "In any case, we once expected our Daniel to marry Jane Weldon. But when the old duke offered for her, Jane accepted in a moment. Who among us can account for feelings of the heart?"

"Are you still speaking of my lovesick cousin?" Mr. Havers returned to them, the lady in white having been claimed by another gentleman. Emily thought his strategy well conceived: he allowed himself to appear diverted but apparently heard every word of conversations in which he did not have a part. "Daniel is very resentful of the duke's triumph. But some believe he merely waits for the old man to die, and then might reclaim his former love."

Mrs. Carroll laughed and tapped him playfully with her fan. "He might not be the only one betting on that horse," she said.

Emily glanced at her hostess and her escort, and realized there was much she had yet to learn about Glenfell society.

And yet, glittering with candlelight and reflecting crystal, echoing with the conversations of many people, Mrs. Carroll's affair was as familiar as anything Emily had attended in London.

As she and Peter Havers came through the tall arched doorway into the ballroom, every person seemed to pause in conversation and acknowledge their presence. Emily guessed they deferred to the duke's grandson, but that illustrious flatterer promptly abandoned her to the company of half a dozen young ladies.

"Why, you must be Miss Clarkson," a sweet voice sang, not waiting for a formal introduction. "I am Beatrice De-Witt, a very good friend of the Lennox family. Lady Gray told me all about you and your noble mission."

"How kind of her to pave my way, Miss DeWitt. But I think it only fair to tell you it was more my mother's mission than my own. I still walk a very uncertain path," Emily said honestly. "But I feel a good deal steadier this night. Mrs. Carroll has been most warm in her welcome."

"Mrs. Carroll always warms to a new source of gossip!" Miss DeWitt laughed. "But she is not alone, as most of us are very happy to greet newcomers. We tend to grow tired of our own company, and heartily desire new faces, new voices, new views. You grace us by providing all three, though there will be some who will not be happy to see how very pretty your new face truly is!"

"I am only the schoolmistress," Emily demurred.

"Ah, yes, I forget," Miss DeWitt said solemnly before adding, "And Daniel Lennox is only a mill owner!"

Emily was not sure she understood why the other ladies found this uproarious, but suspected it had to do with his bright eyes.

"Do not mind these impertinent ladies, my dear," said an older lady with a gentleman in tow. "We are most anxious to meet you. I am Mrs. Cafferty and here is my husband, who once worked with your fine father. He now attends the Duke of Glendennon."

The gentleman bowed neatly. "It is an honor to meet the daughter of Dr. Clarkson. He proved a healer of the highest rank."

"And yet he attended to the lowest," Emily pointed out, a bit put off by Mrs. Cafferty's insistence on her husband's elevation.

"As you do as well," Mrs. Cafferty continued smoothly. "I sometimes wondered why your father bothered so much with those whose lives were of such little value. I might ask you the same."

The question startled Emily into an admission so honest she had not yet considered it.

"Mrs. Cafferty, surely every life is of great value."

Her words dropped into a circle of silence. Indeed, not only had Emily apparently stupefied Mrs. Carroll's guests, but she astonished even herself.

"No wonder Daniel speaks of nothing but you, Miss Clarkson," another lady sighed, astonishing Emily even further. "I am Catherine Milrose, a very old friend."

"Mrs. Milrose; it is a pleasure. I already met your husband."

A titter of amusement followed Emily's comment.

"Have you? Then perhaps you may introduce him to me, for I have so far searched in vain," she said, and the others laughed. "But you must be talking of my brother, Captain David Milrose."

"Of course. I am sorry for the misunderstanding."

"No matter, Miss Clarkson. There is much you do not yet know about our little neighborhood," Miss Milrose answered. "We are not as simple as we seem, nor as provincial as you must imagine. Indeed, some of us have very high expectations."

Miss Milrose raised her chin and looked over Emily's shoulder, giving the impression she gazed upon some distant, imaginary horizon. Emily thought her very precious and fey, until she realized all the other ladies followed her direction.

Emily turned, even as she guessed the source of their interest. She hardly knew him, not really, and yet she already felt the unbidden tingling of her senses whenever he came near.

Standing in the doorway, head and shoulders above almost all the rest, Daniel Lennox looked over the crowd of guests. His bright eyes darted, then lingered, and his ready smile greeted several people who bowed before him. He looked every bit the prosperous merchant, sporting a fine jacket well cut to his muscular frame, and fashionably snug trousers. Eschewing the ornate style of London dandies, Daniel wore a plain white shirt, its only ornament a simply knotted cravat. As he turned his head, Emily saw a raw bruise on his left cheekbone.

And then he turned back, instinctively tuned to the coterie of admiring ladies, and met Emily's eyes.

She did not have to know what he thought of her already standing comfortably among his cronies, for the suspicion seemed apparent in his eyes and his smile vanished at once. Though still at some distance, he studied her with an intimacy belied by the presence of so many others.

"Daniel! Do come here!" called Miss DeWitt and, to the others, "Is it possible he came alone?"

Mrs. Cafferty offered an explanation. "Perhaps there is one he would like to see here, and it best be done without the company of another lady. Poor boy."

No one else seemed to pity Mr. Lennox in the least. As guests in the crowded room opened up a path for him, the ladies in Emily's circle quickly checked their laces and pinched their cheeks. Emily remained still, certain he approached only her.

"Miss Clarkson," he began, and then seemed acutely aware of his very curious audience. He spoke as a distant acquaintance. "I see you managed to extricate yourself from the classroom and your lessons. I hope you have no children in tow?"

"They make excellent company, Mr. Lennox, often surpassing the adults of my acquaintance. And they try very hard to please me, which is more than I can say for many others."

"You think me remiss, Miss Clarkson? I shall endeavor to keep you happy, or else I may find myself tutoring the children myself. It would be a hard business, for I have not a tenth of your patience."

"Nor the time, I daresay," murmured Miss Milrose. "My brother tells me you are uncommonly busy, Daniel, with problems recently arisen at the mill."

"At the mill, and elsewhere," Mr. Lennox answered, his eyes never leaving Emily's.

"Perhaps Daniel takes too much onto his shoulders." Dr. Cafferty returned to the conversation. "Though it looks like something was aimed a bit higher."

Daniel Lennox glared at the doctor and pressed his fingers against the bruise on his cheek. Close as he was, now

Emily could better see the purplish discoloration of his skin, just above the line of his beard. It looked unbearably painful. Even so, Daniel's broad shoulders seemed sturdy enough to take on a good deal more.

"I believe my opponent's aim on target, and not entirely unprovoked," Mr. Lennox said steadily. "But I always defend what is mine. Or what ought to be."

He glanced at Emily, who hardly dared to guess what he meant.

"We will have no talks of fights here, gentlemen," said Mrs. Cafferty, "for this must be an evening of celebration."

"What are we celebrating, my dear lady?" Mr. Lennox asked.

"You should know better than everyone else, Daniel. We celebrate the presence of a lovely lady in our society," said Mrs. Cafferty. "We welcome Miss Clarkson."

The others murmured their agreement and Emily felt flattered. While the neighborhood here was small, its generosity was great.

"There is something else to toast, which Daniel should also know better than anyone else," his cousin said suddenly, his entrance predictable and well-timed. Emily wondered how much of the conversation he had heard. "Our lady, the Duchess of Glendennon, is expectant of an heir."

"I believe you give us stale news, Mr. Havers," Mr. Lennox said and turned to Emily. "Miss Clarkson, would you be . . ."

"But you must think on it almost every minute, Daniel. It concerns you as it concerns no one else," Peter Havers insisted. Emily believed that in that moment she began to despise him.

Mr. Lennox flushed, and his bruise disappeared altogether. Emily thought she had never witnessed such a display of suppressed anger; the suppression was admirable, the anger justified.

"As I am not the lady's husband and as the child is not mine, I suspect the business concerns me not at all. However, it seems to interest you a great deal, Cousin. I wonder why that is so?"

One of the ladies gasped, and Dr. Cafferty took several steps to remove himself from the circle. Emily looked around her in all wonder, shocked by Mr. Lennox's implication. Surely he did not accuse his cousin of the very behavior he himself repudiated?

She waited for his angry words to be handily disputed. But they were not.

Though Miss Clarkson allowed him to believe she preferred his damned cousin to himself, Daniel sensed the shifting tide of her allegiance during the scene in Mrs. Carroll's ballroom. He felt her move closer to his side, and saw her look of repugnance when Peter began his advance. He also saw she remained very much in the dark as to the complicated web of relationships and loyalties in Glenfell. Good, and better.

Better still, she did not seem to mind when he slipped his arm through hers and led her out to the refreshment buffet. They walked away from Peter, who was flirting shamelessly with Cat Milrose, and neatly avoided the company of the Caffertys, who looked at Miss Clarkson with such speculation they would have him betrothed and married by morning. But Emily Clarkson seemed not to notice any of them, and Daniel admired her fortitude.

"Your position seems to be a very dangerous one, Mr. Lennox," she said between tiny sips of her lemonade punch.

He swallowed his in one ungentlemanly gulp, and the acid burned his throat. "If you refer to my quarrel with my . . ."

"I refer to your cheek, Mr. Lennox," she said gently, and reached up to trace the outline of his bruise. It was impossibly bold of her, but he did not mind if they had witnesses, for her soft touch was balm not only to the wound but to his anger. "I cannot imagine how anyone as civilized as you claim to be can partake in such primitive tactics. It sets a bad example."

He was a fool to think she felt concern for him. As always, she thought only about her charges in the schoolroom.

"It would be naive to think a study of Latin or geography sufficient for survival, Miss Clarkson. I wish only for the children to succeed in this life. Some may do it by the pen, and others by their fists. They may perceive how I manage very well on both counts," Daniel said, and waited for Miss

Clarkson to debate him. Instead, she stood pensive and quiet, studying the yellow liquid in her glass. "They may learn a similar lesson from you."

That got her attention, as he had hoped it would.

"My fists, Mr. Lennox? Whatever can you be thinking?"

She raised her right hand, clenching it in a manner she must have imagined appeared vaguely threatening, but which only emphasized her feminine delicacy. Unable to resist, he caught the tight little knot, and raised it to his lips.

"Save your fists for hammering on your classroom desk so your students might observe the rare woman before them, Miss Clarkson. Let them learn a real lady is one whose manners are never compromised by the situations in which she finds herself, and one who is sensitive to obligation and honor. I do not doubt you capable of fighting for what you desire, and for respect due you."

Daniel still held her hand, and felt her fingers stir against his palm. He supposed his words were just what she wanted to hear, but he would have very much preferred to explore the prospect of the things she desired. She parted her lips, and he felt sure she would have answered him, but for a sudden commotion behind them.

It must be Jane, he realized, though the thought of her coming had completely left his mind. All around him, conversation ceased. Mrs. Carroll's guests turned toward the door, so expectant, one might have thought the prince himself arrived, rather than a local girl who some believed had done very well for herself.

Seeing her now, pale and gaunt in the candlelight, he did not think she had done very well at all.

The Duchess of Glendennon wore a high-necked dress which even Daniel recognized as being several years out of date, and several pattern sizes too large. Her hair, the golden treasure he had once caressed in the moonlight on the riverbank, hung lank about her ears. The only spot of color on her perfectly bland figure was the famous Glendennon necklace, encrusted with emeralds and graced with a ruby reported to have belonged to Elizabeth herself. Poor Jane wore it like a yoke around her thin neck.

He glanced down at the woman whose warm hand he still held and wondered how he had ever imagined he preferred waiflike prettiness to such vivid beauty. He had been an innocent; it was his only excuse. He had not known what he wanted until his sisters and the irresponsible Mrs. Clarkson sent Emily Clarkson to Glenfell, to seduce him with nothing more than her patent dislike of him.

And her poised determination.

And her splendid black hair and dark eyes.

And her creamy shoulders and breast.

"You may be excused to greet your lover, Mr. Lennox. She looks disdainful of all the company, and you may give her joy."

And her lofty manner. How had he forgotten that?

"Miss Clarkson, you forget. She is married to the duke. He is the only man who is permitted to give her joy."

"Poor dear. It is no wonder then she looks as if she has not smiled in a very long time. By all accounts—other than your cousin's—the duke is a very cold, disagreeable man."

Daniel watched as Jane held out her gloved hand and was immediately assailed by a throng of devotees. Peter somehow managed to be among the first, followed by Dr. Cafferty. But Daniel had no intention of leaving Miss Clarkson's side.

"How much have you heard?" he asked, genuinely curious. If his servants were gossiping about the Duke of Glendennon, he had a right to know about it.

"Oh, not very much," Miss Clarkson answered coyly. "Not a fraction of what I hear about you."

Daniel put his free hand to his neck and loosened his cravat. Here was not a very comfortable topic either.

"Are you not permitted to go close, Mr. Lennox? Does the duke's censure spread so far as Mrs. Carroll's drawing room, so you are unable to pay his lady her due respect?"

"I go where I please in this town, Miss Clarkson," he said, though it was not entirely the truth. "The duke may despise me, and I have little use for him, but he is a frail old man who still imagines himself powerful. He is not. Therefore, if I wish, I may approach him, and his, with impunity."

"Then you are the better man," she said, surprising him. "He seems a nasty, foolish thing. It sounds as if you have been judged harshly, and the duke deprived of excellent company."

"You amaze me, Miss Clarkson."

She said nothing for several moments and then gently pulled her hand from his. "Sometimes, I amaze even myself, Mr. Lennox."

The Duchess of Glendennon allowed herself to be led through the deferential crowd like a lamb going to slaughter. As she passed, Emily studied her with more interest than she ever would have admitted. Here, cold and impassive, walked a woman whom Daniel Lennox had lost to a man of a much higher social class; it could be no wonder the mill owner resented such distinctions. The duchess seemed pretty enough, but her dreadful gown hung loosely on her slim build, hiding anything of interest.

But Mr. Lennox's blue eyes were all for the duchess as he followed her procession through the room. He took several deep breaths, as if something pained him, and Emily wondered how much his bravado masked an aching heart. He had loved this woman, and wished to marry her.

Emily pressed the hand he had kissed against her cheek, comforted by its lingering warmth. She was a fool. A man who showed a preference for pale, sweet things did not suddenly find attraction in a dark woman who was bent on giving him a hard time.

"The duchess looks very forlorn, even in this cheerful crowd," she said quietly, her voice breaking a little. "Is she without her husband?"

"You are very perceptive, Miss Clarkson. It is an excellent quality in a schoolteacher," he said at last and on a note of sarcasm. "But while the Duchess of Glendennon is without her estimable and ancient husband, I doubt she is ever quite alone."

Emily glanced up at the man who might have been Jane Weldon's estimable and young husband and saw how very deep his pain. But then her gaze returned to the duchess, who seemed very comfortable in the close society of Peter Havers, and Emily realized Daniel Lennox might not have been thinking of the duke at all.

Chapter Six

$\mathscr{E}$mily's next days in Glenfell were marred by rough weather within the classroom, where lightning often flashed and storms arose without warning.

The first squall interrupted a lesson in arithmetic, precipitated when one of the Daniels released an injured starling onto Anne's desk. The little girl leapt from her seat, overturning the bench onto another Daniel's foot, which kicked Nell Worthington on her bottom and left a dark boot-print on her cream chintz dress. The poor bird, terrified out of his tiny mind, left his own nasty mark on Margaret's slate, and scuttled his way toward the bright light at the window.

"John, will you see to the bird? He will beat his head trying to escape." Emily felt a genuine sympathy for the little beast, understanding too well his frustration and desperate need. "Meanwhile, Daniel Whitlow can explain why he chose to bring a bird into our classroom."

" 'Tis a present for you, ma'am," the boy said. The bird squawked in the corner as John tried to catch it. "I didn't know if you ever seen a bird. Being a London lady, and all."

"We do have birds in London, Master Whitlow, and rarely do they enter the classroom," Emily answered patiently.

"But the fox would get him if he stayed outside. His wing is broken."

"Then we shall have to help him, I daresay. I do know something about such things," Emily said, and it was close to the truth. She had watched her father splint broken bones many times; how different could it be to repair the wing of a starling?

A good deal, as it turned out. Humans were less likely to peck at your fingers and pluck at the bandages. They rarely squirmed out of your fingers and fell onto the floor. They did not try to fly into your hair.

Truly, she had not expected the experience of being schoolmistress to be quite so hazardous. Afterward, as she bravely forged ahead, set on her lessons, she could not help but wonder how little intellectual reformers understood the practical realities of the hard work they advocated. Could someone sheltered by every comfort imagine such a scene?

She thought not. She never could have imagined it herself, even before coming to Glenfell.

But Daniel Lennox probably imagined it very well. He had known what such rugged work would involve, and yet he had insisted a gentlewoman be subjected to it. And that children, who perhaps thought knowledge of the natural world far more useful than learning sums, be made to prove the worth of his utopian experiment. Just now, however, the classroom looked anything but utopian.

The children were tired and distracted, and the wretched starling screeched his displeasure from the back of the room.

"Do you think we are quite through for the day?" Nell asked, a little bleakly.

Emily put down her book. "I suppose you would like to spend the afternoon with Noland?" she asked, enviously.

"I should adore it, but Noland would not appreciate the interruption. Nor would Daniel, I should think. I rather thought we might spend the time together, Miss Clarkson."

Emily looked at Nell, feeling absurdly pleased. She enjoyed the woman's company, and relied on her very much for support in the classroom. But she was uncertain what Nell, devoted to Daniel Lennox like everyone else in Glenfell, thought about any woman who made her displeasure with the man well known.

She would like to find out.

It took less than a minute for Emily to dismiss her class, and for the children to make good their escape.

"They all look to you for example, Emily," Nell said as she shelved a handful of books. "And with adoration."

Emily looked up from her desk. "I am sorry, Nell. Did you say . . . ?"

"The girls, especially Margaret, would like to be like you when they are women. In the evenings, in their rooms, they often pretend to be teachers, instructing dolls and the littlest ones in reading and mathematics. Did you not know it?"

Emily felt a little tickle of delight and no uncertain pride.

"Do they really? I am honored to imagine it, but this will make it so difficult for me to leave them, as I must someday soon. Perhaps, if you and I succeed, we might plant the seeds for a continuing line of teachers for Mr. Lennox, so he need not look as far as London for his employees," Emily mused, very easily imagining bossy Margaret as one who might handle the likes of all the Daniels. "But come, must we discuss such plans in the presence of that poor bird? Let us escape along with the children."

As they walked into the hall, Nell continued. "But I do not think they merely wish to emulate your teaching manner. They would like to dress like you, speak like you, know such happiness and comfort in life as you. I cannot say I blame them."

"They know nothing about it. Neither, I suspect, do you, my dear friend. Do you think if I were so very satisfied with my lot in life I would have left all I know to come to Glenfell? My life is hardly charmed." Emily heard her own words echo against the bare walls and recognized the hard truth in them. What had she left behind in London but her Aunt Constance and a placid sort of existence with no expectations to excite either of them?

"I lived very quietly with my aunt and we managed on fairly modest means. We did not know, until recently, how very modest. My father, her brother, died three years ago of some pestilence he contracted in his hospital. And of my mother, you already know something. Freed of wifely obligations, she decided to follow a path of reform and adventure. None of this included me, until she belatedly remembered a promise to Mr. Lennox's sister that she would be schoolmistress here. I came in her stead, but not with her conviction. Certainly you see why I have feelings of resentment for Mr. Lennox's great experiment?"

"But why resent Daniel? Can you not separate the goodness of the man from the things in which he believes?"

"Is that not the definition of the man?" Emily said teasingly as she pulled Nell out the door.

Nell smiled. "Most women would say not. They would consider his height and strength and eyes, perhaps. And I do not think Daniel is lacking in any of those areas."

"I admit he is very handsome. But not the sort to tempt me."

"Do you prefer Peter's blond godliness? For, if you are looking for beliefs in that man, you are likely to be disappointed. Peter has lived all his life in the company of the duke, at Gleneyrie. His only conviction is that he deserves to be the heir presumptive."

"Is it not possible? Perhaps the inheritance is such that the title might pass to him by way of his mother."

"It is not possible if there is already an heir presumptive," Nell said softly, and plucked a bud from a twisting vine.

"Of course. The duchess is expecting and a son would be the heir apparent. But Mr. Havers did not seem so very upset by the news."

"I suspect he would not be." Nell started to walk down a rugged path, one too narrow for them to walk abreast. Emily ran a few steps and caught Nell by the shoulder.

"You are keeping something from me, are you not?"

"It truly is none of my business. But as your friend, I would only urge caution in the company of Mr. Havers."

"Dear Nell," said Emily. "I am not likely to be in his company again. He delivered me to Mrs. Carroll's party but scarcely spent a moment in my company, as he clearly preferred the conversation of the duchess. It was left for Mr. Lennox to stand by me, and you know how we feel about each other." She sighed, wondering how things might have gone if they had started differently. "Consider my social triumph: I attended a party with a man who abandoned me, and spent the evening with a man to whom I must be polite because he pays my wage. Is it not a joke? I am certain I am the very last person the girls should emulate."

Nell laughed and turned in the path. "Not the very last. But I will admit there is some room for improvement."

"What do you suggest?"

"I would suggest you look beyond matters of class. It is possible to find a diamond in the darkest coal," she said cryptically.

A circus came to Glenfell one dusky evening, and by the next morning, Emily knew it impossible to get the attention of her students. They looked out the windows, dropped their slates off their desks, and teased each other relentlessly. The strains of distant music drowned out the sound of her own voice, and two of the boys tried to escape through an open window.

Perhaps Mrs. Bernays sent word of her difficulties to the mill office because Mr. Lennox soon appeared at the door of the schoolroom.

"Pardon me, Miss Clarkson," he said, as he took off his hat. "I hope I am not interrupting anything very urgent."

"We are in the midst of reading about the ancient pyramids, sir," Emily said. "It has not been an urgent matter for several thousand years."

"I see. And yet it is a topic of some current interest, as there are still those who like to build monuments to themselves."

"Such as mills and schoolhouses, Mr. Lennox?"

"Vanity may be forgiven if such buildings serve others." He paused and looked at the blank faces of the children. "I can see how happy your scholars are to be so well served, Miss Clarkson. It will be impossible, I fear, to persuade any of them to patronize the circus this afternoon."

But Emily's students abandoned Egypt without a backward glance as they nearly flew from their seats and surrounded Mr. Lennox. "I happened on this bag of coins on my dining-room table, and thought it might be shared among you," he said, weighing a parcel in his hand.

Emily clapped her hands in an attempt to restore order, but she might as well have been trying to control a hurricane.

Near-chaos broke out as the children broke for the door. Mr. Lennox threw the bag to John and stood aside as the storm blew past him. Nell was far more subtle. As she walked by, last of all, she reached up to kiss his cheek in gratitude.

Emily might have done the same, happy for the reprieve. But she caught herself before giving in to temptation.

"Well, Miss Clarkson? Do I not deserve a kiss from you, as well?" Mr. Lennox closed the door and leaned against the post. "But perhaps you did not see my interference as the heroic business I intended. Will you instead reprimand me? Take me to task for disrupting your lesson?"

Emily sighed and sat down on the nearest bench. "Indeed, I should. But I confess to some gratitude, Mr. Lennox, for I am near exhaustion. It is difficult enough to give lessons to reluctant scholars, but absolutely impossible to compete with a circus. Do you not care to join them, by the way?"

"The reluctant scholars?"

"The children," she said wearily, not sure she felt up to a verbal joust this day.

So she said nothing as she watched Daniel Lennox sit astride a small bench. His jacket and trousers had not the elegance of his evening clothes, but suited him even more. His ungloved hands looked rough, as if he had worked with them recently, and the sweet smell of sawdust surrounded his person. She studied his face, even as she knew he gazed upon her, and saw his bruise nearly healed.

"No, I would not care to join them," he said.

"Not even to see an elephant from India? The boys have spoken of little else," she teased.

"I should like to see an elephant, but will content myself with the wild creatures you harbor in this room. I heard something of a starling wrapped in bandages. Is the poor thing the victim of a demonstration for your studies of ancient Egypt?"

Emily looked at him, puzzled.

"Mummies?" he asked pointedly. "There is nothing I love so well in London's great museum."

"Ah, mummies." Emily nodded. "But the little fellow is quite alive, you know. He has been named Daniel, by the way. It is not terribly original, but all the children seemed to think it an excellent name. And I would not want to ruffle any feathers."

"You are among the few ladies of my acquaintance who can deliver a pun without trying to be clever, Miss Clarkson."

"Perhaps you do not know enough clever ladies, Mr. Lennox. But then, if you prefer to go to the British Museum when in London than to dinner parties and balls, I can understand why."

"I assure you, Miss Clarkson, if I had any idea you attended such wearisome social gatherings, I would have declined the society of the mummies and sought yours instead."

"As you decline the company of the elephant just now," Emily said. "I suppose you intend to flatter me, but I do not consider leathery remains of people nor chained beasts to be real competition."

"They are not. And I do intend to flatter you when I say one would have to search a very long time to find a lady to rival you," Mr. Lennox said, and leaned closer to her. "Of course, you have probably heard such words from other men."

Emily stood, and he did the same. If she had heard such words, she had readily forgotten the gentlemen who uttered them. "I have, Mr. Lennox," she lied. "But the flattery would be greater if I did not already know you would say anything to have me remain in Glenfell. However, I will not be so easily seduced."

"I see," he said thoughtfully, more or less confirming her suspicions. The idea ought to have pleased her, but did not.

He ran the back of his fingers across his cheek.

"Why did you fight, Mr. Lennox? Was it simply to assert territorial claims, as you suggested? It seems a bit primitive."

"Even gentlemen may not find their existence so gentle in Glenfell, Miss Clarkson. We do not hesitate to use our hands, and fists, if necessary. In this case, I daresay you will be censorious when I admit I fought for the most primitive reason of all. I was injured in the defense of the reputation of a lady."

The words hung in the still air, and Emily looked into his bright eyes, searching for some truth to the persistent rumors about himself and the Duchess of Glendennon.

"She is a lucky lady, then, to deserve such a champion."

"She does not know it, so perhaps she does not feel particularly blessed. And, I fear, even if she did know it, she would not appreciate it."

Emily thought of the unhappy-looking lady who had chosen the duke over a merchant, and wondered if it gave her any joy to know that the man she rejected still pined for her. Did she enjoy her life at Gleneyrie and share her husband's contempt for the busy center of industry below? Would a baby, an heir, bring her comfort?

Of course a baby would bring joy. Surely it was one of the reasons for the marriage.

"I have something to return to you, Miss Clarkson," Mr. Lennox said suddenly. He reached into his jacket and pulled from it a narrow length of fabric.

"Ah, the silk. Did you find it did not suit you, sir?"

"The color is good enough and it should make up well into a gown. But it does not suit me, and for a practical reason."

Emily reached out and pulled it gently from his fingers. "Do you not wear silk?" she teased.

"In Glenfell, no one wears silk," he said firmly.

Emily looked at him, surprised their bantering should end like this. "Such a pronouncement seems absurdly autocratic, even coming from you, sir."

"It is not autocratic at all, for it is a sentiment shared by hundreds of people in this town. Miss Clarkson, have you any idea what we do here?" He paced the floor like an impatient schoolmaster.

"You weave fabric?" Emily asked, feeling a little foolish.

"Very good!" He nodded approvingly. "And what sort of fabric?"

"You need not mock me, Mr. Lennox. I see the cotton bolts all around me. I understand very well what you do."

"I did not intend to insult you, Miss Clarkson," he said apologetically. "But as it seems your whole life has been so far removed from the business of the GlenLennox Mill, I thought you might not have a practical perspective on the matter."

Emily would have argued on general principle, if he were not so patently correct.

"The GlenLennox Mill is the largest of its kind in England," Mr. Lennox said, and waited again.

"How very ambitious," Emily said, finally recognizing her cue.

"We provide the cotton fabric for everything from the sails of ships to ladies' garments."

"And truly versatile," came Emily's chorus.

"We supplied our troops with their uniforms during the Peninsular War, and with a heavier tenting fabric."

"And very patriotic," Emily added, wondering what this had to do with the silk scrap.

"And why not? We are a very ambitious, versatile, and patriotic people, Miss Clarkson. Therefore, when many individuals of style and influence in Glenfell decided to cease their purchase of French garments, they were much admired. The deprivation proved even easier when legal trade ended between our two countries."

"And yet, my dressmaker in London continues to provide me with French-made silks and brocades," Emily said.

"I am not surprised, Miss Clarkson. For, perhaps, you did not hear me very well. I spoke only of legal trade. In fact, it is well known how smugglers continue to ply a lucrative trade along our coasts. One's acquisition of bolts of French fabric is only restricted by scruples—and by how much one is willing to pay for an excellent product."

Emily remembered her aunt complaining about the rising costs of fabrics, but had not paid too much attention to her at the time.

"What do you propose to do about it, Mr. Lennox?" she asked, genuinely interested. For the first time, she understood how the well-being of a community could be affected by distant events.

"Ah, you catch on very quickly, Miss Clarkson," he said, returning to the manner of the proud schoolmaster. "I hope to profit by the sudden renewal of interest in English cotton and am currently developing a process by which our simple threads take on the luster of fine silk. You may have seen my sisters wearing dresses made of this fabric while you were in town."

Emily had not taken particular note of the ladies' garments, but customarily considered his sisters very fashionable. They were admired by a good many people and could very likely influence style among their friends.

"How very shrewd of you, sir," she said, not yet willing to concede to his visionary endeavors. Though the success of his mill would benefit hundreds of others, he would be the first to profit from its success. "I believe you try to gain from a war that caused others great unhappiness."

He frowned, and she could not be sure his displeasure derived from Napoleon or herself.

"I see you will grant me nothing, Miss Clarkson. So perhaps I ought to clarify that my profit comes from legitimate means. There are others whose profits are also considerable."

"I suppose you mean smugglers."

"Indeed I do. I continue to wage a campaign against them, and endeavor to put them out of business. And there is why I am so particularly interested in a little scrap of blue silk."

Emily had wondered when he would get to back to that, but now that he did, she still could not fathom his meaning.

"Surely you cannot suggest a child . . ."

Mr. Lennox gave a gesture of impatience. "The child is just a victim. As were her parents. But someone else brought the silk to Glenfell illegally and illicitly and, I already have reason to suspect, stored it in my large warehouse. When in fear of being found out, that person very likely set fire to the place, little caring who would get hurt in the process."

"Your judgment is very harsh, Mr. Lennox."

His face reddened, and Emily saw how very angry he was. "Should it not be?" he demanded. "Twenty-three people were killed that day, healthy people on whom others depended. They all left children behind, children who are now orphans of the mill and in my safekeeping. If anything, my judgment is not harsh enough."

"I daresay you will exercise it fully when the accused is brought to justice? You did say you entertain several suspicions?"

He did not answer at once, but paused to take several deep breaths. "I did say so. I lack only proof. I strongly believe the answer lies with those who are close to me."

Emily suddenly thought of the day when she met Peter Havers and Captain Milrose on the site of the burned building, and dared to wonder if she held a clue to the mystery. Captain Milrose certainly looked a suspicious type, even if his cheerful sister pronounced him a confidant of Daniel Lennox. But did he not consort with someone whom Daniel Lennox did not trust?

Of course, she realized, the same might be said of herself.

But Captain Milrose owned a ship to convey whatever cargo he wished. What better cover than to use Mr. Lennox's cotton over French contraband! Emily grew excited, hoping her employer told her these things so that she might serve as a spy in his own camp. She had never imagined such an adventure.

"Is there anything I might do to help you, sir?"

Mr. Lennox looked as surprised as Emily felt herself when she heard her own words. She must be a madwoman to let her imagination go wild in such a manner. It was a response worthy of Mrs. Clarkson, not her respectable daughter. But Mr. Lennox did not seem censorious, only bemused.

"I did not believe you my friend, Miss Clarkson," he said wryly.

Emily blushed brightly and turned away. "I never said otherwise, sir. I only disagree with your idealistic plans and resent the fact you consider me the means by which to accomplish them. But for that, I bear you no ill will."

"And yet I somehow understood you thought me overbearing and far too proud. Particularly for someone in business. Did you not say you thought me arrogant?"

"I may have said something of the sort . . ."

"Well, no matter. We could very well remain antagonists in certain matters and cooperate in others. It is the very definition of relations between employer and employee; would you not agree?"

"I suppose I do," Emily said thoughtfully.

"And, I confess, I should like you as an ally, Miss Clarkson." He leaned forward, conspiratorially, and Emily saw her own dark reflection in his light eyes.

"In the matter of the fire?" she asked, her dampening enthusiasm once more catching sparks.

"And in a few other things as well."

Emily stiffened, wondering what was to come. In spite of his polite invitations and apparent interest in her affairs, she did not presume to imagine any additional reasons for an alliance between them. Though if he continued to look at her as he was at the moment, she might very well welcome them.

"You need not look so suspicious, Miss Clarkson. I am

not about to ask you to unload barges or anything of that sort. I only wondered if you knew Miss Harriet Martineau has announced her intention of visiting us next month."

"Miss Martineau?" Emily sighed, hoping she did not appear too disappointed. "She will make a great nuisance of herself, sir, and exhaust us all. My mother occasionally dragged me to her lectures, and not one in twenty people could manage to stay awake."

"You shall have to keep the conversation lively and thus help me, Miss Clarkson. Perhaps you might argue the value of a baronetcy over a millinery shop or something of that sort. No, stay. Please hear me out." Emily had not the heart for his teasing. "My friend Jeremiah Colman, who mills mustard seed, will come with her. Miss Martineau will visit him first, and then they both shall come here to Glenfell. It should be very congenial."

"I doubt it," Emily said tersely.

"If not, we shall endeavor to make it so. I plan to host a ball at Shearings in their honor."

"And do you require my help?" After the prospect of espionage, the planning of a ball seemed hopelessly mundane.

"I do not think so. I only hoped you would consent to allow me to escort you, before Peter Havers asks the same." Mr. Lennox reached out to take her hand and traced the lines of her palm with a steady finger.

Emily felt, quite unbidden, a thrill of pleasure.

"I would not think him on your guest list," she whispered.

"He is not but he often appears where he is not invited."

She wondered at that, and all the resentment Mr. Lennox's voice seemed to contain. What must he truly think of his cousin, born to a life of privilege? But then, what did Daniel Lennox know of deprivation? She studied his profile as he caressed her palm, and saw something of Lady Gray in the proud set of his jaw.

"Why do you need to escort me, if you will already be at Shearings?" she asked quietly.

He stopped his teasing touch. "I will then be privileged to ask you for the first dance. Is it not a custom in London?"

"Will Miss Martineau allow it, do you suppose?"

Mr. Lennox laughed out loud, and his face seemed immediately transformed. Emily saw his bright eyes shimmer with delight.

"I hope you have the courage to defy her if she does not," he said, letting her free. "As well as the strength to endure whatever may come."

Although he still smiled, Emily thought his words ominous and laden with some meaning she did not yet understand.

"Is this your way of telling me you are not a proficient dancer, Mr. Lennox?" she asked lightly.

He held out his elbow but she did not think he wished to demonstrate his skills with her. Instead, he pushed against the door and gestured for her to join him. Emily brought her arm through his and felt the hardness of bone and muscle beneath her fingers. His body protected her against the stiff, cool breeze and his warmth somehow soothed her restless spirit. They paused, and he seemed to survey the scene of the mill in the sloping valley before them. Then he turned to walk in the opposite direction.

"Yes. That is precisely what I am telling you," he said at last, though she did not believe him.

Several days later, a purse containing gold coins and a brief message appeared on Emily's desk in the schoolroom. Mr. Lennox thanked her very politely for her endurance of his "lecture" about his business, and requested she use the offering to buy playthings for the children. He explained that his concerns had been all for their health and education until their afternoon at the circus reminded him of other pleasures in life. He hoped the purse contained enough to make all of them very happy.

Emily studied the letter, remarking his neat hand and literate prose, but really searching for some deeper meaning about the afternoon. After all, there were certain pleasures they had enjoyed as well. She had enjoyed their conversation and walk thoroughly. Did she dare imagine he felt the same?

He did not offer a hint of it in his too-polite letter, she finally decided, and cast the crisp white leaf aside. The purse of coins could not be so easily dismissed.

"Margaret? Anne? Would the two of you please accompany me to the shops tomorrow? I am yet a stranger in town and require your assistance for some important purchases," Emily said to the two girls in the front row of seats, after some consideration.

Margaret and Anne looked at each other in amazement, and Emily realized, too late, that they might never have shopped in stores before. Glenfell was not London, and their mothers were not Aunt Constance. But she smiled reassuringly until they agreed, and then she safely tucked the purse into her desk drawer.

By the next morning, it was clear the girls were delighted to walk into town with their schoolmistress and make the most of the rare occasion. Though Emily had already received some guidance from Mrs. Bernays and Nell about which shops to visit and what to buy, she allowed the girls to imagine they directed the whole expedition themselves. It all passed very well.

The people of Glenfell were unusually polite. When they walked into the shops all conversation stopped, and men bowed deferentially. Merchants left customers standing at the desk in order to assist Emily in her business and offered sweets to Margaret and Anne. Perhaps they noticed the heavy purse she held.

"Miss Clarkson?"

"Miss Milrose! How nice to see you again! Have you found anything special to purchase?"

Emily spoke a little too familiarly to her new friend, so grateful was she to see someone she knew.

"I hope to find a new cape, to wear to Mr. Lennox's ball. Our evenings will be very cool by then and we can always expect rain. My brother brought me a very pretty garment from Ireland, but I do not think it will suit," she said, and frowned. "And are you looking for fabric for a new gown? The one you wore to Mrs. Carroll's house would do very well, you know. But I daresay you are accustomed to new ball gowns for every occasion?"

"Indeed, I am not," Emily said quickly. In fact, she had already decided to have something made especially for Mr. Lennox's affair, now convinced her elegant silks would not do at all. But she preferred not to advertise the fact. "And I brought a large wardrobe with me from London."

"Yes, I heard as much," murmured Miss Milrose, merely

confirming Emily's belief that nothing she did went unnoticed. "Then what brings you to town?"

"I am shopping for the children," Emily said, and felt Margaret and Anne peek out from behind her skirt. "Mr. Lennox decided they needed entertainment other than books, and I am hoping to oblige him, and them."

"How delightful! And what have you found?"

Emily felt a little reluctant to admit they had not yet made any actual selections, for she felt even less prepared to purchase children's playthings than she had to teach them how to read. But she had learned how to do that, as she would this. Thus far, she and the girls had only browsed about in various shops.

"Have you looked at these lovely dolls?" Miss Milrose continued, and brought them to a showcase in the corner of the shop. Emily had not noticed it before, but the girls ran to it in an instant. They somehow made selections in less time than it took them to settle into their seats in the classroom.

Fifteen minutes later, their arms laden with packages, the two women and the two girls walked back out into the sunshine. They had purchased dolls for all the girls, and metal soldiers and small cannons for the boys. Several hoops and balls were to be delivered by one of the shop boys, and the storeowner promised to order a new wooden riding horse from London.

"I hope we did not spend all Mr. Lennox's money," Miss Milrose giggled.

"Do you suppose it possible?" Emily asked, more thoughtful than ironic.

"Oh, indeed not! He is very rich, you know. And very generous. Did you know he pays for the upkeep of a small infirmary? And regularly sends food baskets to the elderly?"

"I am not so very surprised. After all, charity has often been the province of the local squire."

"Of course, Miss Clarkson. But do recall Daniel is not the local squire. The acts of charity of which you speak should rightly be performed by the Duke and Duchess of Glendennon. Their lack of goodwill provides an opening for Daniel's generosity."

Emily looked closely at her new friend, searching for some meaning in the intimacy of her words.

"You are very fond of him," she said.

"Indeed. Ever since Jane Weldon married the duke, many eligible young ladies have attempted to engage Mr. Lennox. We have consoled ourselves into believing him now married to the mill. Or at least we did before you came."

Emily did not pretend to misunderstand. "Rest easy, Miss Milrose. Mr. Lennox is as interested in his new schoolmistress as he is in inviting the duke to tea. He treats me as one of his employees, and that is scarcely a basis for affection."

"If you do not mind my saying so, you look a little young to be hanging up your hat, Miss Clarkson."

"It is our mutual preference, Miss Milrose. I am . . ." Emily's voice drifted off when she realized that all conversation in the street had ceased, and that the only sound to be heard was the clacking of the wheels of a large open carriage.

The driver guided his team cautiously, as if it were unaccustomed to town roads, and took the corner at a very slow pace. He wore livery that had been fashionable perhaps twenty years before, and a tall hat that threatened to blow off if he moved any faster. Emily looked at the carriage and saw its elaborate crest.

A solitary figure sat beneath a woolen blanket on a dark leather seat, and there could be no doubt he was the source of everyone's deference and curiosity.

White-haired and bearded, the gentleman surveyed his people with sharp blue eyes that gazed brightly over his large promontory of a nose. His slim gloved hands perched on a walking stick, shaking slightly but otherwise in repose. He looked very grand but even a heavy dark jacket could not disguise his frailty.

Emily knew who he must be, without anyone telling her, but yet wondered why the Duke of Glendennon seemed so familiar to her. Perhaps they had met once, long ago, or she may have noticed his portrait hanging in one of the shops. But she felt she knew him better than could be accounted for by such casual acquaintance, and could not explain why.

Even so, if they had met before, the occasion could not have warranted his stopping his carriage before her, as he now did. Standing on the street in front of the shop, Emily bowed along with Miss Milrose and the girls, and prayed the carriage would move on. But when she rose, it remained, and the old man studied her with a disconcerting scrutiny. She knew she must not speak first, and so could only stare at him in return.

His was a very weary face. Unhappy, angry and stern, it may never have known what it was to smile. It reflected no pleasure in the show of the townspeople and took no joy in the lovely day.

Then, just as unexpectedly, the duke asked his driver to move on, and once again looked as if there were not a thing to interest him on the streets of the town.

"He noticed you most particularly, Miss Clarkson. I cannot imagine what it might mean," said Miss Milrose excitedly.

"Nothing good, I am sure," Emily said quickly.

But before they reached the week's end, a small engraved note addressed to Emily Clarkson arrived at the schoolhouse. The Duke and the Duchess of Glendennon requested the honor of her presence for dinner in several days' time.

Chapter Seven

*E*mily truly enjoyed her time in the classroom, surrounded by the children and supported by Nell. She discovered qualities in herself she had little known she possessed, and wondered how she had ever doubted her ability to accomplish the tasks set before her. And yet the unexpected invitation to the lofty heights of Gleneyrie restored her sensibilities to where they had been when she first arrived at the mill, and yearned to escape to the castle on the far side of the river.

As she read to and lectured her students, her eyes wandered to the window and the expectations of what lay beyond. To be a schoolmistress was very fine, but to be the guest of a duke quite another thing altogether. So distracted was she by the prospect that she did not hear her employer enter the schoolroom in the late afternoon, a signal for her students' departure. Such departures were a habit they had recently acquired, and Nell usually made good her escape at the same time.

Not for the first time, Emily wondered what others thought about her and Mr. Lennox, and how much they imagined things having no substantiation in truth. Certainly, she could not account for his continued interest, save to assume that he wished to have daily reports on her progress with the children.

"Good afternoon, Miss Clarkson," he said and, as always, made himself comfortable on one of the benches as soon as she sat down upon her teacher's chair. "The children seem unusually enthusiastic today. Could the mummies account for it?"

"You need not mock me, sir. They are always very enthusiastic when leaving the classroom."

"Are they not very happy about the prospect of reading, then? Do they not share my opinion that they are to consider it part of their natural birthright as free men and women?"

His light eyes challenged Emily to defy him, but his irony proved disarming.

"Perhaps they do, Mr. Lennox," she said wearily. "But it is no guarantee of happiness. We need look no farther than Gleneyrie for the proof of it."

Mr. Lennox looked up sharply and narrowed his eyes. Here was the very image of a besotted man, and Emily knew with absolute certainty she was not the object of his desire.

"Please explain yourself, Miss Clarkson. And what, in fact, you know of Gleneyrie," he said tersely.

Emily bit down on her lip, so unwilling was she to speak of Jane Weldon, and therefore to allow Daniel Lennox to expose the most sensitive part of his being. But she knew he would not relent until she offered some explanation for her words.

"I believe, for example, the Duke of Glendennon is a

lonely and embittered man, though he surely holds the most enviable of titles. I know almost nothing about him, and yet I feel something in his past made him unhappy."

"I would not credit his emotions," Mr. Lennox said sharply. "And yet I believe him happy with his young wife."

Emily looked at him, feeling much as Catherine Milrose must have felt before relinquishing all hope. To have such a one as Mr. Lennox wear his longing for all to see was a sobering sight indeed. The woman who so afflicted him might even take pleasure in it. But Emily, the heir to her parents' compassion, and her aunt's loving kindness, thought it would grieve her to be the woman who had spurned Daniel Lennox.

She did not pity him, but she believed she understood something of his pain.

"I do know something about it, Mr. Lennox," she said gently. "And I understand why you alone, of all the people I have met in Glenfell, will not speak of your eminent neighbor."

He straightened and rubbed his hand against his forehead, making his hair stand on end. "I doubt it, Miss Clarkson. I do not speak of the duke simply because he and I share little enough in common for me to find him a subject of any interest. But you must feel a bond, for I understand he invited you to dinner at Gleneyrie."

"I did not realize it a matter of public knowledge but . . ."

"It is not public knowledge. But there are those who thought it something I should know."

"Indeed? I cannot imagine why, unless you intend to lecture me on your obligations as my employer. It is a tired theme, sir," Emily said. "I surely am allowed to come and go as I please."

"In principle, I could not agree with you more. But in practice, there are more pressing considerations. I ask you to take great care in the presence of the duke, Miss Clarkson. He is a very bitter man. And bitterness often makes men dangerous."

"You profess to know a good deal about it. Could it be the feeling is mutual? And what, precisely, should I fear?

Do you imagine the duke might stab me in his dining room?"

Daniel Lennox looked pretty dangerous himself at the moment. One of his hands abandoned his hair and balled into a fist while his other tapped on the wooden bench. He drew a deep breath and twice looked as if he might issue a suitable retort.

"I am sure I shall survive to report on the furnishings, the meal, and all those other things Mrs. Bernays and Miss Worthington are so anxious to know. And if the duke draws his saber or attempts to poison me, perhaps Peter Havers will protect me."

That got the desired result.

"He is another who does not deserve your trust, Miss Clarkson. Though he has made Gleneyrie his home, my cousin is not the heir presumptive. There is another who owns that distinction, but Peter foolishly thrives on false expectations."

"So everyone seems to believe. But is it not Mr. Havers himself who is confident the duchess will soon produce an heir?"

"One hopes the lady will manage it. The duke has been married four times, and two babies died young, along with their poor mothers. The first duchess was made of sturdier stuff, but produced only daughters."

"Do the daughters still live?"

"They do not. Nor does their mother, who died nearly thirty years ago."

"You seem to know much about it." Emily said what she had been thinking all along.

"I do," he said. "But then, all the town has been watching and waiting for the birth of a son of the duke."

"Perhaps the fault is not so much the wives', as his," Emily said wryly. She then silently berated herself for even suggesting she knew about such things.

Mr. Lennox did not look at all put off by her boldness.

"So you now understand why Peter Havers nurses his delusions."

Emily wondered, ungenerously, if Mr. Lennox was more than a little jealous of his cousin's good fortune. How could he not be?

"They may not be delusions, Mr. Lennox. For, as you just pointed out, there is some basis for his optimism. He is a relation, and the duke is both elderly and childless. Mr. Havers may very well inherit through the natural course of events."

"If he inherits, it will not be through any natural events. Mr. Havers is very capable of acting on his baser instincts."

"Poor Mr. Lennox," Emily murmured, and smiled, thinking he went too far. "You are so bothered by Mr. Havers' happy expectations, you imagine everyone a villain. Am I now an enemy because I dare to consort with them at Gleneyrie?"

"I hope I will never say so," he said gently.

"And yet you would have both the duke and his relations murderers and thieves. You must admit it sounds a little absurd. If you think they are plotting against me, perhaps I ought to ask for your protection instead of your cousin's."

Something flared in his eyes and Emily thought, for just a moment, that he might oblige her. He suddenly stood up, and she rose to meet him.

"I am happy you finally recognize where your loyalties must lie," he said very seriously, though her words had been spoken with no other intent than to tease him. "But it is another matter I came to discuss with you, one precluding my intervention in your affairs."

Emily wondered, for one bleak moment, if he had managed to find another schoolmistress after all. And in that same moment admitted to herself, for the first time, that she did not want to leave him or his schoolhouse. How had it come to this? But what would she do with herself in London, bereft of the children and her new friends? Would she wander the vast British Museum, hoping to catch a glimpse of him among the mummies?

"I am about to embark on a short journey," he said, looking at her strangely.

"Oh," Emily said, immeasurably relieved.

"You look very pleased, Miss Clarkson. Is my presence so painful to you?"

She could not even begin to explain why his company gave her both pain and pleasure at once, before she understood it herself. She only knew she would not be leaving the mill just yet, and that while he was gone something would go missing from her life.

"Do you travel for business, sir?" she asked.

"Indeed. You have probably read of New Lanark, the mill where my good friend Robert Owen is owner. He recently ordered new machinery and desires my judgment on it." Mr. Lennox studied his sleeve as he spoke and brushed off some imaginary lint. "But you have not answered me, Emily."

Whether it was the use of her first name, or the fact he stepped closer that caused Emily's heart to thump so erratically, she could not say. For surely, she could not be anything but indifferent to the fact that he traveled soon to New Lanark; he could circumnavigate the globe, for all she cared. But still he came forward, expecting an answer to what she scarcely dreamed would be a question.

She stepped away from her desk, and dropped her hands gracelessly to her side. She knew where she would like to put them, but did not dare.

"I have read of Robert Owen's work," she said evasively.

"I am happy to hear it. But I did not ask you about Owen. I wondered if my company proved difficult for you to bear."

"As our affairs have intersected, it is necessary for us to occasionally be in each other's company," she said primly. "Whether the experience is painful could not possibly matter."

"But what if it did?" he asked, and came so close Emily could have reached out and touched his chest. Treacherously, she wondered how the white cloth of his shirt would feel and if his heart beat as roughly as hers.

"I . . . do not know."

"You are a teacher; I thought you knew everything," he mused, and then seemed serious again. "What if we choose to ignore the circumstances bringing us together, and the differences in our stations, and behave as two individuals, unattached and intrigued?"

"It would not do," Emily answered desperately, and tried to fix her eyes on anything but him. "I belong in London. I have a suitor waiting for me there."

"Ah, yes. The London lover. He must have made quite

an impression on you, as you do not recall whether you are on or off. But why, I might ask, would you belong in a place when your heart lies elsewhere?" He reached out for her. "I will not believe it is still in London."

Before Emily knew what he was about, she felt his hand on the small of her back as he pulled her closer to him. His mouth came down tentatively, and then with assurance, on her lips and she closed her eyes, savoring his taste as if she were a starving woman. She suddenly knew she wanted more, much more, and pressed her body into the shelter of his. His response was immediate and startling and she moved her hip against him in wonderment. He said something into her lips, but she did not want to hear it, lest sanity return. And she was not yet finished.

Nor was he. The hands she had considered calloused and rough brushed against her skin with the gentleness of feathers, caressing, soothing, awakening parts of her she had scarcely known existed before this moment. His mouth, silent now but for his drowning gasps of breath, followed a path made by his fingers on her face and neck, but with a greater urgency and far less gently. And all the time, his body stretched long and hard against hers, moving in a rhythm he urged her to follow.

"My heart is not in London," she gasped into his collar, intoxicated by his earthy scent of pine and something indefinable.

He held back a moment and looked into her face. His lids were lowered, shading his light eyes, and yet she saw something there so new and unexpected her heart ached with happiness.

"No, I should think not," he said as he started to pull her closer again.

"But it remains mine," she sighed, trying to hold back and put her hands between them, against his chest. But it was the wrong—or very much the right—thing to do. Through the stiff white cloth she could feel springy curls on his chest and a heat threatening to burn her to cinders. She dared to explore, moving on to savor the hard muscles along his arms and shoulders. His was not the body of a gentleman. Emily wove her arms under his jacket, over his hips, pressing her breast against him so she might run her hands along his back. And she did not feel very much a lady.

Daniel shifted his stance and held her chin so he could see her face. He brushed a finger over lips Emily knew were swollen, and she gently bit down on his nail.

"That is enough, Miss Clarkson. We shall leave your heart—and everything else—where it is," he said in a strangled voice. She ignored him, and caressed his rough chin, enjoying the sensation. "Aside from which, I think you may kill me."

"That would surely defeat my purpose. But perhaps I misjudge you, Mr. Lennox. Is this the manner by which you bid farewell to all your employees?" she asked after a moment, and saw the unholy gleam in his eyes.

"Clearly, you have not met most of my employees. They will have to be content with a nod and a wave of my hat."

"I see. And you did not think I would be so satisfied?"

"I did not presume to guess what would satisfy Miss Clarkson," he said, holding her at arms' length. "I only knew it would not satisfy me."

"You are a selfish man, Mr. Lennox. You would do such things to me, and leave?"

"I will return in three days' time, my lovely Emily. When I made my plans I did not think there would be any reason to hurry back. But that I will. I always finish what I start."

"You make it sound very businesslike," she said, trying to keep her voice steady.

"And I know how much that offends you. I am sorry for it. But it is who I am." His wonderful fingers fumbled with his cravat.

The fact of his business would always stand between them. And yet, Emily thought there might be ample compensations if one were the lover of Mr. Daniel Lennox. Her thoughts, wanton and wild, came thick and fast and she could not help rubbing her tongue across the surface of her dry, swollen lips.

He swayed towards her, and then took a step back.

"You surprise me, Miss Clarkson."

"I always insisted I was not a schoolmistress."

"I meant in other ways."

"Well, you surprise me too, Mr. Lennox. I thought you were very protective of your employees, and would do nothing to compromise their safety. Or reputation." She folded her arms across her breast and leaned against her desk.

"I should like to keep you safe, Miss Clarkson. It is why I want you to stay away from Peter Havers."

"And was that the object of your little demonstration? But I am not a Glenfell lady, who might easily be swayed by a kiss and a promise," Emily said, wondering if this was about power and domination, and not about her at all. "Do you not think me a willful, feeling lady with my own interests?"

Slowly sanity returned, as Emily considered the enormity of what had just passed between them. She was wrong to insist she could not be swayed by a kiss and a promise, for she suspected she would have bent shamelessly to his will. An hour ago she would have insisted she did not even like him. But then something mystical and quite extraordinary had been cut loose from where it had been captive almost all her life and she had behaved in a way she would not have imagined. She should be mortified. She was not. But to Daniel Lennox, for whom this might be a habit among the ladies of his acquaintance, she could not reveal the state of her emotions.

"I will not scorn an invitation so graciously extended by a gentleman and his wife," she said, watching his face. "But I will take heed of your words and not do anything reckless while you are gone. Can you say the same of yourself?"

He stood for a moment, gazing down at her, while Emily prayed he would renew the passions that burned just beneath the surface. But instead he just reached for her, and pulled her close into his embrace. His lips came down hard and rough. And before she could catch her breath he turned on his heel, and walked from the room that now felt as empty and cold as once her heart had been.

"Sir?" A man's voice broke into Daniel's dream.

He rubbed his eyes, realizing he had fallen asleep over a thick accounting book. It appeared he was paying for his little visit to Miss Clarkson with more than whatever punishment she might eventually devise for him, for it had cost him valuable time during his workday. Now there were matters demanding attention before tomorrow's journey to New Lanark.

He looked across the broad table, through the smoke of his oil lamp, to Noland's amused face.

"Is the work getting to be too much for you, old boy?" the American asked, and smiled.

"Nolly, it is neither the mill nor its running getting to me. More to the point, it is the business down at the school-house, and its new mistress."

"My Nell tells me Miss Clarkson is the best of all women, and the children seem absolutely devoted to her. She knows when to have a good time and takes special care with them who need it. But then, I suppose it is not her manner towards the children currently concerning you?"

"You speak like a man of experience, Nolly. I can only say I wish Mrs. Clarkson had abandoned her scheme of going to your native shores and come to me instead. Then I should be employing a lady who might tempt me with the reading aloud of an excellent book. I would feel perfectly satisfied in paying a visit to hear her, and occasionally escorting her to a dinner party."

"Surely you need not do any more with Miss Clarkson, if you prefer not."

"Of course I need not! I am not obliged to do anything more than pay her wages! But it is not to the point: I will not be satisfied to do just that. A man capable of it is more than human."

Noland Haines raised his eyebrows and studied the point of his quill. "If you do not mind my saying so, Dan, there are many who consider you so."

Daniel accepted the compliment with gentlemanly modesty.

"Ah well, I have been lucky in my investments. And have tried to act responsibly in the face of misfortune. Anyone might have done the same."

"One in your position . . ."

Daniel held up his hand.

"The only position I desire just now is to be prone beneath the covers in my bed. Your responsibility is to keep me awake, Nolly, until our work is done."

Noland Haines stifled a yawn and returned to his books. Daniel attempted to do the same but neither read nor comprehended the words on the page, for he only saw Miss Clarkson's delicate features before his eyes and thought about her hands on his body. So unexpected, so devastating, so hopelessly enticing it had been, he could scarcely imagine how an innocent like herself dared to be so bold.

Perhaps she wanted him as much as he did her.

Dare he think it? He closed his eyes, but his daydreams were not of the sort to induce sleep.

"Shall I keep an eye on her?" Noland asked, though he still studied his page of figures.

Daniel opened his eyes.

"On the mill? I should hope so."

Noland laughed. "You are far gone. I thought we were speaking of Miss Clarkson. Do you wish me to watch her comings and goings while you are gone?"

"You mean, spy on her? It is not my business to know where the lady goes, unless it affects the welfare of our children. She would not appreciate your kindness in looking after her. Nor does she desire our protection."

"Will she need it?"

"I hope not. But her very presence could cause sufficient concern in some quarters where they would wish to see her gone. I am not happy about her visit to Gleneyrie. Surely the duke means something by it, for he never entertains."

"Nell tells me the duchess is expectant of an heir. Perhaps her husband merely wishes for her to enjoy some company."

"I doubt the man thinks any company so worthwhile as his own. And if I were the duke I would take care with my invitation list. Not everyone will be happy with the prospect of a new heir."

"Certainly not," Noland agreed, and then put a finger to his lips. The sound of footsteps echoed in the hallway. "Who would come so late?"

Daniel did not answer, but quietly opened the top drawer of his desk, where he kept a knife. He ran a finger over its sharp edge, drawing strength from it. He could think of several people who would come to him in the night, believing him alone, and hoping to accomplish what the burned building and other acts of treachery had failed to.

The footsteps paused at the doorway, and several moments passed as Daniel's hand tightened around the handle of the knife.

The latch rattled and lifted, and the door opened noisily in the still air.

"Mr. Lennox?"

"Oh, it is you, Parker," said Daniel, recognizing the voice of the elderly worker. The knife clattered to the bottom of the drawer. "What keeps you awake on such a quiet night?"

Alsop Parker stepped into the office. Judging by the condition of his clothing, he had already slept in them. He cleared his throat, and seemed surprised to see Noland Haines.

"I had just settled in to sleep when I realized I did not know your plans, sir," he said. "Seeing the candle still burning in the window, I thought to ask you about it."

"You must have very excellent vision. Allow me to ease your rest and tell you I shall be leaving tomorrow, at full light. I will depart New Lanark just as early in three days' time."

"And will you be taking the carriage, sir?"

"I think not. The season is fine, and a ride on horseback should be greatly gratifying. I will probably follow the river to Lewiston, and the old Roman road from there."

"It is a good route, but somewhat deserted," Parker said.

"I do not intend to make any social calls along the way, my friend. Some time to myself might be just what I need."

Alsop Parker made some grunting sound.

"But inasmuch as your concern for me has aroused you from your sleep this night," Daniel continued cheerfully, "pray remain with us and lighten the load of our work."

Nolly smiled good-humoredly but Alsop Parker looked as if Daniel suggested murder itself.

It seemed to Daniel, as he once again resumed a study of the books, that one's face revealed far more than one could imagine. Unless one was Miss Emily Clarkson, whose face, and hands, and delectable body remained as tantalizing and mysterious as a sphinx.

Several days later, Emily walked out of the schoolhouse on Peter Havers' arm, and was assisted into the carriage of the duke. She did not think it the same grand vehicle in which he stopped all traffic in the street, but it proved just as elegant.

"I did not think to expect you, Mr. Havers. Is this also one of your responsibilities to the duke?"

"To be perfectly honest, Miss Clarkson, I do whatever he tells me. And I certainly would never question a mission in which I spend time with you."

Emily smiled and looked up at him. He certainly was very handsome in his dark jacket and elegant cravat, but something about him reminded her more of several boys in her class than of someone who would be emissary to a duke. There seemed a look of recklessness about him, of mischief that could be troublesome, and of restless frustration. If she had not encountered such emotions on a daily basis, she could not have been so sure about recognizing them.

"You are very kind, sir. But we are not very well acquainted, and I fear the antagonism between our households is destined to discourage our changing that. I suspect the duke invited me only because he knew Mr. Lennox would be away."

"You are a very forthright woman, Miss Clarkson. But let me assure you the duke allows no one to stand in his way; he would have me bring you to Gleneyrie even if Daniel stood guarding the schoolhouse door." Peter Havers settled back in the seat cushions, and Emily saw a little cloud of dust rise from the fabric. "However, I knew Daniel would be away, and informed His Grace."

"Do you spy on Mr. Lennox, then?" Emily asked, emboldened by Mr. Havers' confession.

"No more than he on the duke. We all of us know who is about in the town, though the duke remains more isolated than most. He is not in very good health and rarely leaves his home. Therefore it is the responsibility of others to bring Glenfell to his door."

"I am glad to go, for I am very interested in seeing the great house, as well as its inhabitants," Emily said conversationally.

"It is truly a splendid house, built over ages of time. The title is a very ancient and honorable one, as befits the owner of such an estate. Queen Elizabeth herself granted her blessing on the grounds, and she gave the house its name. She stopped here on her way downriver on a great barge, and desired a respite on dry land. Of course, the duke's ancestor happily obliged his queen, and was rewarded with a gift of the barge itself."

"Vastly inconvenient for her retinue. How did they continue on to London?"

Peter frowned in the darkness, and Emily could see the difficulty had never occurred to him before.

Emily took pity on him. "They undoubtedly borrowed several carriages, for I cannot imagine Elizabeth walking the rest of the way. And what did the duke do with his new barge?"

"A most wondrous thing. It was brought up from the river after many years of proper usage, and made into one of the rooms of the house. You shall see it tonight; it juts out from the East Wing, and affords the best view of the river."

"How remarkable!" Indeed, Emily felt intrigued by such a spectacle. "And how very clever. The duke and duchess must enjoy it very much."

Peter said nothing. Emily, remembering the dour expression on the duke's face, wondered if the man enjoyed anything.

Suddenly the carriage made a sharp turn and Emily fell against Mr. Havers' side. She righted herself, feeling embarrassed, and then realized how the closeness of his lean body did nothing to excite her at all, nor prompt any improper thoughts. She did not wonder about him, as she did about another.

"Here are the gates to Gleneyrie. You see the fine ironwork of the crest and the ornate scrolls on the bars," Peter said coolly, and she suspected he did not feel aroused by her either.

"You seem very proud of it, Mr. Havers," Emily said a little waspishly.

Surprisingly, he laughed.

"Why should I not? I have lived all my life here, and it is very much my home. My mother's family·has ever taken matters of class and social position very seriously and with pride. It is a responsibility to society and to civilization."

Emily caught her breath. Once, not too long ago, she had felt the same way. She knew few people beyond those who were acceptable to her family and their friends, and felt the pull of titles and position in the men she met socially. And yet now she realized a good deal had changed, while she had scarcely noticed the transformation. It was not merely her association with an arrogant mill owner whose industry gave his name power and respect. It was also her daily concourse with children who had lost nearly everything, and honest laborers who earned every shilling they owned. Most people did not rely upon inheritance or great expectations. For all of them, and now for her, life was an active affair.

"Do you feel obliged to serve him for society's sake?"

"Something like that, yes," Peter said quietly, and then, "Behold! Your first glimpse of Gleneyrie!"

Emily, of course, had already glimpsed the great house from the level of the road, where one could see its gray stone towers and lacy ironwork on the roof. Smoke rarely blew from the chimneys and never did one perceive any other signs of life from within. But such sightings hardly prepared one for the greatness of the house, for its broad asymmetrical lines and imposing beauty.

In the stillness of the evening, one could hear the cooing lullabies of the birds nestled in the surrounding trees, and the rushing sound of some tributary of the Fell cascading down the hilly terrain. At the base of the great marble stairway, large torches crackled as they lit the entranceway, and a mastiff waited expectantly as the carriage pulled up.

No one else came to meet them, nor did Peter seem to expect it. He pulled the step from the carriage and offered Emily his hand as she stepped onto the irregular bricks of the drive.

"Welcome to Gleneyrie, Miss Clarkson," he said and bowed very low. By his manner, he might already have been the proprietor of the estate, rather than a suppliant of its owner. "I hope you enjoy your visit with us."

Emily said nothing as he drew her up the stairs and into a dark hallway.

"The duke and duchess await you in the parlor," he said, and continued to lead the way. For this favor, Emily felt particularly grateful, for she could scarcely see a thing. They passed beneath large portraits and landscapes and imposing statuary, but all this Emily perceived in very dim light. Whatever the worth of the duke, he clearly did not intend to squander it on candles and oils.

Mr. Havers pushed against a large door, which opened into a room only slightly brighter than the hall.

"Miss Emily Clarkson," he intoned in a voice that reverberated in the cavernous room.

Emily knew her hosts must be seated within, but it took several moments before she could find them. Seated in a corner near an unlit fireplace, in seats so huge several people might well have fit within, were the Duke and Duchess of Glendennon.

She curtsied properly and waited for either of her hosts to extend a hand. When it did not come, she straightened, hoping her blue gown not too lavish for a dinner at Gleneyrie. Indeed, for all their eminence, the duke and duchess looked far more modest than she did herself.

The duke wore a cream-colored jacket of a cut rarely seen in the stylish arenas of 1819. It looked overly large, as if it did not belong to him, and made him appear dwarfish in form. His spindly legs stuck out from his chair, encased in dark pantaloons, and the buckles on his shoes looked tarnished. Daring to look upon his face, Emily thought it seemed as weary as the rest of him, with lines of care drawn deeply into his cheeks, and sparse gray hair dropping down onto his forehead. His eyes alone, bright blue and intensely curious, belied the evidence that he must be a man of at least threescore and ten.

The duchess, by contrast, could not have been older than Emily herself. She, too, dressed unfashionably—in a gray wool dress, modestly cut and close-fitting. Her flaxen hair appeared plaited under her matron's lace cap and her heavy-lidded eyes studied Emily with barely concealed antagonism.

I should not feel so very generous myself, Emily thought, if I had given up the love of one such as Daniel Lennox to marry a man old enough to be his grandfather.

"You had a comfortable journey, I trust?" a hoarse voice ground out.

"Thank you, yes, Your Grace. Mr. Havers proved most solicitous," Emily said, and turned around to acknowledge her escort. Surprised, she realized him gone.

"I demand him to be so," the duke said. While it might have been true, Emily did not think his words sounded like those of a man contemplating his heir.

It seemed to be enough, for a while, and the duke and duchess continued to study her in silence. They neither asked her to be seated nor offered refreshment, and Emily wondered how long she would remain standing under their scrutiny.

"You are related to Dr. Leicester Clarkson, I understand," the duke asked, and the duchess edged forward on her seat.

"Yes, Your Grace. He was my father and taught me a great deal. I thought my heart would break when he died."

The duke laughed. "You need to be stronger than that, my girl! I have taken many losses, but only one broke my heart."

Emily wondered how much of a heart he owned to have been broken but wisely said nothing. Intuitively, she guessed his hardest burden might have been the death of his infant heirs.

"Perhaps Miss Clarkson is not very strong, Your Grace," the duchess said in a soft childish voice. "Ought we ask her to sit?"

Emily gave the lady a look of gratitude but it was not acknowledged.

The duke waved again, an act Emily took to mean his assent. She looked around her, and chose a low needlepoint chair at a comfortable distance from her hosts.

"I am dismayed to learn a young lady with connections as yours would accept such an offer as the one made by Lennox. Teaching the common children of the mill is a degradation," the duke said.

Emily felt a stab of indignation.

"I beg your pardon, Your Grace, but honest employment must never be considered a degradation. One may have advantages of birth and wealth, but the former might be useless without the later. I accepted Mr. Lennox's offer on behalf of my mother, and because I chose to make myself useful to my family. And as to Mr. Lennox, while his connections may not be as elevated as my own, his sister is married to an earl. Surely the association cannot be so very reprehensible."

The duchess leaned forward, and of course Emily knew her sudden interest must have to do with Daniel Lennox. She wondered if the lady ever thought her earlier connection "reprehensible."

Her husband's face seemed to have hardened into a

mask, frowning and severe. Emily hoped the poor duchess' child would inherit nothing from the father but his title, and then realized that the old man might have been handsome before age and bitterness affected his visage.

"Shall we eat, Your Grace?" his lady asked and rose. The gray fabric of her gown fell down in straight lines.

"I suppose we must," the Duke of Glendennon said grudgingly.

"You may follow us in, Miss Clarkson," said the duchess, careful to remind Emily of her precedence.

Nevertheless, Emily could not help but feel some rising resentment as she walked behind them into the vast dining hall.

It had been built for another age, for a time when knights assembled before their lords, and then supped and slept and made merry in the most public of exhibitions. The shouts and groans of those long dead seemed to reverberate throughout, to the heights of the arched, timbered ceiling. Emily looked up, thinking the structure very much like that of an inverted ship, and thought she saw a bat, or a bird, flutter among the rafters.

She followed her hosts to a rustic oaken table, very likely another vestige of happier days. Three settings were placed upon it, in the brightest corner, and Emily realized Peter would not be a guest.

A servant held out a chair for her, and Emily faced the young duchess. In the candlelight, the young woman looked younger and rather elegant, and Emily appreciated how Daniel Lennox might still pine for her. There also seemed something rather tragic about her lot, as if she were a figure of fairy tale, her youth and vitality kept captive in the castle of the ogre.

The ogre said nothing as he sat down at the head of his table, but rapped on his glass for the service of a drink. He sipped it cautiously, as one might do very hot tea, and Emily wondered if he feared he might be poisoned. She noticed that her hostess did not have anything at all.

"The rooms at Gleneyrie are very grand," she ventured. "You must take pride in them and great pleasure when you entertain."

The duke nearly spilled his glass. "Our pride is a matter of record, for generations of my family have protected

Gleneyrie from villains and pretenders. It is long our history, and this century is no exception. But there has been no party here for at least thirty years, nor likely to be unless there is a reason for celebration." He looked accusingly at his lady, and Emily did not have to possess a sixth sense to know what he meant.

"Surely you celebrated your own nuptials," she said artlessly and smiled brightly, encouragingly.

The duchess looked into the flame of the candle, her eyes half closed. "My family rejoiced in the match, and hosted a very fine feast in their home. We do not open Gleneyrie to those merely curious and vulgar and certainly not to those who do not wish us well. We have, however, desired to note an exception in your case."

Emily certainly recognized an insult when it came at her, but felt rather more curious to know of which of the two offenses she might be guilty and why, in fact, exceptions were noted. She could only guess the duke and duchess had been even more curious to meet her than she to meet them, and their curiosity undoubtedly had to do with Peter. Indeed, it seemed the best explanation for his sudden absence; if he desired their approval before he accompanied Emily on any more outings, they might more readily grant it without his interference.

"You are most kind, Your Grace. And I do assure you I only wish you to be well and happy. As one so new to the neighborhood, I have scarcely formed loyalties and bear no ill will toward anyone."

Emily saw the look that passed between the duke and duchess and wondered of what they must suspect her, if of anything beyond her apparent friendship with Peter Havers. If he were the heir presumptive to the dukedom, it might matter to them if he planned to pursue a modest schoolmistress. Aside from that, she could not imagine why her association with Daniel Lennox or with others in the town might be made to matter.

"We are a town divided, young lady," pronounced the duke. "There are none who can walk the line between Gleneyrie and Shearings and manage to remain upright. One must choose, and chance the consequences."

"I hope Your Grace does not imagine I might be able to have success where others have failed. I came to Glenfell because of the generosity of Mr. Lennox and necessarily owe him some allegiance. But I never presume such gratitude precludes friendship with others, particularly those worthy of deference."

The duke grunted. "You sound like a very clever young woman. And a clear-eyed one. That is why I invited you to Gleneyrie . . ."

Emily smiled, feeling no uncertain pride.

". . . To ask you to leave Glenfell."

Bewildered, Emily stared at him over the glass of cider. Surely he did not ask her to his table so he could request her to depart from it.

"Forgive me, Your Grace. I do not believe I heard you correctly."

"I heard no reports of your deafness. What did you not hear? It is in the best interests of this neighborhood, and your own happiness, that you leave at once."

"Your Grace, I am under obligation to stay until Mr. Lennox pronounces my services no longer necessary. As you must know, I am an employee at his mill."

"The mill, and all who associate with its operation, are corrupt. For the sake of your esteemed family, who value you, I ask you to leave before it is too late."

Emily wondered who, aside from her aunt and mother, were so connected to her that they feared for the reputation of the Clarkson name. And why the duke, whose contempt of everything beyond the walls of Gleneyrie seemed potent, would champion their cause.

"And my lady? Are you acquainted with the Clarkson family wishes as well?"

The duchess looked at her husband, as if asking for his approval to speak. He gave her no notice, no encouragement, no indication he even knew she sat there. Instead, he rapped on his glass for the first course and watched as a brown broth was spooned into his bowl.

"My lady duchess does not know the Clarksons, nor could it concern her to ever meet them. Her reasons for bringing you to Gleneyrie are not so very different from my own. She wishes to warn you away from Lennox."

Emily looked toward the duchess and this time met her eyes. It was not her business to know what separated this lady from the mill owner, but she had heard enough gossip to believe the young woman had been swayed by the prospects of title and position. But who really knew what had gone on between Daniel Lennox and the woman he had hoped to marry? He could be arrogant and proud, and demand too much of one. He associated with some rough types, and did not appear anxious to assume the role of a gentleman. He worked in trade, and measured himself by its success. What else might have diminished his suit?

"He is not an honorable man, Miss Clarkson. He prays for no one's happiness but his own. And cares not for the welfare of this neighborhood."

"If he were so very indifferent to the welfare of others, I am sure I would not have been brought here in the first place. Though Mr. Lennox is a practical man, he was persuaded to open a school for the children and is responsible for their care. He seems very interested in the happiness of his workers and never shows me anything but kindness."

"Is that all, Miss Clarkson?" the duchess asked. Her husband seemed preoccupied in finishing his broth.

"I suppose not, Your Grace. He also attempts to add progressive improvements to . . ."

The lady laughed, a curiously hollow sound that reverberated in the room. "I do not care to hear his qualities repeated. I wished to know if kindness is all he shows you."

Emily looked at the duchess levelly, thinking her question crude for one in so elevated a position. But perhaps such things did not matter if they spoke as one woman to another and, more particularly, as two women involved in the affairs of Daniel Lennox's life. Of course, they did not share intimacies in private; they sat at table with the husband of the duchess.

Emily glanced at the old man, and understood why his lady would be so bold. He already seemed to have lost interest in their conversation, in their company, in everything save for the meal in front of him.

"He shows me polite kindness and an occasional interest in my affairs. I expect nothing else," Emily said. She blushed thinking of their intimacies a few days before, but felt it no concern of the duchess.

The lady nodded in satisfaction. "You must endeavor to remain so. Otherwise I would fear for you."

"Your Grace cannot imagine I have anything to fear?"

"I can imagine a good deal, Miss Clarkson," the duchess said, and picked up her soup spoon.

The meal proved a dreadful affair, not only in the steady diminution of what passed for conversation, but also for the general tastelessness of the food. Boiled vegetables followed the weak broth, and the stringiness of the beef made it virtually inedible. The duchess seemed to attack it with some spirit, for otherwise she would surely have starved to death. But Emily, having known no deprivation in her menu since her removal from London, politely pushed the food about her plate.

No one seemed to take notice.

The platters, only partially filled, did not take very long to finish. The duchess looked wistfully into her empty bowl of broth and wiped her lips very prettily.

"I am sure the ladies wish to retire to the parlor." The duke made a formal pronouncement, more in keeping with an audience of a hundred than the women on either side of him.

The duchess assented by rising and curtsying to her lord. When she walked from his presence, Emily quickly followed.

"My husband will sleep now," the lady said. "He requires a great deal of rest."

"Is he not well?" Emily asked politely.

"He is always well, Miss Clarkson. How can it be otherwise?"

Emily had never supposed the lofty to be exempt from illness, or unhappiness, or death, but the lady seemed to think otherwise.

Silently, the duchess led Emily through the labyrinth of rooms of Gleneyrie, in which beauty transcended mustiness and the odor of decay. Finally they entered a curiously-shaped chamber, with windows on three sides, and Emily recognized the royal barge of Peter's description.

"You surely must see why I felt drawn to this place, why I believed it must be my home," the duchess said softly.

"It is very lovely, indeed. But I think it is the people who make a home, who draw us in."

The duchess looked angry, but her words were calm. "You see only what you wish to see and cannot pretend to know another's reasoning. Only a few individuals understand the spell of Gleneyrie. I am one . . .''

"And I daresay Peter Havers is another."

The duchess smiled. "Peter has every reason to be drawn here, as he is related by blood."

And desire, Emily thought, instinctively aware of what lay beneath the surface. Could the lady, aware of the weakened state of her elderly husband, already have her second husband waiting in the wings? How convenient it would be never to leave her chamber, and to welcome an uninterrupted succession of dukes to her bed.

"Daniel Lennox did not understand my desire to be here," the lady continued.

Indeed, he would not, if his beloved jilted him so painfully.

"And we shall never be reconciled."

"Then why should it matter to Your Grace if Mr. Lennox spends any amount of time with me? Although I have assured you our relationship does not extend outside the classroom, you neither seem happy nor convinced of the fact. I cannot understand why."

The Duchess of Glendennon started to walk away, and Emily guessed their conversation—and perhaps the evening—at its end. She watched the small figure advance on the draperies and pull one section aside to look out the window in the direction of the river and Daniel Lennox's mill.

Just as Emily thought she should withdraw from the room, the lady turned back to face her, and Emily was shocked by the look of utter desolation on her features. Her eyes, so fine, were red-lidded and teary, and her small mouth seemed to pull in several directions at once. Her pale hands were clasped in front of her and moved as if she held a captive, wild thing within them. For the second time in a matter of minutes, Emily was struck by a revelation.

"Do you still love Mr. Lennox, Your Grace?"

The lady's face colored and then went pale. "Your impertinence is not welcome here, Miss Clarkson. Kindly consign it to the classroom, where I am sure it is an asset. Daniel must have thought it admirable, or he would not have kept you there."

"I believe he did, Your Grace," Emily said tersely.

The duchess turned back to the window, and Emily wondered if she should make good her escape. But then she heard a choking sound and realized her hostess sobbed as she looked out into the night.

"I most certainly could not love Mr. Lennox," she gasped. "How could I in my position?"

Never did a denial so absolutely confirm Emily's suspicions.

"Of course you could not, Your Grace," Emily said softly. "A woman made a duchess must necessarily own such joy as to make cares insignificant."

"You are right, of course, Miss Clarkson," the lady sniffed, and hastily wiped her cheeks on the dusty draperies. "There are compensations. But they cannot erase pain."

Emily now believed she entirely understood the reason for her invitation to Gleneyrie, the duke's abrupt manner toward her, and the lady's emotional outburst. It all hinged on Mr. Lennox himself: the duke thought he protected society's interests by preventing a liaison between Emily and the man he despised, and the duchess thought to protect her own interests by preventing the same between Emily and a man she still loved.

Jealousy could prove a demanding taskmaster. And perhaps it had intensified, if the lady had not entirely abandoned her first lover at his mill, but continued to meet him. Then it might be Daniel Lennox who waited to marry her and be a father to the baby she already carried, rather than Peter Havers—who would be usurped in all his expectations. The heir apparent might have been already conceived. Emily remembered the strangled conversation between Mr. Lennox and his cousin and realized that a death might be as much anticipated as a birth.

She sighed aloud, and regretted even the little part she played in such desperate affairs.

"You need not fear for me, Your Grace," she said softly, knowing herself the most insignificant cog in the machinery. "Nor do you have anything to fear from me."

"Will you leave, then?" the duchess asked.

"I cannot, Your Grace. I am as obliged to remain in my modest schoolhouse as your ladyship is to stay in Gleneyrie. We both are bound to promises and decisions we have made."

The duchess closed her eyes, though Emily could not know if the gesture confirmed or disputed Emily's pronouncement. She rather suspected the latter, since the lady did not speak more than ten words to her for the rest of the evening.

Chapter Eight

*P*eter Havers did not show himself to Emily again at Gleneyrie, although she caught a glimpse of him as she departed, unescorted but for the coachman, down the long drive. There, revealed in the flickering light provided by the torches burning at the bottom of the stairway, she saw him engaged in animated discussion with an older man whom she thought she recognized from the mill. Another person, draped in a dark cloak, witnessed their exchange but said nothing while Emily's carriage passed.

It could be no concern of hers. Perhaps the men tended to some business on the property, or were managing the affairs of the duke. He undoubtedly needed help. Indeed, on this evening the old man had never awakened from his place at the dinner table.

Though Emily could scarcely wait to escape, she felt an inexplicable sense of loss when the carriage began to roll down the steep hill toward the mill. She doubted she would ever see Gleneyrie again, nor would she ever discover the ancient mysteries it wore with grace and style. If a house could be said to have a character independent of its occupants, this surely was it; that seemed its most defining feature. She could no sooner see Peter Havers doing its grand history justice than the embittered duke.

As such, she felt saddened, and possessed of an uncommon weariness of spirit.

Within minutes, however, the Fell came into view, and Emily realized how very little distance actually separated the two great houses of the town. Their owners stood worlds apart, but the domains were more similar than either man would admit to.

Emily told herself, as severely as any schoolmistress, how she must ignore any advances on the part of Daniel Lennox, no matter the pleasures they afforded. If his heart and concerns were elsewhere, he only trifled with her, and perhaps acted with the expectation that she would depart shortly. Indeed, if something happened to the duke, and Mr. Lennox married the widowed duchess, Emily would leave on the first stage.

Before she could reason why she should feel so strongly, the solid structure of the schoolhouse appeared against the gray sky. Emily longed for the sanctuary of her room, but the sight of its dark, austere facade made her feel shut out. Not a single light burned within.

Apparently, the duke's driver did not think anything amiss, for he stopped abruptly in the unlit drive. A moment later, he appeared at the door and reached for her hand.

"It does not look as if I am expected," she said.

He turned away. "My instructions are to return you to the door," the man said stubbornly and nearly pulled her out of the vehicle. Without anything further, he climbed back onto the bench, urged his horses to go forward, and left his charge standing in a little swirl of dust on the drive.

Emily watched him leave, faintly bemused.

Gathering up her stiff skirts, she walked over the grass to the front door, expecting it to be opened by a waiting servant. When it was not, she pushed against it, and was disheartened when it did not budge. Her knocks went unanswered, and she only succeeded in bruising the side of her hand.

She knew the schoolroom would be locked, and decided her most promising portal would be the kitchen. Mrs. Bernays often remained awake until the late evening, keeping the cook, Mrs. Lashley, company while she kneaded the bread for the next day. On several occasions, Emily had wondered when the two women ever slept.

The rushing waters of the river grew louder as Emily turned the corner of the building to approach the herb garden and kitchen. Even in the cool temperatures of the autumnal evening, the pungent aromas of sage and rosemary blessed the air. Unable to resist temptation, Emily reached down and caught a few leaves between her fingers. Curiously, they felt sticky and wet.

She ran to the door, nearly tripping over a prone body on the walkway. Gasping in fright, Emily felt only partially relieved to recognize one of the dogs from the mill. The poor thing whined plaintively.

"Are you also locked out, boy?" Emily asked, wondering if the animal could be sensitive to the agitation in her voice. "And will you not sleep at Shearings, where you belong? Ah, but Mrs. Lashley's kitchen is a comforting place."

Emily groped for the handle of the door in the darkness. The same sticky substance covered it, and Emily did not even want to guess what a wretched state her gown and body would be in.

The door opened at her urging, and the dog dashed in ahead of her. Almost as desperately, Emily stepped into the anteroom, and waited for her eyes to adjust to the darkness. Baskets of onions and potatoes lined the stone walls and their earthy scent provided some steadying comfort. Emily stood still, gathering her wits.

A sliver of light at the base of one of the doors provided the slightest beacon. She heard voices, at least one of them feminine, and the flickering light on the floor suggested movement in the main room of the kitchen. Surely Mrs. Lashley would be within, and might even be happy to have a little talk.

Emily smiled and opened the door to the larger room.

Mrs. Lashley, it seemed, already enjoyed enough help to bake bread for an army. Several people huddled around the long wooden table, working away, entirely preoccupied with their chore. As one man wore the muddy clothes of a river man, Emily could only wonder why Mrs. Lashley would allow him to come so close to the dough and hoped that at least he had scrubbed his hands.

Suddenly, two of the people parted slightly, and Emily could finally see what lay upon the table. She could not comprehend the strange vision until the sight of a dark boot dripping with weed and water jolted her into acute understanding.

"Good heavens!" she cried and put her hand to her lips.

"Miss Clarkson!" scolded Mrs. Bernays, turning around, and once again blocked Emily's view of the body on the table. "Away with you! This is not for your eyes!"

For the briefest moment, Emily felt like running right out the door and all the way home to her aunt's house. But circumstances—not to mention her own curiosity— conspired to make her a participant in whatever wretched events had occurred this night, and she would not listen to any warning.

"You gave me no choice, Mrs. Bernays, as the other doors were closed to me. I know not what mayhem is afoot, but I seem destined to be a part of it. You must at least be honest with me: is there a dead man on our kitchen table?"

Mrs. Bernays sucked in her breath and leaned closer. "There is not, though he will be if he is not tended to, or if no one sends for Dr. Cafferty."

"The doctor is the duke's man," one of the men muttered.

"Perhaps I can help," Emily said calmly, gaining strength from the desperation of the others. "My father was a surgeon, and often allowed me to assist him with his patients."

It was a bald-faced lie, but she doubted anyone would dispute her just now.

"You do not want to be a part of this, miss," said Mrs. Bernays firmly.

Emily raised her chin as she untied the bow on her cape. "If a man dies because I did not come to his aid, I should regret it for the rest of my life," she said with equal conviction.

"Let her," said one of the men, and no one denied him, or her. Emily steadied her nerves and walked bravely to the table.

"Oh!" she cried and fell back. If Mrs. Lashley had not been just behind her, she would have found herself on the hard floor.

"Whom did you expect?" The woman rasped into her ear, and pushed her forward.

"I . . . expected some wretched soul pulled from the

river," Emily said, so faintly the others must have strained to hear her.

"He is a wretched soul pulled from the river," echoed one of the men.

"Wretched" scarcely did justice to the bloodied and broken form of Daniel Lennox, who lay stretched out on the table before her. Weeds matted his dark hair, and blood from a fierce cut dripped from his temple onto a rag someone had placed beneath his head. His lashes cast a shadow on his cheeks, rough with the growth of his beard and discolored by a bruise. Emily looked at his open mouth, so accustomed was she to hearing his tart words, and was sickened to think him silenced.

Someone had already ripped apart Mr. Lennox's soaked and filthy shirt to reveal a tanned and muscular chest nearly bisected by a deep gash running from his collarbone across his breast and disappearing beneath the nasty remnants of his garment.

Shaking so violently she thought she would fall again, Emily nevertheless reached out to run her finger along the ridge of the cut, stopping only briefly at its lower extremity to unfasten a button. Out of the corner of her eye, she saw a hand reach out, but Mrs. Bernays brushed it away.

"Let her," she said firmly. Emily gained strength from the woman's confidence in her ability: an expression surely misplaced since Emily possessed no ability at all. If any of them had thought about it, her lie would have been recognized in a moment, for no gentleman would ever have allowed a young daughter to witness the horrors of the surgery.

Emily laid her palm flat on Daniel Lennox's cold stomach and only then felt the slightest vibration of his breathing. She offered a silent prayer of gratitude, and pressed down harder in an effort to revive him. But for the slightest flickering of his eyelashes, he appeared dead.

"We must act quickly," she said in a renewal of determination. "Mrs. Bernays, I will need five or six of your finest sewing needles and some black thread. Mrs. Lashley? Will you boil several pots of water? Quickly! I also must have washing cloths; old ones will do if they are clean. And blankets, as many as can be spared. Do you not feel how cold he is?"

Emily's orders recharged her troops and even before she finished, she realized she stood alone over the body of Daniel Lennox, retaining only his loyal dog for company.

Without the circle of servants surrounding him he must have grown even colder, for she thought she saw him shiver. Looking quickly around her, she reached for her woolen cape and pulled it over him to his shoulders. Protected though he now was, he looked even more vulnerable.

Emily leaned over him, close to his face, and felt futility of the most painful sort. Had her father ever known such a feeling when confronted with a patient too ill to be helped? He, with all the skills of his profession, must have known hopelessness. What was she—with none of his talents and tools—to believe?

"I will not leave you," she said to him. "I will do everything of which I am capable, and remain by your side."

Then, ever so faintly, she felt a warm breath on her cheek, and thought she heard him speak. She turned her head quickly, and saw his mouth now closed; the smallest gesture reviving the greatest spark of hope.

"Should we not call the doctor?" she asked, her lips close to his ear. His eyelashes fluttered, as if he struggled to awaken.

"No." His voice was hoarse and only a whisper, but she did not mistake his word.

"He will know what to do," she persisted.

"So I fear," came the answer, with just a glimmer of the familiar irony. "Must be secret."

Emily frowned, doubting his words and intention, and then realized an obvious truth.

"Was this an attempt at murder?" she asked.

He said nothing, but startled her by opening his eyes. And her answer was there, as clear as any message she had ever received.

"You are safe here," she said, and before she could reassure him further, the room suddenly filled again with people.

"Here's hot water, Miss Clarkson, and more will be boiling soon," said Mrs. Lashley, with no more fuss than if she had been making soup. Mrs. Bernays joined her, and opened a felt cloth to which several shiny needles were affixed. Heavy woolen blankets filled the arms of the groom, and one of the other men had thought to find a pillow. The anxious group surrounded her, and Emily realized they awaited her orders.

She cleared her throat. "We must wash him," she said a little doubtfully. When no one moved, she repeated, more firmly, "We must clean him, or his wounds will become diseased."

"He came up from the river," offered the groom.

"Indeed. And we have ample evidence of the purity of the water," said Emily grimly, and waved her hand over the mud, the weeds, and the putrid drippings off the table. She reached for a cloth, and soaked it gingerly in Mrs. Lashley's bucket of hot, soapy water. As it cooled in one hand, she gestured with the other for Mrs. Bernays to remove the cape from around Mr. Lennox's body and replace it with one of the blankets.

She started on his brow and felt immensely relieved when the dirt and blood washed away, and his bruises did not look as dreadful as they had at first. Carefully, gently, she worked, intent on her operation but never indifferent to its intimacy nor to the feel of his bones and flesh beneath her probing fingers. He moved once, startling her, but she soothed him with a few words.

Looking up only once at her open-mouthed audience, she continued her awful task. Mrs. Bernays held a pot of water at hand, replacing it quickly when its contents turned red. Emily reached for a succession of cloths but knew the prospect of cleaning all the dirt from his wounds was nearly impossible.

The deep gash across Daniel Lennox's chest followed the line of a soldier's sash, and looked very raw and deadly. The edges of skin, yellow and dry, could not be persuaded to come together even after soil and sand had washed away, and would need to be stitched. Emily moved her fingers over the dark hair tapering toward his stomach, and wondered how on earth she would manage it.

"You better let me handle this, Miss Clarkson," said a gruff voice, and a man reached for the cloth.

Understanding she had moved too close to indecency, Emily dropped the linen into the pot and allowed herself to be drawn away from the table by Mrs. Bernays and Mrs. Lashley.

"This is no job for a lady, Miss Clarkson," the housekeeper said. "I do not know how your father let you loose around his surgery, but you look like you are about to faint dead away."

Emily rubbed her fingers along her brow. Behind her she heard the sound of ripping fabric and the thud of a dropped boot, and dared not imagine what she would see if she turned around.

"Then you must give me strength, Mrs. Bernays. I know not what else to do." Emily bit down on her lip, afraid she would cry. "We cannot let Mr. Lennox die."

She looked from one anxious face to the other, and realized the two kindly ladies loved him as much as she did herself. For if she knew nothing else at this dreadful, fateful moment, she recognized an emotion she had scarcely felt before and would not abandon now. She needed Daniel Lennox to live so she could share that awakening with him.

"We will not let him die, Miss Clarkson," Mrs. Lashley said. She held up a corner of her apron and wiped Emily's face as if she were a little girl. When she brought her hand away, Emily saw the stain of blood—Daniel Lennox's blood—on the white fabric. "Now calm yourself, for I do not know who else can do the deed."

"I confess: I myself do not believe I can do it."

"You must, Emily," said Mrs. Bernays, shaking her by the shoulders. "You must and you will. We all depend on you, but no more than the master."

Still grasping her shoulders, the housekeeper turned Emily around. There seemed no hope but to try to remember things her father had said, and act with sense and reason as her guide. They needed to be summoned, for they had abandoned her at the door.

Sick at heart and stomach, Emily returned to the long table and felt some relief when her patient slipped into unconsciousness again. The business seemed bad enough; she did not imagine for a moment she could pull a needle through the flesh of a man who would be able to feel every sting. She thought she ought to start at his collarbone and work her way down the length of his torso, and loosened the blanket at his neck. His skin felt cold and clammy, as a corpse's would be. But as her fingers moved over his neck they met the quickening pulse beneath his skin.

Her hands shaking, Emily tried to thread the fine needle until Mrs. Lashley hastened to do it for her. She dropped it into a small dish and instructed Mrs. Bernays to pour boiling water over it, thinking to wash away any dirt picked up in the room. Possibly this was an unnecessary precaution, though she remembered her father insisting upon it.

Finally, with needle in hand, Emily leaned over her patient and prayed she would not be sick. She tried to imagine herself at work on a bit of embroidery, but it proved very difficult to convince herself that Mr. Lennox's muscular body shared any similarities with a scrap of cotton. Aside from the tanned strength of his form, the tantalizing pattern of dark hair, and the slightly fishy smell of him, she knew that—with any success—he would bear the scar of her workmanship forever.

"He is a fine figure of a man," said Mrs. Bernays calmly.

"Thank you for reminding me of the fact," Emily said wryly, without looking up from his wound. "If you intended to intimidate me even further, you have succeeded admirably. Now I know I shall answer for this to his wife one day."

"She will show you nothing but gratitude, my dear."

"Then let us pray I do not sew his arm to his neck or something of that sort," Emily added, and marveled how her absurd show of humor somehow bolstered her flagging confidence. She seized its advantage.

Necessarily positioning one elbow upon his bare chest, she began to apply the needle to his skin, remembering the admonitions of her governess to use small and even stitches. If the dear lady had ever imagined her student would apply her lessons while ripping through human flesh, she would have had a seizure.

Emily's fingers moved just ahead of the needle, pushing the ragged edges of the skin together, and keeping the line even. Three times she accepted a newly threaded needle and allowed Mrs. Bernays to cut away the old one. And once she looked up at the cook, who wiped tears from her eyes so she could see.

And so she worked, for the better part of the longest

hour of her life, until she reached the lowest extremity of the wound. Here her awkwardness increased, for she could only stitch by his waist if she balanced herself on his thigh, and she hesitated.

"You cannot stop now, Miss Clarkson," said the groom encouragingly.

"It is not proper," Emily said in a voice scarcely recognizable as her own.

"My dear, no one will think less of you for it. Indeed, only we in this room shall know of Mr. Lennox's indebtedness to you. If you prefer, we will not speak of it even to him."

But as Emily pressed against Daniel Lennox's body, she knew he had awakened and seemed as aware of her as she was of him. His skin by now seemed flushed and warm and she saw a tightening in the muscles of his stomach. He shifted where he lay.

"Mr. Lennox, please!" cried Mrs. Bernays. "John, Michael . . . hold his shoulders! You must not move an inch or you will disturb Miss Clarkson."

Emily did not think it possible to be more disturbed than she already felt, but decided not to press the point.

"Must not disturb Miss Clarkson," she heard him say, and in spite of her difficulties, she smiled. Then, without warning, one bare arm snaked out of the nest of woolen blankets and caught her wrist. The needle went into her finger instead of his side, and in an instant, her blood mingled with his.

"You must let me finish, Mr. Lennox," Emily said, through a painful lump in her throat. She leaned down and rubbed her cheek against the back of his hand, having nothing else free to offer any sort of comfort.

He grunted, which she took for assent, and released his hold.

The last few stitches were no match for her first painstaking ones, but Emily knew only a very few people might ever get to see them. If the duchess did not like his scar, she could look elsewhere for consolation.

"I believe I am done, Mrs. Bernays, so we will have no need of that final needle. Unless . . ." she looked questioningly at the men, almost dreading their reply.

"Just some small cuts and bruises, miss. They need not concern you."

Indeed, thought Emily wearily, they did not. For all her sudden warmth of emotions toward her employer, she knew she only played a small role in the drama of his life, after which she would undoubtedly move on to another role. And when Mr. Lennox woke up to realize the intimate part she had performed in this night's events, he might never wish to look upon her face again. She knew she would not be able to bear it.

"I am glad to hear it. Nevertheless, I am concerned about the events of the next few days, for they will reveal whether we can expect for him to recover. I suggest we bandage him in some of the mill's fine cotton and bring him to his bed in Shearings."

"No!" The simultaneous answer from everyone else in the room startled the speakers as much as Emily. As they looked at each other sheepishly, she folded her arms over her breast.

"I think I have earned your confidences," she said sternly. "Is it not time to tell me what happened to him?"

John looked the most guilty. "We don't rightly know, Miss Clarkson. He probably was attacked by a highwayman."

Several heads nodded in agreement.

"I see," Emily said as she looked at them. "Then why could Dr. Cafferty not be called? Do you suspect him of being the robber? Or, even worse, do you suspect the duke? I distinctly heard someone say Cafferty is one of the 'duke's men.' "

"You must understand, miss, here in Glenfell there are them who are loyal to the duke, and them to Mr. Lennox."

"So I have come to understand. But why should it matter to the duke if Mr. Lennox is attacked upon the road?"

No one answered, but Emily saw how they all expected her to reason it out for herself.

"The duke would want Mr. Lennox dead?"

"We have reason to suspect it, miss."

"What has Mr. Lennox done to the duke to provoke him so?"

Mrs. Lashley cleared her throat. "It is not so very much what he has done, as who he is, Miss Clarkson."

Emily glanced back at the kitchen table where, mercifully, Daniel Lennox slept under a mountain of blankets. They rose and fell with each breath, a fact of infinite reassurance. He did not look like a man who could arouse wrath in anyone.

"A mill owner? The duke seems to wear his rank even more heavily than does the prince himself."

"He is a very proud man. And a dangerous one."

"I have heard the same said of the unfortunate Mr. Lennox. But it did not seem to have served him well in this misadventure." Emily thought of the viciousness of the slashes on Mr. Lennox's body, and how he undoubtedly had been left to die. "Do you believe it anything but an accident?"

"We will not know until he is well enough to tell us what happened."

Emily's shoulders slumped in weariness and she supposed she should leave it all until the morning. But she already knew she would not sleep until some of her questions were answered.

"How did he get here? Did you find him in the river?"

"He came through the very door you did, Miss Clarkson," said Mrs. Lashley. "Walked right in on his own two feet. He was in the river by the look of him, and for some time. But he came in and up to the table where I worked on my bread, and collapsed where he stood, poor boy. I called for Mrs. Bernays, who sent Pamela for the men. I knew mischief was afoot, so we put out the candles and locked the doors as soon as they all arrived. Begging your pardon, miss, but I forgot you were still out."

"No matter. There were more important things on your mind. But if you believed me upstairs, why did you not summon me?"

Mrs. Bernays looked guilty. "Because you were with him, Miss Clarkson. We could not know you were to be trusted."

Emily had not known it herself until this night. "I hope I managed to convince you. You know my loyalty is to Mr. Lennox."

She stopped as her voice broke. She might profess her loyalty, but would not wish her new friends to speculate on any deeper feelings. In the light of morning, her heart would undoubtedly settle into a more temperate rhythm as she went about her business. Mr. Lennox might wish to avoid her altogether.

On the table, under the flickering light, their patient started to kick away at his blankets, revealing a large foot.

Emily gave a little laugh, in spite of her weariness. "I thought he might have broken a leg, so twisted did his body seem when I first saw him. But he disproves my fears."

Mrs. Bernays hugged her. "Do not worry about Mr. Lennox, dear Miss Clarkson. I have known him since he was a boy, and nursed him through enough injuries to fill a surgery. I daresay he will insist on being up and about by tomorrow."

"Oh dear! But he cannot, Mrs. Bernays! The stitches will be very painful and may open if he aggravates them. He could run a fever, and we shall have to worry about the onset of infection. He should not move at all."

Mrs. Lashley looked over Emily's shoulder and grimaced. "Would you have him on my table?"

Emily's laugh was so much at odds with the bloody scene around them, they must have thought her mad.

"And have him help with the daily baking of the bread? I would not think Mr. Lennox very domestic and he would be in the way. Let us find a sturdy board, and bring him to my bedroom."

Emily spoke in a perfectly reasonable manner, and yet, even as she uttered her words, she realized how shocking they were.

"It makes perfect sense," she continued. "He must stay hidden, lest he be attacked again. Where better than in a place where no intruder would think to look? Until Mr. Lennox is able to tell us what happened, and whom he suspects, we must not let anyone know his condition or whereabouts. We must protect him, not only from illness, but from further physical harm." Emily bit down on her lip, and tasted blood. "I suggest we say nothing. The attacker might then believe he succeeded and abandon his mission."

"I do not like the arrangement," Mrs. Bernays said primly.

"You need not look so censorious, Mrs. Bernays! Mr. Lennox hardly seems a threat to my virtue! Indeed, I already know him more intimately than could ever be considered proper. And I should rightly have the care of him while he recovers. What could be more convenient than that he be put in my bed and I sleep in the dressing room? Only Pamela and yourself enter there and no one should suspect anything amiss."

"I am not only thinking of your virtue, miss, but of your

own health," Mrs. Bernays argued. "You, yourself, have undergone an ordeal tonight, and look like one in need of several days' rest."

Emily spared a glance down at her stained gown and ripped lace. Her hair already hung about her head in stray wisps and her fingers had her blood, and Daniel Lennox's, upon them.

"Then I had best retire at once," she said. "I daresay Mr. Lennox will prove a most difficult patient when—and if—he awakens and I should need all my strength."

Mrs. Bernays could scarcely conceal her smile as she put her hands upon Emily's shoulders. "I wondered about this for several weeks, my love, and now I am certain. You have been sent to us to heal him," she said, and turned her towards the opened door.

Chapter Nine

On the day Daniel Lennox's father died, a messenger came down from Gleneyrie and remained closeted with the prosperous mill owner for several hours. Daniel, only eighteen years old at the time and home from Oxford on holiday, feared the arguing and shouting coming from the mill office would tax Francis Lennox's strength and felt it his place to stand with his father against this unexpected assault. But Laura, his sister, pulled him away from the locked door and shuttered windows.

Later, the visitor made good his escape, nervously looking over his shoulder as if expecting an attack from the rear. And Francis Lennox, pale and silent, emerged from his office and looked at his four children—for by now Eleanor and Miriam had joined their older brother and sister on the stone wall facing the closed door—like a stranger.

The warmth and affection with which the widowed man customarily greeted his children was gone and he turned from them to walk down the path toward the river.

Daniel had only seen his father look so once before, in the days after their mother died, and then the company of his bereft children had seemed his only comfort. Without a word, Daniel reached for his sisters' hands and pulled them along after him.

For reasons he could no longer fully justify to himself, he held them at a respectful distance from their father and stopped short when the man climbed atop a large rock overhanging the falls. It was a popular spot for local lovers and small boys; a depression had been worn into the stone and the place proved somewhat safer than it looked.

Therefore, Daniel could not have been more shocked when his father suddenly clutched his heart, bowed from the waist, and slipped headlong into the Fell. Laura cried out, and held tightly to her brother's arm, knowing as she must how Daniel would plunge into the swirling waters after him.

Daniel shrugged himself out of his jacket and his sister's frozen hold, and dove in from the embankment. His clothes hindered him, but no more than the crashing water and the complete lack of visibility. He floundered a bit, though never thinking himself in danger of drowning, and searched for his father's dark head.

Francis Lennox never had a chance. Where the great wheel of the cotton mill thrust out of the foaming river, the body of the mill owner was pulled into its crushing grip, and he remained caught beneath the surface of the water until his son drew him from the depths.

Dr. Cafferty determined the incident an accident, but nothing would ever dissuade Daniel Lennox from the firm belief his father's heart stopped as he stood over the river and he may have already been dead before he hit the water. And Daniel knew it had been no accident: The duke's messenger had given their father so much pain with his errand, he had brought on the attack. In all the years since, highest on their list of grievances against the old man, the mill owner's children listed their father's death.

An eighteen-year-old man could scarcely assume the care of three unmarried sisters, and so the girls were sent to their mother's cousin in London, where they went on to make successful and agreeable matches. Daniel Lennox hastened to finish his studies, and then returned to Glenfell, determined never to forget the grievances of the past, to improve the conditions of the present, and to ensure the continuity of the mill's success in the future.

Now he knew he had failed.

He remembered his battle in the river, where he had struggled to keep afloat in water so dark it might have been ink, and where rocks and floating debris had hammered his body unmercifully until he could feel no more.

Even yet, the effects of the ordeal wearing off, he could think of little else but the searing pain in his chest, the horrible tautness making him feel as if his body would split apart, and the certainty that, for all his efforts, he nevertheless would be tortured in hell for all eternity.

He opened one eye and saw a shaft of light on a white ceiling above him. Perhaps there remained some ounce of hope, after all.

He shifted slightly, sending spasms across his tight chest and stomach, but gaining much from a changed perspective.

It appeared he was laid out in a room, where flowered curtains billowed against open windows and where the fresh smell of grass and leaves wafted in the cool air. A basin stood on a small table near his head and a damp cloth draped over its edge released droplets of water to beat a gentle tattoo onto the floor. Daniel moved his hand over those parts of his body bared to the hazy sunshine and tried to move his legs. They seemed intact, and yet something hindered his left leg, pressing gently against his thigh. With considerable effort, he raised his head, and saw the glossy black coat of his favorite setter close to his side.

This, then, was heaven.

He did not know how long he dozed again, but he awoke to the sound of men's voices from outside, and the twilight. The sigh of a satisfied woman sounded very close by and, startled, he pulled himself up against the headboard of his narrow bed.

Now he saw he did not share his bed with his setter but with someone infinitely sweeter. A lady, her chair pushed up to the very edge of his mattress, bent at the waist to lay across his legs, her arm stretched nearly to his foot. Her hair, a mass of loose and wild curls, reflected a burnished light even in the darkening afternoon. Suddenly, almost unbearably, another part of his anatomy felt as tight as his chest.

"Miss Clarkson?" he asked in disbelief, but made no sound at all. He cleared his throat, an act which would have awakened a dead man by its pain, and repeated her name.

She gave another sigh, and, through the curtain of her curls, he could see she opened her eyes. They blinked and her lashes caught on a strand of her glorious hair. Abruptly, she pushed herself up off his thigh and tugged her curls away from her face.

"Mr. Lennox!"

"You sound surprised to see me here, but surely no more than am I," he croaked. "And yet I do not think I managed to rise from the Fell to this dry and warm place on my own accord."

She seized upon his words immediately, and surprised him with her fierceness. "You remember, then. You must tell me what happened to you."

"I . . ." he stopped and closed his eyes. He recalled the darkness of the river, and felt the current pain of his heart, but nothing else.

A gentle hand moved over his face, and Emily gave him water to drink. Goodness knows, had he not drunk enough of the Fell to satisfy his thirst for a lifetime? But then she pressed a cool, damp cloth to his forehead and eyelids, and the argument left him.

"You must remember," she insisted, like a schoolmistress taking one of her charges to task.

"I remember the river," he said firmly, wishing she would continue to provide comfort without taxing him.

"How did you get in the river?" she asked.

Suddenly, the full import of her words hit him, and he realized something must be amiss. He did not yet know how long he had slept, or what went on outside the confines of this chamber, but he had regained enough of his senses to know others waited on his word. Miss Clarkson, whose connection to this business he did not yet fathom, seemed to be one of them.

He started to pull himself up but felt firm hands on his shoulders pushing him back against the pillows.

"I suppose I fell in, like my father. Perhaps it was my heart . . ." he said, but without any conviction.

Emily Clarkson's next words explained why his instincts, now alert and aware, doubted it.

"You did not fall in, Mr. Lennox. Nor do I think there is anything wrong with your heart. Another inch or two closer by your assailant and I daresay it would have been sliced in two, but you have my assurance it remains intact. Its stubborn beating proved the only thing to give us hope when you arrived in Mrs. Lashley's kitchen three days ago."

As she spoke, her eyes followed his hand as it delved beneath the warm wool blanket. He started at his shoulder, where a cloth seemed stuck to his bare skin, and ran unsteady fingers across his chest and down to his hip, following the line of his bandage. He felt scratches and bruises along the path, but nothing of the injury that had so clearly threatened his life. Still watching her, knowing she hoped to anticipate his moves so she might arrest them, he pulled the bandage from his shoulder.

"You must stop, Mr. Lennox," she protested, and her hands were once again upon him. He wondered how he might continue to provoke her thus for some time to come. "Your injuries need to heal."

"I will not rest until I realize their extent, Miss Clarkson. If I am to be maimed, or crippled, I wish to know it at once."

Her eyes widened, making him suspect the worst. But then she nodded, and slowly pulled the blanket from his shoulders, down along his arms and chest, to his waist. He told himself not to be aroused by her simple, impersonal action, though something in her large brown eyes suggested she knew what she did, and what effect it would have on him.

Wordlessly, she continued to work her way along his body, peeling off one layer of bandage after another, pausing only to draw in deep breaths, and fuss with parts of the cloth sticking to his skin. Her actions proved more painful than erotic, but by the look on her face, he knew she did not torment him unnecessarily.

"Do not be surprised by what you see, Daniel," she said softly, and she looked as if she would begin to cry. "It proved an awful business, and I cannot imagine how we survived it."

He noticed not only the use of his first name, but also her presumed partnership in the affair. But as the cool air on his skin seemed to tighten his chest to a new level of pain, he did not pursue the wonder of their changed relationship, but used the opportunity to examine himself.

A track of dark, even stitches bisected his chest, following a line that began at his collarbone and ran straight down to his hip. Miss Clarkson did not exaggerate the proximity of the cut to his heart, and he knew himself lucky to have survived the attack.

The attack. Unbidden, the image of his assailant rose up before him and he saw a hooded man wielding a saber. He remembered dropping from his horse, and hearing the creature crash through the underbrush along the edge of the river. Turning to confront his attacker, he reached for his own dagger, and knew it would be as effective as a butter knife against a man still on horseback. The man cursed viciously, held the huge blade aloft against the night sky like some avenging angel, and brought it down across Daniel's chest, ripping the cloth of his jacket and shirt. Falling to the ground, Daniel grabbed one of the man's legs and brought him down—painfully and hard—on top of him. His hands probed for his attacker's eyes, and he heard the man roar in pain when he found his target. As the villain pulled himself off Daniel's prone body his hood fell back, and pale hair shone in the moonlight. The man grabbed a rock and smashed it into Daniel's shoulder. Seizing the gift of a crude but effective weapon, Daniel picked up the wet rock and threw it at the man who would have him dead. He missed his mark, but aimed well enough to catch the man at the side of the head, and hear him stagger back through the bushes.

And then, knowing himself at the end of his strength and his resources, Daniel rolled down the embankment and plunged into the cold river, believing the mill and safety lay downriver.

He knew not how he came from the river, or into Mrs. Lashley's kitchen, or into Miss Emily Clarkson's bed, but he believed he knew who wished him dead.

"Daniel?" Emily said softly. "Are you all right? I assure you, it will look better in time."

He looked up into her beautiful face and the concern etched on her features gave him hope where all else seemed desolate. Her lips remained open and her eyes never left his.

Finding himself short of breath, he finally returned his gaze to his bare chest and he could not prevent himself wincing at the sight of his injury.

"I do not doubt it," he said cheerfully. "The doctor did an excellent job. I always thought him a blind fool."

"So he might be, sir. But he did not tend your injuries, nor does he even know about them."

Daniel frowned as he met her eyes again. "Then who . . . ?"

She did not answer, but bit down on her lip, and started to reapply his bandage. When he shivered, she hastened her task, and soon had covered him up again.

"It is not possible," he said, daring her to dispute it.

She did not.

"Indeed, I do not think it possible myself, and yet it did happen. There seemed no one else who knew what to do, and I felt sure you would die."

From above his head, where Emily seemed very much concerned about the plumpness of his pillows, fell a drop of salty water. He arched his back to glimpse her face, but she quickly turned away.

"I think I have much to live for," he said.

She did not look back, but began to gather up cups and plates from a table near the door.

"Emily," he said, and thought the word as dear a caress as ever he had uttered. "I owe you my life."

"And I owe you the satisfaction of my present employment, sir. So consider your debt entirely paid."

"Is that all?"

Suddenly she looked quite angry, and folded her arms across her breast. He held a sudden vision of Emily Clarkson in a formal gown, stained with blood and water, and knew he now remembered something of his unexpected homecoming three nights before.

"What else would you have, sir? I have given of my time,

my care, and all my energy. I needed to discard my favorite evening gown, for your blood stained all of the bodice and much of the skirt. I hurt my own finger in the effort to sew you together." Here she held up her second finger, which looked perfectly fine. "And I have sacrificed the lessons of the children, which should always be my first concern."

"And is that all?"

"What more do you wish?"

"I would wish to hear you say it worth the effort."

She came several steps closer and he saw she knew precisely what he meant. He also saw it did not give her any pleasure.

"It must always be worth the effort to save a life, regardless of any reward. Someday you, and Mrs. Lennox, might thank me."

He saw the tears well up in her brown eyes and the lines of grief in the corners of her lips.

"Might it not be you?"

"You are very likely delirious and know not what you say, Mr. Lennox. Circumstances have brought us together more closely than could ever be considered decent, but you are not obliged to save my honor merely because I saved your life. Now that you are awake and as willful as ever, I shall resign you to the care of Mrs. Bernays. You need not see me for some time and, if you are fortunate, will not even recall the words you just said to me."

"I am not out of my mind, my dear Emily. I know precisely of what I speak. And might my desire also be yours?"

"It is not possible. I have been warned to stay away from you and Glenfell, and it cannot be coincidence someone tried to murder you," she said as she picked up a tray. "I am sorry, but it is certain someone does not wish us to be together. No one could have an argument with me, truly not. So they would come for you again. It is too much to ask of anyone, Daniel. I did not struggle to save your life just so I could lose you again."

She slipped through the open door with barely a glance back at him. Undoubtedly, she thought she had the final say in the matter.

But her argument gave him nothing, if not reason to hope.

*   *   *

"Miss Clarkson!"

Mrs. Bernays ascended to the top of the long stairway and took the tray from Emily's trembling fingers.

"Whatever can be the matter? Surely the master . . ." Mrs. Bernays' voice broke off in a little cry. ". . . He is dead?"

The older woman dropped to the step and pulled her starched apron to her face.

"What will become of us all?"

Emily dried her own eyes with the back of her hand. The housekeeper had come upon a wretched scene, to be sure, as Emily found herself incapable of anything but to cry her heart out in the hall near her—now Mr. Lennox's—bedchamber. After days of practical, even-tempered control, the sluice gates had suddenly opened, and Emily felt more upset about her circumstances than she had even imagined she would.

"He is not dead, Mrs. Bernays," she sniffed. "In fact, I believe him as rude as ever. I ought to have run from Mrs. Lashley's kitchen as fast as my legs would have taken me, and allowed the man to suffer the consequences."

"You are too kind to mean it, my love," said Mrs. Bernays, and hugged Emily to her. "And care too much for Mr. Lennox to do anything other than what you did."

"I do not care for him at all," Emily sobbed. "He loves only his mill and his precious cotton, and pines for a lady he lost to a better man."

"There is no better man," Mrs. Bernays said firmly. "When you accept that, you also may understand why you acted as you did, and why we are all so grateful for it. He will be too, when he is well enough to hear the whole story."

"So might he be already," Emily said, and waved her hand carelessly in the direction of his closed door. In the sudden lull, the two women heard something that might have been a chair falling, and a well-articulated curse.

Mrs. Bernays laughed out loud. "I pray some day the master will find good purpose to remaining in bed. Surely there is nothing to keep him now." She rose to her feet and patted Emily on the head. "Away with you. Let me restore him to his senses."

Emily fled to the parlor, leaving the tray to the kind housekeeper, but took along her tears to nurse through the long night ahead.

Washed, brushed, and sobered by a morning spent in the company of her neglected students, Emily postponed an outing by the river so she might return to her bedchamber and its temporary resident. Mrs. Bernays reported Mr. Lennox had spent an easy night, and that he begged a brief audience with his schoolmistress to discuss the progress of his children. Even if the good lady had not accompanied her message with a wink, Emily would have known the excuse to be a lame one. But as she had spent part of the morning in conference with Mr. Haines and Miss Worthington, with whom she trusted their secret, she felt she could manage a short visit with some degree of composure.

When she knocked on Mr. Lennox's door, expecting to be answered by either of the men who spent the day with him and helped him bathe and manage other necessities, she heard nothing. Assuming they slept, she turned the knob to open the door, and found it locked.

Emily's blood ran cold as she envisioned another attempt on her patient's life. Somehow the murderer, knowing he had not succeeded, had accosted Mr. Lennox here and finally carried out his mission. If she walked away now, she might be called back hours from now when Mrs. Bernays used her key to open the door and they all entered upon another scene of horror.

Emily clenched her fist, prepared to beat down the door. However, the moment she lowered it, it was caught by a strong hand pulling her into the room.

"Mr. Lennox," she said, scarcely disguising her relief. "You look to have made a full recovery. Were you planning to step out, or are you afraid your stitches will pull quite apart?"

"They already have," he said wryly and then put his finger to her lips when she gasped. "Fear not, my guardian angel. There seemed little enough bleeding and I patched things up as best as I could. John came in this morning, and helped me restore some semblance of my self-esteem. I fear the situation hardly seemed decent, and I felt sure you would not come to visit me again."

"Indeed, I should not. But I understood there were matters of business you wished to discuss." She hesitated, and noticed someone had already shaved him and brought him clean clothes to wear. The sour smell of blood and fever had been replaced by sandalwood and she felt immensely grateful she had not arrived earlier and intruded upon his bath. "Do you really feel well enough to be up and about?"

He paused as if considering the question, and flexed the muscles in his right arm. "I confess, I do not know how long this respite will last. I do know it feels infinitely better to move about and stretch the skin where you practiced your needlework upon me, and exercise my sore muscles. But I did not think so much upon these things as the necessity of seeing you again."

"Oh," Emily said.

"And I feel infinitely better now that I have succeeded," he said, watching her closely.

She averted her eyes, and focused instead on his chest. Through the linen of his shirt, she could see the thick outline of the bandage.

"Would you like to walk with me, Miss Clarkson? Emily?"

"Of course. Perhaps we ought to take a turn about the hall."

He looked up and down the long corridor. "Very promising scenery, to be sure, but I rather thought you might accompany me to the mill office."

"To the office!"

"Of course. You may have already noticed I spend much of my day there. Do you not think there will be those who will find it suspicious when I do not make an appearance in several days?

"Fear not, Mr. Lennox. We have already set it about you are delayed in your return from New Lanark. And Mr. Haines assures me all is running smoothly in the operation of your mill."

"You continually impress upon me your many abilities. I hope you do not consider it too rude a compliment if I say you would make an excellent woman of business. We are a low class, I know, but we do exhibit certain qualities."

Emily smiled, and realized she had not thought about his social position since the night she went to Gleneyrie. Then it had seemed to her that Mr. Lennox proved more worthy of deference than her boring and disagreeable host. And the events later in the evening surely had nothing to do with matters of class.

"Stamina must be one of them, Mr. Lennox. Are you quite sure you can make it all the way to the mill?"

"To be truthful, Miss Clarkson, I am not. I should not put on a very good show if I need crawl across the yard on my belly. May I impose on you one more time? Will you accompany me?"

Emily hesitated, though she wanted nothing more than to see Mr. Lennox safely at his desk. But what danger would she expose him to if an enemy saw them walking arm in arm, with her solicitous and attentive to his every need?

"I assure you, we will not be presenting them with anything they have not already guessed," he said, reading her mind.

"Even if it is not true?"

"Who knows the truth in our confusing little society? I am sure I do not," he said, and buttoned his jacket over his shirt. Emily had admired the close fit of his wardrobe on more than one occasion, and wondered how many people they met were likely to think him gaining some weight. His additional bulk did not appear unflattering and, in any case, they would be more likely to take note of his black eye than his muscular chest.

Patiently, he allowed her to straighten his cravat, and then opened the door. But for the slowness of his pace, and her fear that he might collapse dead upon her, they managed the stairs and hallway very handily, and finally walked out into the sunshine.

"Did you mean what you said about the truth?" she asked.

"You sound as if you are about to tax me on it, Miss Clarkson." He paused and spoke to two young women who pulled a cart between them. They giggled and preened and greeted Emily with a knowing nod.

"Do you really not know the truth about your circumstances? About who is to blame for the deed?"

"I entertain a keen suspicion, but I suspect you have figured it out already."

Emily did not altogether appreciate the submission in his

tone, believing it could not be genuine. She felt a little burst of impatience.

"I have not troubled myself to figure out anything, sir, but rumor and innuendo came my way even as I arrived in your town. I know the Duke of Glendennon is your avowed enemy, though I cannot guess why, and he is one who wishes you harm. Therefore, I assume you believe he set upon you in the woods and tried to murder you. However, let me assure you I sat with him on the very night you were attacked, and the man does not seem strong enough to climb the stairs to his chamber, let alone inflict the sort of injury you sustained."

"At last he and I have something in common," Emily thought she heard him say. And then, more clearly, "The duke would never condescend to greet me in direct confrontation, and employs others to do his dirty deeds. Did Peter Havers join you that evening?"

Emily had known he would ask her the question, and wished she had more closely followed Mr. Havers' comings and goings.

"As a matter of fact, Peter escorted me to Gleneyrie. He shows an uncommon amount of pride in the place, and would prove a worthy heir if the duchess does not produce a child."

"Do you truly think so?" Daniel Lennox asked, and Emily thought she heard a touch of jealousy in his tone. Did he think himself a more worthy recipient of the duke's largesse? And then, as they continued to walk for several minutes in silence, she realized, with a shock, that he most certainly would be. She looked up to study his profile, so noble and so very dear to her. "He may come to prove himself some day, for I understand the duchess miscarried her baby several days ago."

Emily nearly stumbled in her path. How came he, a half-dead invalid, to know more of what went on in the town than she did herself? Why would news of the miscarriage reach him so quickly, and why could it matter? Unless . . .

"Mr. Lennox, do you have a personal interest in the affairs of the duchess?" she asked rashly, because she knew she did not really wish to hear him profess love for the lady.

"I do have a personal interest, and there are those in town who undoubtedly speculate on a relationship even more intimate," he said. "I suspect you have heard some very lively rumors. Therefore, I hope it will not insult your sensibilities if I assure you the baby was not mine, nor do I wish to marry the duchess in the eventuality of her husband's demise, nor would I seek to dishonor the names of two families by committing any act that might be reprehensible. The duchess and I were friends—once. When she chose the duke over me, she forfeited the possibility we could ever meet again as friends, or as anything else. I am sorry to hear she is unhappy, but there is little I might do to alleviate her pain."

"She seems so very lonely. Do you not think the company of old friends might bring her comfort?" Emily asked gently.

He twisted to face her, and the movement must have pained him. "I daresay my cousin provides a good deal of comfort. In doing so, he invests in his own expectations," he said.

"Of course," Emily reasoned, thinking about all the things she had ever heard said about the affairs of Daniel Lennox's enemies. Suddenly Gleneyrie came into view as they turned the corner, glorious and majestic atop its hilly ledge. "It might prove very worthwhile. If anything should happen to the duke, there should be no impediment to a marriage between Mr. Havers and the duke's widow. If he is the heir presumptive, then she might regain possession of the title."

"I doubt it," Mr. Lennox said and seemed uncommonly cheerful. "Married they may be, but they should have to conquer some tenacious problems."

He quickened his pace, pulling her along, and she wondered at his great show of strength.

"What do you hope to accomplish at the mill this day, sir?" she asked. "You seem very anxious to arrive there."

"I am always anxious to be among my workers, for it gives me great pleasure. I prefer to believe they will be happy to see me returned as well. But I know I am remiss in certain matters as a result of my absence, and one of them directly concerns yourself, Miss Clarkson."

"And will you not tell me what it might be?"

Mr. Lennox stopped suddenly and pulled her around to face him. She saw that the color had returned to his face and his usual good humor was now etched around the lines of his mouth. A person unaware of the recent circumstances of his life might not notice anything at all amiss.

Unless Daniel Lennox collapsed from sheer exhaustion.

"Why, do you not recall Miss Martineau's promise, or threat, to visit us? She does not trust me, in spite of my honorable connections, and believes I am abusing you most shamefully."

"In light of the events of this past week, she would have every reason to believe her suspicions well-founded."

"I hope we need not speak of it to her, Miss Clarkson."

"Of course not, Mr. Lennox. But if you should die before she arrives, she might very well demand an explanation. She is very fierce, you know."

"Well, so am I. I will not die. Did I not already say I have much to live for?"

"So you did." Emily blushed, scarcely daring to imagine what he meant, and turned away. "When is Miss Martineau expected? I may wish to anticipate when I might catch up on my sleep."

Emily tried to speak calmly, but felt a little nervous about Harriet Martineau's visit. In recent days, the schoolmistress had given less than her full attention to the children and they might not show Mr. Lennox's school in the best light.

"In a few weeks' time, if I am to believe Mr. Jeremiah Colman's letter. It just arrived. And it seems as if my old friend and yours have taken to traveling together. Jeremiah must not mind taking time away from his business and Miss Martineau must not mind the odor of freshly milled mustard."

Emily laughed, attracting the attention of several passersby.

"But I do not see how we can be ready for them, Mr. Lennox."

"Will the children not be prepared? I know their education must be uppermost in Miss Martineau's mind, but Mr. Colman seemed more interested in what dinners I shall be hosting and with whom. Can we expect the young lady to lecture us at the table?"

Emily sighed. "I believe we must. You shall have to endure it the best you can. Harriet is very right-minded, and just goes on even as her companions are slipping under the table. I hope you will spare me."

"My dearest Miss Clarkson. I wished to ask you the very same thing." He stopped at the gate to the mill office, as if the business in which they were currently engaged remained quite independent of whatever went on within. "But I suspect our fate is sealed. I shall entertain my guests with every comfort and indulge their whims. But I cannot succeed unless you assume your place opposite me at the table in Shearings. I feel as if you quite belong there."

Absurdly, Emily felt the very same thing. It seemed as much her place as the side of Mr. Lennox's bed, where she had nursed him through all the long and dreadful hours during which she feared she would lose him.

Thus her heart spoke to her. But reason, ever a spoiler, reminded her that believing she would forever be at his side was a very dangerous thing.

Chapter Ten

*D*uring the course of the week, it appeared Emily's intuition proved stronger than Daniel Lennox's constitution and his foolhardy determination to go on as before. Twice she saw blood seeping through his starched shirt and knew his stitches had ripped and were healing roughly. And once Noland Haines reported finding Mr. Lennox clutching the edge of his desk, bathed in a cold sweat, and unable to continue with his work. But these setbacks were dealt with in secret, since Mr. Lennox insisted as few people as possible need share their concerns, and his attacker should never guess how close he had come to success.

Emily did not pretend to understand her employer's position, except that he believed his continued frailty would be a weakness he would be loath to reveal. But she did not argue with him. She volunteered once to examine his stitches, and then almost immediately regretted her impulse, for the sight of his bared chest completely shattered her composure. But she managed to pronounce him whole and safe, and suggested someone else might cut the black threads off him in a week or so. He agreed, making her guess he felt as awkward about the whole thing as she did herself.

Nevertheless, when she began to be summoned regularly to his study at Shearings, she offered no protest or refusal.

Mr. Lennox, apparently believing his obligations to appear at his mill office fulfilled by mid-afternoon, would make good his escape by claiming some business to accomplish in his home or elsewhere. Mr. Haines readily covered for him, knowing full well why his employer needed to remove himself, and reported only Alsop Parker's complaint about the master's irregular hours.

Every afternoon Emily walked up to the large, sunny library at Shearings, usually armed with some article on reform or the occasional letter from London. Daniel always stood to greet her upon arrival, but then sank into his large leather chair, where he would remain for the course of their conversation. Emily could see his first days of recovery required an extraordinary effort on his part. And so she walked about the room, finding the books he required, and serving him his tea when Mrs. Winters, his housekeeper, delivered the tray to Emily's side.

And he gave Emily something she desired: a better understanding of the business that defined his whole life.

"Will you wear silk to the ball next week?" he asked one day as Emily sat scanning a map of the Fell Valley.

She looked up and realized her answer somehow mattered a great deal to him. She thought about the lovely yellow silk gown in her closet, and knew it would remain hidden for now.

"I thought the wearing of silk not permissible in your company, sir," she said.

She waited for him to tease her, or at least minimize the severity of the sin. But he did not.

"Enough human life has been wasted in pursuit of so paltry a thing as bolts of fabric. While the manufacture of cloth remains the lifeblood of this town, I never considered it worth the sacrifice of even one person. And yet, we have lost so many."

"You are thinking of the people burned in the warehouse, Mr. Lennox. But surely accidents . . ."

"I am thinking most particularly of my father, Miss Clarkson. Who has come to haunt me frequently since my accident. My ancestors worked this land for generations, surely since the time of the Conqueror. The Lennoxes were ever subservient to the Dukes of Glendennon, ever reliant on protection, ever careful to publicly demonstrate the correct degree of obedience. But by my grandfathers' time, the balance seems to have shifted somewhat, and my father went on to create his own little empire in defiance of propriety and tradition."

"I do not see it as a very bad thing, Mr. Lennox," Emily said, quietly. "I may have felt that way once, but my opinion has undergone a transformation. If your father possessed the resources and the wit to improve the situation of his family, and bring so many others up with him, why should he not defy the rather staid balance of life in Glenfell? You seem to live very comfortably, sir. And your sisters have married well. Are these not the very measures of success?"

"To some, Miss Clarkson."

"Is it really necessary to reform the whole world, Mr. Lennox? Might progress start in one small corner and spread throughout the room? Might my mother have done more good to come here and help her own people than venture to America?"

"But then I would not have met you," he said.

"You came fairly close to missing it, as it is." She sat still, in the warmth of the room and his presence, and thought about the very extraordinary events of the past few weeks.

"Miss Clarkson?"

Emily looked up, startled out of her reverie. Daniel watched her closely, as if waiting on her very words, his light eyes hooded but missing nothing. He always seemed so sure of himself, so very certain his needs would necessarily be met and his desires made real. Even the attack of a villain could scarcely deter him from his path, as he had fought his way home, determined to live. Why could it possibly matter to him what a gentlewoman of few expectations thought about the dynamics of his small society?

Of course she knew. She did not possess any great talents in understanding the desires of young men, but she knew why he looked at her so, and why her answer made every difference to him. If he doubted her esteem, she must needs reassure him.

"I . . . almost did not come, you see. And you do remember how tempted I was to turn on my heels and get back into the carriage. You pulled me back out and having done so, I believe you pulled me out of a certain degree of complacency. What did I know but the life I had lived for twenty years? My father and mother were great deed-doers, but their lives were apart from my own. Indeed, because their charities separated them from their home and only child, I came to resent the things that really mattered to them."

"Hmm. Are you telling me you did not have vast experience in your father's hospital? There seems to be much regard for you in certain small circles here. John thinks you a doctor."

Emily looked down at her lap. "I confess I exaggerated a little when I came into the kitchen at the schoolhouse. But, in my defense, I did not even know it was you injured."

"Would it have made a difference?"

"I suspect it would if I had killed you."

"I see." He rotated his shoulder, wincing a little. "I have not yet complimented you on your handiwork. But I seem to recall my sisters' embroidery usually had little rosebuds on it."

"Perhaps I have not their skill."

"Perhaps. But you certainly surpass their courage."

"I have no ambitions to be a heroine. Circumstances conspired against me." He could not know how deeply.

"Poor Miss Clarkson. Such has been your plight since ere you met me. But can no good come from this misadventure?"

Emily felt her heart racing and knew her face grew warm. She thought she knew what he wanted to hear, but resisted every impulse to say it. The danger was not yet past, his safety was still at risk, and she did not know what parts others played in the deeds of recent weeks. Thus, she evaded him by giving him a different sort of truth.

"I think good has come of it as your schoolmistress learned an important lesson. I seem to have grown disdainful of the trappings of title and inherited wealth, seeing them now for false values. There is merit in proving one's own worth."

His mouth twisted, and she thought he might be suppressing a smile. But his next words had no humor in them. "This is quite a radical turnabout for you, Miss Clarkson."

"It is. But I have given much thought to the elderly man at Gleneyrie and even more to his wife. I can think of nothing more grievous than being the Duchess of Glendennon."

Daniel Lennox sank back into his seat, looking more pained than Emily had seen him in days. Perhaps the strain of leaning towards her hurt his stitches, or the thought of his former lover in a pitiable position bothered him overmuch.

"My father professed similar beliefs," he said. "And paid for them mightily."

"As you almost did yourself," Emily pointed out quickly. "But all your efforts would be in vain if you abandoned your hopes now. Too many people rely on you, and look to you for example."

Emily felt dampness on her cheeks, and put up a trembling hand to wipe away her unbidden tears. How absurdly vulnerable she had become, how far she was from the sheltered girl who lived a quiet life with her aunt in London!

The gentle pressure of warm hands upon her shoulders startled her into remembering she had an audience consisting of the last person on earth who ought to witness her distress. But, with him, she already felt beyond embarrassment, for they had shared too much. She looked up into Daniel's face, surprised he had managed to move around the huge desk so quickly, and wondered at his recklessness.

Later, in the privacy of her own chamber, she would wonder at her own.

She rose up out of her seat in a moment, standing nearly breast to breast until he pulled her into his arms. He fell back slightly, leaning against the edge of the desk, which now supported the weight of both their bodies. As Emily's hands pressed against his chest, trying to create some buffer for his injuries, she felt his hands on her back, on her waist, on the exposed skin at the nape of her neck and, finally, on her face.

"Hush," he said, his mouth very close to her ear. "I promise you, I will not die, I will not leave you."

Emily blinked away her tears and, without thinking, pushed away. He winced, but did not relinquish his hold.

"Why do you demand less of me than you are willing to give yourself?" she asked indignantly.

"Because you do not know the whole story, nor yet understand the dangers ahead."

"Have I not yet proved myself? Will you treat me like a child, as one needing protection?"

Daniel Lennox smiled and a tantalizing dimple appeared in his cheek. "You do need protection, my dear Miss Clarkson. But I will not treat you like a child."

Nor would she be treated like one. She had come to Glenfell a lady but had been drawn into service as a woman. Though her abused sensibilities would not allow her to believe anything enduring would come of her relationship with Daniel Lennox, she knew with absolute certainty she wanted a partnership. She wanted to understand what drove him, and made others despise him enough to try to murder him, and why he seemed so different from every other man of her acquaintance.

As she ran her tear-wet finger along the uneven line of his nose she heard him suck in his breath, as if in pain. But she did not withdraw, for she was woman enough to know this pain was of the most delicious sort.

His lips tasted her mouth, and moved over her nose and eyelids as if he would devour her. Emily clung to him, and pressed against his body as closely as she dared, and made mischief of her own. She arched her back and felt the bulky line of his bandage through the thin fabric of her dress. Her fingers continued their assault upon his face, and she ran her nails over the raspy hairs of his beard. No stranger to the lines and contours of his features, she followed an exercise begun when he had lain still the week before, unaware of her ministrations.

How very much more gratifying it all seemed just now. He finally stilled her hand with his mouth and brushed his tongue over her fingertips. Emily rose up on her toes, until her shoulder just fit under his arm, and nestled her head near his chin. She would have desired to stay just so forever.

Nor did Daniel Lennox seem to desire otherwise, for he wrapped his arms tightly around her. Through the bandages, Emily felt his heart racing like a runner's.

"I must confess," he said, and she heard not only gratification, but also humor in his voice. "I thought you had promise when you first arrived in Glenfell, Miss Clarkson. But it appears your abilities exceed even my fondest expectations."

"I believe you are insulting me, sir," Emily said slowly, trying to match her tone to his. "For a lady would never own to such skills as those to which I believe you refer. But I learn very quickly, you see, and just wanted for an excellent teacher."

"Ah, my dear. Have we taught you too much of our provincial ways?"

She ran a gentle, teasing finger along the white scar on his chin. The rough, chapped skin of just a week ago had healed so smoothly she felt tempted to sample its texture with her tongue.

"Do you think my Aunt Constance would have allowed me to come here if she suspected something of the teachings you had in mind? Lady Gray should have warned me."

Daniel looked as if he would say something, but a quick rap at the door put them apart in an instant. As Mrs. Winters entered the room, he casually picked up a book and fingered one of the pages. Emily folded the linens by the serving tray and greeted the housekeeper quite as if nothing were amiss.

"The tea must be cold by now," the older woman grumbled. Daniel did not even look up as he waved the tray away. But Emily smiled sweetly, praying Mrs. Winters would not wonder why they stood so close, or why her cheeks burned bright red.

"It was delicious, Mrs. Winters," Emily said.

The housekeeper nodded as she looked at her, and reached out to straighten the lace at Emily's breast.

"I am sure it was, Miss Clarkson," she said, and busied herself with the tea service.

Emily looked amused, but Daniel realized he was putting her in harm's way. If the knowledge of their intimacy spread beyond the privacy of his home, into the hands of his enemies, she could very likely become the next target of their venom.

He must marry her, for surely he had already compromised her most shamefully. He might then keep her under the sheltering arm of his protection, and insure no harm would come to her. There would be very practical sides to such an arrangement, but he knew he would not even consider such a thing if he did not truly love her. But love her he did, realizing he had never felt such selfless devotion toward another, even as he did not know how and when it had come upon him.

He only remembered that when he awakened in his narrow sickbed, and felt her lying upon him, there seemed nothing more natural in all the world, nothing more redemptive in heaven. Somehow, she had been a part of his life even before he knew her, for she restored him to a belief in the future and a justification in his past.

He owed her his life. He owed her his gratitude. But he could not, as a gentleman, give her more than that until he told her the full truth about the circumstances in which she found herself, for he also owed her the truth.

It would not come easy; if it could have he would have revealed it all when she had first arrived in Glenfell. Then, it had seemed altogether adequate for her to understand the tensions governing the town, and the great disparity between the lives of those in Gleneyrie and those at the mill. Such glimmerings should have been enough if she had remained but a schoolmistress.

But Emily Clarkson had almost immediately become much more to him. Her beauty, her wit, and her natural grace with the children were the sweet nectars enticing him to drink, and so nearly intoxicated him as to make him forget himself and who he was. But she never seemed to forget it, even when she came so willingly into his arms, and gave him her trust.

He needed to tell her the truth.

"Thank you, Mrs. Winters. Mr. Haines brought up some of the importation books from the office, and Miss Clarkson and I are going over them together."

"I did not realize Miss Clarkson understood the cotton business."

"She is a woman of many talents," Daniel said tersely.

"You would not know it to look at her," Mrs. Winters shot back, and winked.

Daniel savored a few moments in doing just that: looking at her. But for the pink glow on her cheeks, one would not have guessed Emily bore any souvenirs of their passion. She looked very calm and collected, and her pale blue dress suited her curves to perfection. It suited him, too.

"Thank you, Mrs. Winters," Emily said, sounding very much the lady of the house.

The housekeeper, accepting Emily's authority, gathered up the tea service and marched from the room. Though she closed the door behind her, Daniel suspected she waited in the hall for some excuse to break in on them again. Whom, he wondered, did she think she was protecting?

Emily laughed a little nervously and tucked an errant curl behind her ear. Daniel realized that his housekeeper wanted the same thing he wanted himself: to keep Emily safe. But then she raised her dark eyes to his, and he knew how hopelessly lost he was, how much he needed rescuing himself.

"I suppose we should be grateful to Mrs. Winters," he said softly, "for I believe I quite forgot myself, Miss Clarkson."

She continued to study him. "I doubt you ever truly forget yourself, Mr. Lennox. But if you required an antidote to our behavior, I might have provided one just as readily. I have a letter here from Harriet Martineau."

Emily was quite right; the woman's name had the same effect as having a barrel of icy water thrown over his head.

"Ah yes, the paragon. If she has not entirely incinerated my old friend Mr. Colman, I daresay we shall expect them here in a few days' time?" Daniel spoke quickly. "What else does she say?"

Emily selected a small straight-backed chair and pulled it close to his desk, and rifled through a small pile of papers she had brought with her. "Miss Martineau reports her work at Stoke Holy Cross nearly at an end, having converted Jeremiah Colman to her objectives. She stays because she formed an alliance with the man himself, and hints at some personal happiness."

"I suppose it is to the advantage of reformers like Miss Martineau to marry rich men so they might finance their various schemes?" he said, without thinking.

Emily dropped the papers and stared at him. "I am a reformer like Miss Martineau."

"You were not until you met me!"

"You are quite right, Mr. Lennox. I scarcely knew my own mind until I came to Glenfell. But now you put me in mind of an intriguing notion. Perhaps it is not enough to marry a man of wealth. If I married a man both titled and wealthy, I surely would be able to exert more influence in society."

He knew she was teasing him, testing him, stretching him to the limit of his endurance.

"Then find your happiness with Peter. He seems to be in expectation of a title," Daniel said, watching her reaction.

She shrugged in a gesture of indifference. "So he is. It would be very grand, I daresay. But I do not love him."

Daniel thought his heart would burst in his damned scarred chest. But before he could speak, Emily went on as if she had not said anything of import.

"Miss Martineau wishes to know what she might wear. She says she understands silk is an odious fabric to you, sir. It seems your opinion on this matter has spread very far."

"I am not without influence," Daniel said carefully, still watching her. "But I do not expect to overthrow the fashion houses of London. Miss Martineau could wear burlap, for all it matters."

"Perhaps I might wear burlap as well," she said softly.

"Although you would still look an angel, I would rather you wear armor if it might protect you. Indeed, you would be safer to wear your damned smuggled silk, lest my enemies think you were too closely connected to me."

Emily rose from her seat, and urged him down as he started to do the same. To be certain of it, she settled herself on his lap. He looked down into her face and saw she knew very well the effect she had on him. Perhaps he himself should call on Mrs. Winters for protection. But then he should receive all the blame, for no one would believe their levelheaded Miss Clarkson a seductress.

"And are you connected to me, Mr. Lennox? Would the 'damned' silk not put you off?" she asked quietly, caressingly.

"Do not doubt I am connected to you, my dear. You captured me the very first morning in the classroom, when I envied no one as much as the unruly boys who could spend the whole day staring at you. The prospect seemed like heaven itself."

"Even when I punish them?"

"Why, especially when you punish them," he said wickedly.

"I see," she said, and touched her tongue to his chin.

"That was not what I had in mind for the boys."

She laughed softly, a sweet song in his stuffy room.

"And you have punished me enough as it is."

She leaned back and the music ended. "Why would you say so?"

"Because you have given me an additional reason to worry. We should stay aloof until a murderer is discovered and punished. If I were a man of sense, I would return you to London at once."

"Then why do you not?" she said against his ear. "It is what I wanted, after all. You need only dismiss me, and I will return to my own home. And then your great problem would be solved."

Daniel shifted. "Agreed. You will leave Glenfell tomorrow."

Emily looked at him in shocked disbelief. "I will not."

Daniel threw up his hands, nearly dropping her.

"I will not," she repeated. "If we are connected, as you say, I insist on staying here to fight your enemies with you. I believe it is fair to say I have demonstrated my worth on the battlefield, and I can come and go in this town with impunity. Only the duchess suspects something, and that sad woman would do me no harm."

"You do not know, Emily . . ."

"Then tell me! Have I not earned your trust? You have not been entirely honest with me and do not dispute it!"

"I have not and I will not. But I have reasons . . ."

"Who tried to murder you?" she interrupted.

"Peter Havers."

She winced, as if he had slapped her.

"Who set fire to the warehouse?"

"Peter Havers."

"Who would come after me for my association with you?"

He did not say it, for he saw she already knew the answer. He merely nodded and took her cold hand.

"You are certain?"

"No."

She looked sharply at him and tried to pull her hand away. He would not release her.

"Then you have not told me the truth."

"I have told it as best as I understand it. My suspicions are justified. And you would do me a great service by not spending time with that man."

"I see. And I thought you jealous. I flattered myself."

Daniel kissed her hand. "I was jealous."

"He is your cousin and he stands in the duke's graces. Would that not be enough to make you jealous? You do not need additional provocation."

"I do not envy his position there, only with you. You should never have agreed to go to Mrs. Carroll's party with him."

"You should have asked me first," she said gently, "and then I would not have accepted him when I met him in the field."

She paused and he wondered what was disturbing her.

"Daniel, I saw Peter Havers looking for something in the field that day, in the area near the fire. He was in animated conversation with your friend, Captain Milrose. Is it not possible the captain is your infamous smuggler and a murderer as well?"

Daniel felt both amused and intrigued by the workings of her logic. "You may leave David out of this."

"Indeed? I am glad to hear he inspires confidence. For my part, I think he might make a tidy profit by bringing smuggled fabric to Glenfell, even using your own warehouses for storage. Why not? He would not be suspected, as he is your friend. His sister would surely warn him of any rumors about his behavior. And the duke, urged on by Peter Havers, might finance his operations. I think it very plausible."

Daniel looked at her appreciatively, knowing he had not misjudged her cleverness. She was close to the mark on some of her musings and she suggested some possibilities he had not yet considered. But for all he desired her, he would not have her a part of this.

"Miss Clarkson, I fear we have corrupted you. Are you drawing conclusions as a women of business might?"

"It would not be so very bad, I think." She smiled up at him. "And it is true you have corrupted me."

He did not answer, as her wandering hand rendered him speechless. He caught it as it approached his shoulder, molding the muscles of his arm beneath her fingers.

And then he proceeded to show her what a very bad influence he might continue to be.

Chapter Eleven

The next days passed in a flurry of preparations and excitement, suspending the afternoon sessions in the library at Shearings. Emily missed them terribly, but her more rational thoughts cautioned her how dangerously close she had come to Daniel and how inappropriate a relationship it truly seemed. She recalled how readily her hands had reached for him, and shuddered to think of the liberties already taken. Of course, Daniel Lennox was at least an Odysseus to her Circe, but censure so rarely applied to the man. If gossip about them should ever come out, it would most certainly be she who would be damaged in reputation.

Assuming there remained anything of her reputation to damage.

Mindful of her responsibilities, and of the work remaining to be accomplished, Emily became a strict taskmistress.

Harriet Martineau most certainly would wish to see some progress, some evidence that Daniel Lennox's educational experiments had succeeded, and the schoolmistress at the mill would need to produce children who could read and write. Most of them were already reasonably prepared, and could read aloud from some rudimentary texts, but Emily hoped to polish them until they glistened.

Much of the same endeavor towards perfection also governed the two housekeepers on the mill estate. Mrs. Bernays and Mrs. Winters led small armies of servants, equipped with soft cloths and oils, and left no surface untouched. Although both Mr. Colman and Harriet Martineau had been invited to stay in the far more elegant Shearings, Miss Martineau had declined, requesting to be in the schoolhouse dormitory instead. She would not be denied.

But on the day the two eminent visitors were expected, Mr. Lennox requested Emily's presence in his parlor, where they might greet their guests in a great show of unity. After days of necessary estrangement, Emily felt some awkwardness, but recognized his logic and came at the appointed hour.

Daniel Lennox also would not be denied.

"Are you quite prepared for Miss Martineau's assault, Miss Clarkson?" he asked. He stood at the window, looking better than any man deserved, and the light silhouetted his broad frame. He studied her, undoubtedly satisfying himself that she wore an appropriate dress fabric, but surely lingering on her form longer than strictly necessary.

"I hardly think I need to be prepared, sir. My students will be under scrutiny, and I believe them quite capable."

"I am glad to hear it. But you will be under some scrutiny also, and I am happy to see you looking so well."

"You are looking well yourself, Daniel," she said.

He raised his eyebrows. "No mean feat, if you heard about yesterday's events."

"I did not." Her voice was not calm.

Daniel smiled, which did not reassure her at all. "John and Michael removed the remnants of your handiwork on my body."

Emily blushed mightily.

"And were they successful?"

"If by success you mean, did they manage to get it all out, I daresay the answer is yes. If you mean, did they manage it without nearly bludgeoning me to death, my answer is not unqualified. They made a mess of it; I would have welcomed your hand."

"Surely you see it would have been impossible?"

"Why so? You managed the initial work. You checked on the healing several days ago. And are we not very good friends?"

Emily felt a heartache so intense and sweet she thought she would die for lack of breath. She closed her eyes, recalling the intimacy of lying across his chest as she stitched his wound, the casual way in which he had bared his torso to her so she might examine the bloody tears in his flesh, and always, always, the tantalizing feel of skin and hair and bone and muscle. A few days ago, she had assured John and Michael they were quite capable of the task, and now she felt guilty to hear they had not been. But did her own need to heal not count for her excuse?

"Emily?"

She opened her eyes and knew he understood something of her treacherous feelings. She did not ask to feel this way, to finally feel a devotion so intense it made her beaux back in London seem like preludes to the symphony. And still she was denied a promise that they might see the music through to the end. Daniel said they were connected and allowed her some access into his life. They shared stolen moments of intimacy when the children were out of the classroom and Mrs. Winters was out of the library. But it was not enough.

She looked into his face, at the clear, fine features so rarely troubled by the crises in his life. She knew he wore his troubles within, not allowing others to see the doubt and grief and pain mixing in their own poisonous brew, because too many people relied on him for their own protection and looked to him for support. Such a burden could scarcely be borne alone, and yet Daniel Lennox carried it with dignity and grace and the great illusion of confidence. Emily imagined she lived among the rare individuals who saw the occasional cracks in his veneer, and recognized his enduring humanity.

She loved him all the more for it.

"We are friends, Mr. Lennox," she said very quietly, and turned away from him. "It is a pleasure I did not expect when I came to work at your school. But what you ask demands more of me than just friendship and I am not sure I am able to handle it with any degree of equanimity. The paths of our lives have intersected, but I do not believe they are destined to run smoothly together. You hold a very privileged position in your neighborhood and are quite set on your course. I am only the schoolmistress, managing to stay a few days ahead of my students, and hoping to earn enough to support the Clarkson home in London so I might return there."

"Is that what you want, Emily?"

She heard his words in her ear as he came up behind her and pulled her against his chest. His arms folded just under her breast and his tongue played with her earlobe.

"My sisters urge me to come to London," he continued. "They think it is time I presented myself in formal society and to several ladies who are anxious to meet me. I suspect it is more for their own gratification; they may wish to show their friends their brother is not the loutish provincial he is reputed to be."

Emily could scarcely contain her smile. "They may be disappointed. You will have to behave very well."

"They will be disappointed, because I informed them I am not coming anytime soon. My responsibilities preclude my leaving."

"Could not Noland Haines manage your affairs?"

"Some of them, yes, but you know there are things to concern me beyond the operation of the mill."

They stood for some time in silence, Emily aware of little but the beating of his heart against her shoulder blade. Outside, in the park around Shearings, several starlings quarreled in the trees, and carriage wheels crushed the gravel in the drive.

"Emily, there is a matter I wish to discuss with you. I pray it may be of great importance to your future and to your happiness," Daniel Lennox said with a note of urgency in his voice. "There is some delicacy about it, and I did not know how you would respond. But now, with Miss Martineau and Mr. Colman close at hand, I feel any pretense at secrecy must be abandoned."

Emily closed her eyes and leaned against him. Did she dare imagine he would make a declaration to her? Might she greet their guests with the certain knowledge she would soon be the mistress of all this? Harriet Martineau would think she had purposely played into such a strategic position. Daniel himself spoke of such things, and made reformers sound heartless in their pursuit of rich men. Is that why he yet hesitated? He could not possibly doubt her love. Yet he asked her about London, and told her he would not travel there while he dealt with problems in Glenfell.

She suddenly realized his intent. What could his words suggest but that he would send her away, convincing them both it was for her own safety? He feared for her as much as she did for him. But he had the power to dismiss her from her position, and she had nothing but her love to influence him.

"Emily, are you well? Am I holding you too tightly?"

He was not. If he would only hold her and never let her go. If he would only crush her against his body and keep her close to his heart.

She gasped, and even though she brought her hands up to place upon his, he loosened his hold. She felt painfully bereft.

"I am well," she said, and turned within the circle of his arms. She looked into his face and saw her own reflection in his eyes. "But must we speak of such things now? Will there not be time enough in the weeks ahead, when we quite settle back into our routine? Let Harriet Martineau observe the school and my students. Let her assess what needs be done."

Daniel Lennox narrowed his eyes and bent closer to her, and Emily instinctively braced for an assault.

"Your guests have arrived, sir," Mrs. Winters barked from the doorway, with all the subtlety of a terrier. She cleared her throat, demanding their attention. Emily felt, rather than saw, Daniel turn his head, but he did not release her. Mrs. Winters, presumably, saw a good deal more, and drew her own conclusions. "Shall I have them wait in the hall?"

"After coming so far? Indeed not, Mrs. Winters. Miss Clarkson and I are very anxious to be reunited with old friends."

Emily could think of few things she desired less.

"Of course, Mr. Lennox," she said agreeably. "Harriet Martineau proves herself an indomitable force and would be through the door in a minute if she suspected we kept her out."

"I see. Like someone else I know?" he said, for her ears only, and Emily suppressed a giggle. He dropped one hand, and caught Emily's elbow with the other. "We shall greet our guests, Mrs. Winters. Thank you for letting us know of their arrival."

"My duty and my pleasure, sir," the woman said, and Emily could not help but wonder how Mrs. Winters' polite choice of words reflected the conflicts in her own confused life.

Harriet Martineau loved nothing so much as an audience. She sat to Daniel's right, her thin hand covering the bowl of her wineglass as if to drink from it would be against her lofty principles, and sought to intoxicate those who gathered at the dining table in Shearings. Her gown seemed very grand, but it added weight to her very thin frame. Perhaps it was the effect she desired.

She also desired the good opinion of the men at the table. Daniel, who knew some things about ladies' corsets, found himself wondering what sort of apparatus managed to shape her breasts into such a position and contain them within the confines of her gown. Perhaps later he might ask Colman what he knew of the business.

His old friend, the man whose livelihood consisted of mashing the seeds of the mustard plant into a fine yellow powder, must have tasted of some powerful potions capable of pulling him away from his mill operation. The man usually was seen in the midst of a yellow cloud, writing in his ledger, or testing the strength of a piece of machinery. The sharp smell of mustard settled on his clothes, on his hair, on the bedding in his guest room. Daniel remembered returning from a visit and requiring his shirts to be boiled in pine water.

But Miss Martineau proved of sterner stuff than he. Already she had worked her influence on Colman, making him improve the conditions in which his workers lived and setting up a school similar to the one at the GlenLennox

Mill. She must have offered other compensations as well, for as Colman looked across the table at her, he smiled like a man well satisfied at his feast.

"Do tell them about our new harvest baskets, Miss Martineau," Mr. Colman prompted.

"Why yes, of course!" Miss Martineau's voice rose to new excited heights and she very nearly toppled her neglected wineglass. "It is of the most clever design, one I conceived while on the coach between London and York. First I noticed . . ."

Mrs. Carroll, to whom Daniel owed at least a year's worth of dinner invitations, slept through much of the discourse. Polly Drummond, her sister, nudged her periodically, presumably to keep the older woman from falling off her chair. John Drummond ignored the little drama to his left, seeming rather more interested in the rise and fall of Miss Martineau's breasts.

Noland Haines and Ellen Worthington demonstrated a more creditable interest in Miss Martineau, but one not as great as their apparent fascination with each other. Daniel's heart swelled to see them so happy, so content, so settled in their affairs. Some day he hoped Nolly would take over many of the responsibilities at the mill, as knowing in its business as Nell seemed to be in the running of the school. He would look no further than her door when Emily's successor would need to be found.

For he knew with absolute certainty Emily must occupy a more important place in his life than that of his schoolmistress. He wanted her presiding at his table and he wanted her in his bed. He could imagine no one else as the mother of his children, nor as his partner in all the matters of his life. In her presence, Shearings became a sanctuary from pain and difficulty, a home.

Daniel watched her run a finger over the rim of her glass, and grew edgy remembering how that divine finger had trifled more purposefully with his own anatomy. But Emily sat in her place, cool and poised, and had scarcely paid him any heed since dinner began, though he had given her ample opportunity to do so.

"Do you think Miss Martineau's plan ought to be implemented here, Miss Clarkson?" Daniel asked, barely able to contain himself. He was not altogether sure what point

Harriet proposed, but to presume there was one seemed a safe wager.

"That we send the children out to hunt for new strains of wild mustard, Mr. Lennox?" she replied cheerfully.

"But it would harm Jeremiah's business, Miss Clarkson," Miss Martineau protested. "I believe . . ."

Whatever she believed could not signify, for the only responses that mattered to Daniel were Emily's. She sat still, smiling, looking for all the world like a satisfied lover.

And yet she held back from him.

Why would she not let him speak in the drawing room, when he so strongly felt his resolve to do so? What did she already know of his history that she would shut him out so quickly?

He reminded himself he should be cautious before he put all his hopes and dreams on the exquisitely contrary lady.

But, indeed, it already was too late. For he knew he loved nothing so much as Emily Clarkson.

Some time later, Emily led the other women into the parlor, as if it were the most natural thing in the world for her to do so. Mrs. Carroll looked very knowing and self-satisfied and said something about her own important part in introducing Emily to Glenfell society; Mrs. Drummond hushed her up very quickly.

Nell stayed close to Emily's side, and seemed intent on protecting her from the voracious Miss Martineau.

"Would you like to hear about our progress at the school, Miss Martineau?" she asked sweetly.

"I am sure there is time enough for such things, Miss Wellington," said Harriet, studying the carved mantelpiece.

"My friend is Miss Worthington," Emily corrected her impatiently. She doubted the great reformer ever heard anyone but herself. At the moment, she most certainly did not, as she ran a finger over the woodwork. "You can be assured, Harriet, Mr. Lennox is not only a successful businessman, but possesses a very fine taste. If you require evidence of his worth, you need only ask anyone in this town."

"Excepting the Duke of Glendennon," Mrs. Carroll added.

Harriet did not seem to care about the duke. "I am sure

he acquired his taste from his sisters, and endeavors to impress those who doubt him. Surely he sets an excellent table." She paused to lick something off her finger and nodded in approval.

"I daresay Mrs. Winters had as much to say about it as he, but I will not deny the excellence of his governance," Emily said, a little tartly.

"How lucky you are, then, Emily. For my own Mr. Colman is a bit of a Philistine, and requires my guidance in everything from managing his mill to putting down the proper napkins at table."

Emily winced, hoping the other ladies had not caught Harriet's rather obvious implication.

"However did he manage all these years? Indeed, I thought you were acquainted only briefly."

Harriet stuck out her lower lip, looking like a recalcitrant child. "It is not so much the quantity of the time that signifies, but its quality. In any case, I know in a minute if a man is worth cultivating. And I have decided to cultivate Mr. Colman."

"I am very happy for you, Harriet. Let me be the first to wish you joy, for the gentlemen seems very ardent in his affections," Emily managed to say with some composure. "But will it not interfere with your great plans for reform?"

Still pouting, Harriet plumped herself down in the closest chair, and nearly loosened her left breast from the bodice of her gown. She beckoned the rest of her audience to approach her.

Emily held back, leaning against a case filled with some of Mr. Lennox's collection of books. If he could not be here to support her, at least his possessions brought some comfort.

"Nothing must interfere with the great plans for reform. You should be committed to the same ideals, Miss Clarkson."

"I never professed the same level of commitment as my mother, Miss Martineau, though I have some respect for your endeavors. I share your belief that education might be the great equalizer; to that end Miss Worthington and I work very hard at Mr. Lennox's mill school. I pray we will give the children a better future."

"And what of your own future?" Harriet asked, her finger pointing accusingly.

Emily wondered whence such vehemence derived. She

glanced toward her companions, suspecting an enthusiastic gossip among them, but saw only the faces of the curious. She knew herself the object of speculation, but then so might any young and reasonably attractive woman be who came into Mr. Lennox's sphere. A handsome and wealthy man could not remain a bachelor past the age of twenty-five and not inspire many hopes and dreams.

"My future is very much undecided, Miss Martineau. I look to nothing past my work at the school and returning to my home in London. I have not been in Glenfell very long and am not even certain Mr. Lennox is happy with my progress."

Out of the corner of her eye, she saw Mrs. Carroll nudge her sister and exchange a gleeful smile.

"He is forthcoming with Mr. Colman," Harriet said.

"Pray, will you not share your information? I am sure there is not anything the others may not hear," Emily said, sounding more confident than she felt.

"I am not so certain I ought," she said. "I will say, however, Mr. Lennox has the very best intentions."

"His intentions are excellent," Emily agreed, "and he is absolutely trustworthy. He is everything he appears to be."

But while Emily expected a chorus of agreement from his other constituents, her words were followed by absolute silence. She looked to Mrs. Carroll, who promptly turned away, and Nell, who suddenly found something of great interest in the folds of her gown.

Something insubstantial but insistent started to tickle Emily's memory, and she felt the most curious and undoubtedly unreasonable suspicion begin to take hold. A miscast word and a vague image suddenly infected her imagination, and seemed sufficient for Emily to believe others knew something of which she remained unaware. But it seemed too impossible to contemplate.

And if she must contemplate it, this was not the time to do so.

"It is some years since we have seen a ball at Shearings," Mrs. Drummond said. "Not since Laura's betrothal to Lord Gray has the house been open to all the neighborhood. And now we welcome Mr. Colman and Miss Martineau."

"Of course," Harriet said grandly. "As you can imagine, I am well accustomed to such affairs."

If her general manner had not been enough to make the other ladies bristle, her present implication aroused the greatest defense.

"I assure you, Miss Martineau, we have many such events ourselves, though not often enough at Shearings. We danced the waltz before it gained hold in London," Mrs. Drummond said.

"However so?" Harriet asked.

"Princess Lieven herself came to Glenfell. Oh! It was such a time!" crooned Mrs. Carroll.

Harriet sat up in her seat, her eyes wide. "And what might have brought . . . ? Oh, I suppose it was to see the duke."

"I do not recall their meeting. Rather, she came to see the children of her old friend, Mrs. Lennox. The girls were quite dependent on their brother, you see, and the princess did not think him anxious to spend the Season in London. Even then, he devoted all his energies to the running of the business."

And if he had not, Emily thought, if he had joined his sisters at parties and balls in London, then he might have become another of the colorless gentlemen who were obliged to pay court to young ladies thrust before them at every turn in a ballroom. He would not be the man he had become, thrumming with the energy that drew others into his wake.

But Harriet did not have reason to waste her time on romantic tales if the discussion did not involve social reform.

"I am most interested in this relationship, Mrs. Carroll, for I ever believed the princess an aristocrat of the most unforgiving kind. And yet you tell me she condescended to sponsor the daughters of a common mill owner? I am profoundly impressed; I shall write to her at once and give her my approbation."

For all Harriet's fame as a reformer, Emily did not think her letter of approval would be greatly appreciated by the princess.

Polly Drummond sat up straighter in her chair and narrowed her eyes. "The Lennox daughters are well connected," she said haughtily. "You could not imagine they could be so well married if everyone shared your prejudice, Miss Martineau."

For the second time in a few moments, Emily felt the tickling of some unbidden knowledge, and groped for the elusive key to a locked door.

"Why, I am ever the optimist, Mrs. Drummond. I always preferred to believe that Laura, Miriam, and Eleanor charmed their eminent husbands by virtue of their own accomplishments," Harriet said, and Emily thought it the most applaudable thing she had uttered since arriving in Glenfell.

"Do tell us about your own accomplishments, Miss Martineau," Nell said earnestly. "Mr. Haines tells me you frequently travel to his homeland."

Harriet required nothing else. She spent the next half hour describing the horrors of life in America, pausing only to catch her breath when the men's voices sounded outside their door.

Daniel looked for Emily as soon as he entered the parlor and was surprised to see her lost in thought. Miss Martineau somehow engaged the attention of the others, though her voice sounded as if it had been overused in the past hour, but Emily's dreamy brown eyes gazed elsewhere, on the portrait of his mother.

He wondered what she saw to interest her on his mother's imperfectly painted face, in a portrait revealing all the prettiness but none of the character of a singularly independent and defiant lady. Did she note certain family resemblances, or the richness of the dress? Did she see the wound in the canvas, where a tree branch had caught the painting when its unforgiving owner tossed it into the Fell? His mother and her portrait had quite a colorful history, and he prayed Emily did not yet understand it.

But then she turned her gaze upon him as he stood in the doorway, and he feared she began to understand the truths of which he could not bear to speak.

"Have you enjoyed your respite from our boorish company, ladies?" he asked gallantly when Harriet paused to take a breath.

"But your company is never boorish," Mrs. Carroll answered cheerfully. "I daresay the same is true of the two other gentlemen as well."

"But we are sad fellows when you put us together, Mrs.

Carroll," Daniel continued, still looking at Emily. "We have little to talk about but business and matters of economics, and no fair ladies to distract us."

He hoped to provoke Emily into some retort, something to arouse her from her obvious brooding, but the answer came from Harriet Martineau.

"We are very happy to distract you now, Mr. Lennox. I have only just heard of your family's connection to Princess Lieven and am so anxious to hear your thoughts on the great lady."

"I wonder whom I have to thank for imparting such knowledge," he said wryly and was rewarded when he saw Mrs. Carroll blush to the roots of her gray hair. He also wondered what else she had seen fit to share with Emily and the others. "But I thought it well known that the princess sponsored my three motherless sisters for their Season in Town. She is a relation, in fact. They could not have asked for a more influential patroness, though I believe my estimable brothers-in-law fell in love with them for their own merits."

"And were you not tempted to follow them, Mr. Lennox? To protect the interests of your sisters?" Emily asked.

"I had other interests to protect here, Miss Clarkson," he said carefully. "You understand, we were not only motherless, but fatherless as well. In the event my sisters did not succeed, it would have fallen on me to ensure their livelihood. Besides, I believe there is only one thing I missed by not going to London."

He thought he saw Emily blush.

"But to resist the lure of Almack's, Mr. Lennox! For if the princess had held you in tow, you would have gone every night!" Harriet edged forward excitedly. "And then you would have become an accomplished dancer and made a famous match!"

He held the tails of his jacket and sat down with the ladies, nodding for Jeremiah and Nolly to do the same.

"I still hope to make a famous match, Miss Martineau. And, if necessary, I shall demonstrate my dancing skills on the night of our ball. I promise, I shall not step on your toes."

Harriet giggled, abandoning the stiff facade of the reformer and looking more like a little girl. For the first time, Daniel wondered how old she was.

"Will you stand up with me first?" she asked.

Near him, Jeremiah shifted in his seat.

"I would be honored, Miss Martineau, but certainly Mr. Colman claims his right to the opening dance with you. And I . . ." he slanted a glance toward Emily and saw her twist her linen handkerchief into little balls in her lap. "I am already promised to Miss Clarkson. She understands all my limitations, but agrees to my request in spite of them."

Or because of them, he said to himself. With Miss Martineau's apparent fascination with the waltz, it now seemed impossible to withhold it from the program. And by acquiescing to her desire, he obliged himself to stand up with Emily for each of them. Any other lady, dancing so close, would wonder at the bulk of the bandages beneath his jacket. And Harriet Martineau would probably insist he undress in the ballroom so she might see them for herself.

He would dance the waltz with Emily and hold her as close as he dared. And, of course, if she insisted he undress, he would be very happy to oblige her.

"Why do you smile, Mr. Lennox?" Polly Drummond asked, and he quickly recovered himself. "Is it because you have secured Miss Clarkson's favors?"

"Oh no, Mrs. Drummond. If I had already secured Miss Clarkson's favors, I should think I would have no patience for a ball at all. I should want to spend every minute in her delightful company."

"But then we would be so sadly deprived," Mrs. Carroll said.

Daniel smiled graciously, and patted his dear old friend on the hand. But a small and unexpectedly selfish part of him felt like protesting. Indeed, why should he be the only person to have something of Emily's attention and still believe himself the sad victim of deprivation of the acutest sort?

Chapter Twelve

"*H*onestly, Emily, if I were not so enamored of my own dear Mr. Colman, I should make such a play for Mr. Lennox as to embarrass myself throughout the countryside." Harriet bent at the waist to look at her reflection in Emily's dressing mirror and came so close her hair caught on Emily's brooch.

As Emily disengaged herself from her enthusiastic friend, she reflected upon how Harriet had already given an excellent imitation of one pursuing Mr. Lennox, having played the part very aggressively throughout the past few days.

"I am glad you warned me of his dislike for silk and brocade," Harriet continued. "My dressmaker made this gown up just before I left London, and you see how very plain it is in fabric."

"But it is so very lovely, Harriet," Emily said, truthfully.

Harriet bit down on her lip. "But not half so pretty as yours, Emily. No wonder he cannot resist you."

Emily blushed, for here was the very first compliment her friend had ever paid her. Throughout the hours spent in the classroom, in discussions over strategy and lessons, in interviews in the company of others, Harriet had never given Emily the least intimation she felt at all grateful for Emily's work at the school. She still did not. Yet here came praise of a different sort.

"Of course he resists me. Have we spent more than a few hours' time in the gentlemen's company?" Emily said lightly.

"Oh, if you could just see him, Emily! You are always looking down into a book, or examining the portraits on the walls, or doing something equally evasive, so you do not notice the way he looks at you!"

"And how is that, dear Harriet?" Emily dared to ask.

"As if to catch your smile would be grace itself."

Emily let the words linger, to savor their sweet taste.

"How I should like to think so," she answered, "though I came to the mill without any intentions of pursuing its master. But we have shared many things in the time since I came here, and I consider us allies. It is well and good for a business partnership, but I am not sure it will ever go beyond such an understanding. Just before your arrival, he asked if I wished to return to London. Those do not sound like the words of a man longing for my notice."

"Are you quite sure?"

"Dear Harriet," said Emily, displaying all the wisdom of her twenty years. "I have spent sufficient time in London society to know the signs of infatuation by now. Mr. Lennox shows pleasure in the society of women; that is all."

"Do not belittle him by saying so. Nor yourself for thinking it."

"You are kind, Harriet. But surely you see it is not to be? He is married to the mill; he told me as much when I first arrived. I own he has some affection for me, but it seems to get in the way of his pursuits. I am not sure he desires a wife."

Harriet sighed, the sound a fair reflection of Emily's own frustration. She tucked a curl behind her ear, and adjusted her thin lace. "Shall we walk to Shearings, Miss Clarkson? Or will we damage our slippers on the drive?"

"I daresay we shall, but we travel with too large an escort to arrive by carriage," Emily said. "The children are all invited to come, you see."

"To the ball?" Harriet cried, and did not sound very like the great republican she professed to be.

"To the house," Emily amended. "They have fine new clothes."

Harriet recovered herself enough to ask, "And where will they go? They cannot attend the servants' party."

"Of course not, for it would be most inappropriate. Mrs. Winters prepares a special dinner in the upper hall, at Mr. Lennox's insistence. They will be able to watch the arrival of all the guests from such a vantage point, and enjoy the musicians."

As Harriet Martineau reached for her cape and allowed her friend to tie it tightly under her chin, she sighed wearily: "Is he not the best of all men?"

Already surrounded by the promptest guests, Daniel glanced anxiously out the window, wondering why Emily and Harriet were delayed in coming. Though there were a multitude of very prettily dressed diversions happy to engage him in conversation and ask him his opinion of the weather, the prince's new home at Brighton, and the current style of gloves, he passed them off to Jeremiah Colman, who seemed infinitely more knowledgeable on such matters.

More than a hundred guests were expected this evening, with invitations having been sent as far away as York and as close as Gleneyrie, but there was no one whose company Daniel desired as much as Emily Clarkson's. Jane would be here as well, escorted by Peter Havers, and for the first time in several years, he felt he could look upon her with complete dispassion. Almost disinterest. Yielding to custom, Daniel had sent an invitation to the duke and duchess, even though all such previous overtures had been absolutely ignored. When Jane announced her intention of attending, he had felt surprise, some curiosity, but no particular stirrings of emotion.

"She will not come any faster if you ignore your other guests to watch for her, Daniel," said Catherine Milrose. "Perhaps she wishes to make a grand entrance."

Daniel turned from his place in the window.

"You cannot know her very well if you think it, Catherine. She is a fairly modest lady, for all her London ways. I suspect she does not consider herself above any of the others."

"And do you?"

He looked at his old friend in surprise. "If you ask it, you cannot know me very well, either. Have I not endeavored . . ."

"I know you better than anyone, and understand perfectly well how your stubborn pride prevents others from giving you your due. But you willfully misunderstand me."

Daniel frowned.

"Do not be so thick, Daniel, for it scarcely becomes you," Miss Milrose scolded. "I only asked if you considered Miss Clarkson above the others."

"Does it matter so much to you if I do?" he asked gently.

"If you have not married me in all the many years we have known each other, I hold no hopes you will do so at any time in the future. Miss Clarkson is a fine lady, and very beautiful. I only hope she is never a cause for your pain."

"That seems a very cryptic blessing."

"Not at all. You have been injured before, and not only by a beautiful lady. Glenfell is not as safe a place as it has always seemed to be."

"You exaggerate the situation," Daniel said gently.

"You forget, my brother shares a great deal with me. And I know you did not get that nasty bruise on your cheek by bumping into a closet."

"David forgets himself."

"Just so you do not, sir." Miss Milrose put her hand to his cheek. "You have too much at risk."

Daniel felt a tightening of his chest and the now-familiar pain of his healing wound.

"Why, what is this?" Catherine asked, excitedly, and looked past him to just outside the window.

"If it is the duke's carriage you see, do not be surprised," he said as he turned.

"Of course not. The whole neighborhood knows how Jane condescended to accept your invitation," Catherine said hurriedly. "But there is something else."

Daniel looked to the edge of the drive, where the peculiar line of foliage now emerged as a small band of people. At the fore, leading the way through the steady stream of carriages and horses, walked two of the oldest boys. And just taller than all the rest, including the diminutive Miss Martineau, stood Emily, her face nearly hidden by her voluminous calash.

"Is she so devoted to her charges she cannot leave them for a moment?" Catherine asked. "Or do they provide protection?"

"Of course not. I asked Mrs. Winters to prepare a repast for the children, so they would not be left out of all the gaiety. Though I confess, I do not know why Miss Clarkson and Miss Martineau have chosen to walk with them, instead of riding in the carriage."

"Then you do not know Miss Martineau very well, my friend. Perhaps she hoped to pick up a field hand or two along the way, and redeem their characters in time for her entrance."

Daniel laughed, wondering if he should set Miss Martineau on his wicked cousin.

Emily put two nervous hands to her face, warming her cheeks. Undoubtedly the brisk walk had done more to give them color than any amount of pinching in the hall would have, but she would not appear to great advantage if her teeth did not stop chattering.

Only part of her chilled state could be due to the weather, for she and Harriet had dutifully delivered the children to Mrs. Winters and stood for several minutes warming themselves in front of a large fire. But soon the housekeeper hurried them off and up to the ballroom.

Emily and Harriet entered together, but Mr. Colman waited just inside, and immediately removed his favorite so he might show her off to several acquaintances. And Emily was left quite alone.

"I thought you would never arrive."

She felt warm hands upon her wrists, pulling her hands away from her face, and looked up at Daniel.

If he only knew how the sight of him looking thus would have brought her to him at any cost. His bright eyes were no longer shadowed by the pain of his injuries, and the bruises and scratches on his face were virtually gone. His hair looked recently trimmed, but his valet had brushed some across his forehead to obscure the sight of his recent scar. Lips no longer swollen were slightly apart, revealing his very straight teeth.

Remembering the taste of his mouth, Emily quickly looked down, to gaze upon the buttons of his fine blue worsted jacket. Just over its lapel, she saw the outline of his bandage.

"Do you feel quite up to this evening, sir?" she asked.

"More so since your arrival, my dear. I began to fear Miss Martineau had engaged you in some discourse, or needed to see your plans for lessons for the next few years."

Emily laughed. "It would not be unlike her. But I fear I must dispel a popular myth—put about by Harriet herself—and let you know she is as excited to be here at your ball as any girl in her coming-out Season. I suspect she did not have such a Season herself, and comes upon these pleasures belatedly."

"Whereas you are quite an expert, I suppose?"

"I believe I am, sir. I have had more than one Season, and believe it is enough to try any woman's tolerance."

"I hope your indifference does not make you regret coming this evening? There are many people I would wish for you to meet, and they are very anxious to make your acquaintance."

Emily raised her eyebrows. "Did I not understand this event was to honor Mr. Colman and Miss Martineau?"

"I would much rather honor you," he said.

"Oh," she said, and closed her eyes, fearing she would awaken from a dream.

"You do not look very happy at the prospect, Emily," he said in a teasing tone, but there seemed to be an underlying urgency in his voice. "Are you afraid to dance with me? I promise I will not bleed all over you."

"Nothing could be less amusing, Daniel! And as I am promised to you for the first dance, I shall have to endure it."

"A pity. But then, there will be at least three waltzes, and I believe you must dance those with me as well."

She sighed. "I shall have to chance the consequences."

"Excellent. And then there will be several quadrilles."

"You will give everyone reason to gossip."

"I believe I already have. What say you, Emily?"

Emily smiled. "As you are my employer, I fear I must not refuse you."

He laughed. "Happy words! I should like to remind you of them for many years to come!"

Emily studied his face, utterly bemused. She felt sorely tempted to charge him with his meaning when the musicians suddenly changed their tune and a happy cheer rose from the crowd. Emily looked around her, surprised to see so many new arrivals since she had started speaking to

Daniel, and even more surprised to realize they looked expectantly at her and her partner.

"It appears as if you must fulfill your first obligation," he said, and offered her his arm. Emily put her hand on his elbow and allowed him to lead her through the warm and receptive crowd.

Though a stranger among them, she felt very much at ease. Was she not given a place of honor at Daniel's side? Had she not already dined with the duke and duchess? And was not her little school already destined for some success? She owned every reason to hold her chin up and walk proudly.

Daniel marched her to the very center of the floor, and as twenty or more couples fell into place around them, she finally took stock of their surroundings.

"Do you like this house, Emily?"

"Why, very much, sir. It seems all designed for comfort."

"Such might have been the intention. Many years ago, there was a smaller home on this site built as part of the Gleneyrie estate, for a dowager duchess still young enough to enjoy entertainment and parties. Her son, a very generous young man by all accounts, would not have her totally displaced."

"How kind of him. But how came it into your family, sir?"

"My paternal grandfather bought it from my . . . lord. I believe it the very beginning of their emnity."

"It seems rather petty. The Duke of Glendennon would not have been the first to lose a piece of property to one prepared to pay a fine price for it."

"Certainly not. But it was not all he lost."

Just then the opening notes of the dance sounded, and Emily almost missed a step. But she caught herself in time to turn Daniel's corner and find herself facing Mr. Colman, who looked uncommonly happy.

It seemed a feeling shared by all the company, if one might judge by the looks on everyone's face and the delighted greetings passing from one dancer to another. Emily recognized nearly everyone, from some of the more illustrious guests at Mrs. Carroll's dinner party to Mr. Fallon, who owned a very fine shop in town. Noland Haines and Nell Worthington stood between a rather elderly lord and his lady and Mr. and Mrs. Drummond, and gave every appearance of knowing they belonged there. Indeed, Emily reflected as Daniel circled her, who was she herself but the schoolmistress of Mr. Lennox's children?

But even as she thought it, she admitted herself too modest. He might have asked this dance of any of a dozen ladies who would have been perfectly delighted to accept him, but he asked it of her. He might have chosen someone of long acquaintance, raising no speculative eyebrows, but he had chosen her. He might have looked to Miss Milrose and saved his old friend the embarrassment of stepping out to the first dance with her brother.

But he had not.

Emily did not doubt the warmth with which the people of Glenfell regarded the handsome and generous mill owner.

Now, for the first time, she wondered in what light they regarded her.

"You dance very well for a London lady, Emily," Daniel said, when the music brought them close. "You outshine every woman here."

"I suppose you mean such words as compliments, sir. But you make me now think your guests have three reasons to despise me."

Daniel looked puzzled. "That you come from London, I perfectly understand. That you are beautiful would be a natural cause of resentment for some. But pray, what might be the third?"

"Why, that you chose me at all," Emily said, somewhat breathlessly, and returned his intense gaze. She saw, by the satisfied expression there, that he had known precisely what she would answer. "Surely there are those who are surprised, or even upset."

"There could not be above twenty," he said very seriously. "But then, there must be a good deal more who are perfectly delighted. I have been reminded, and not only by my sisters, how I spend an inordinate amount of time engaged in my business."

"And what would they have you do instead?" Emily asked, and then realized she might catch herself in a trap of her own making.

"They would have me marry, of course. And live like a gentleman of leisure," he finally answered.

"Is it not a contradiction? If one marries, and expands one's household, I should think the goal of a gentlemanly life must be necessarily deferred."

"So it would seem, Emily. But, like Mr. Havers, I too have expectations."

The musicians chose that unfortunate moment to sound the final notes of the dance. All around them, the guests re-formed groups and hurriedly exchanged partners. But Daniel did not escort Emily from the floor, nor did he express his gratitude with a bow. Instead, he stood silently, his hand on her arm, and waited for the others to assemble around them. When the musicians started up again, he stepped forward and caught Emily by the waist.

"I do not recall you asking me for this dance," she said.

"Perhaps it is among my expectations that I should not need to do so," he answered in her ear.

"You sound very lordly to say such a thing," Emily said, and waited for his denial. But he surprised her.

"Do I indeed? And do you fancy it suits?"

It did, uncommonly well. Not for the first time, she reflected how much more in command of his people, of his community, of his holdings he seemed than the tired, ailing duke at Gleneyrie. All the people who gathered at Shearings paid homage to Daniel Lennox by coming here, and looked to him for example and guidance. He seemed the full worth of a nobleman.

"As a matter of fact," she said, "I believe it does."

She watched his features very closely, purposefully looking for his response. She saw him nod, almost as if he carried on a dialogue with himself, and straighten his back.

"Emily," he began, "we have not yet finished a particular discussion."

"Is this the place to do so?" she asked, rather pointedly.

He looked around him, looking for all the world as if he had forgotten they danced at the very center of a large crush.

He grinned a little sheepishly. "It is not," he admitted. "though there may not be one here who would not guess my words."

They continued to dance in silence until Daniel missed a step, and brushed against her bare arm.

"Are you well?" she asked anxiously. Whatever else he

was to her, he yet remained her patient. "Your injuries? Are they worse?"

His hand slipped between the buttons on his jacket and moved along the lines of his bandage.

"I do not think they are. Why do you ask?"

"You seem suddenly distracted, sir."

He smiled, a little ruefully. "I am sorry. It is only the arrival of another guest."

Emily guessed her identity, though not with any degree of pleasure. She felt a fool, waiting for the words from him she would wish to hear, even though he always seemed to pick an inopportune moment for wanting to utter them. Surely, proposing marriage to a new love even as the old love entered the room would be considered vastly inappropriate.

"It is a very fine party, Daniel. It would be a pity were anyone to miss it," Emily said.

When the music stopped, he said, "I would not care who missed it, if I could only have one person in attendance."

For one brief moment, Emily's heart fluttered in anticipation, in defiance of her reason. But common sense prevailed, as it always must, as soon as she heard one of the servants call everyone's attention to the doorway behind her. Daniel looked past her shoulder, his expression inscrutable.

"The Duchess of Glendennon," announced the servant in a voice that reverberated through the room. As the company bowed in deference, he added in a lower voice: "Mr. Peter Havers."

Emily turned, knowing she could not escape the inevitable, as the man she loved made his way through the crowd to greet his neighbors. She could not see his face, but she could see the lady's, and saw a rare flash of joy across her drawn features. The duchess pouted prettily as she stood in the doorway waiting for him.

Emily looked then upon Mr. Havers, a man whose intimacy with the duchess had proved the cause of so much speculation. Indeed, he seemed a suitable match for her this evening, looking very much like a gentleman of the highest aspirations.

His pale hair gleamed like gold in the candlelight and it looked as if he had begun to sport a brief mustache, which suited him. His jacket looked a close match to his lady's gown, though his leggings were a shade darker. Taller than any man in the company save Daniel, he towered over the duchess like an oak over a poplar.

Soon, blocking Emily's view of the newcomers, Daniel's broad back edged between the other guests. He bowed low before the duchess, a gesture surely causing him some discomfort.

Emily hoped it killed him.

She turned on her heel and made her way to the buffet tables beyond the arches of the ballroom, little caring who saw her blatant discourtesy toward the most esteemed lady of Glenfell.

Chapter Thirteen

*D*efying everything Aunt Constance had taught her about ladylike manners, Emily gulped down a glass of ratafia and felt its cooling sweetness wash over her heated spirit. A surprised servant, interrupting as he arranged a tray of cold meats on the table, quickly refilled it, but Emily nursed her second portion between her hands.

She might have regretted her hasty retreat if anyone had witnessed it. But aside from a few servants whom she did not recognize, only a dozing gentleman in the corner stood her company, completely oblivious to the great honor afforded the guests by the arrival of the Duchess of Glendennon.

How little the grand lady deserved the adoration of her community, Emily thought ungenerously. Any other lady who scorned a worthy suitor would have met with censure—or, at best, disapproval—but the duchess' lofty title made her exempt from such harsh judgment. Of course, Emily admitted to herself, she too had once been influenced by the nobility and seduced by its inherent power. But in recent weeks she had come to appreciate how, like deference of any other sort, respect needed to be earned. In any case, she would not be disposed to be gracious to Daniel's previous lover, even if the lady were a match girl.

But she was not. Nor was there anything Emily could do about it. It was one of the reasons she did not wish to be exiled to London, even with the excuse of her safety. Daniel seemed intrigued by the duchess, by her position, by her relationship with his cousin. The duke was frail and ailing. Peter Havers was Daniel's enemy. Might Daniel consider the winning of the duchess after the duke's death a triumph over those who would defeat him?

Emily sipped her drink and leaned against one of the columns supporting an arch. She might as well have been invisible, for the lady and Mr. Havers captured all the audience, and Daniel stood in the front row.

"Miss Clarkson?"

The whisper came so softly, Emily felt sure she had imagined it.

"Miss Clarkson?"

Instinctively, she ducked back into the shadow of the arch before she turned to look for her mysterious companion. At first she saw nothing, just the reflection of the candles in the large windows. But then a form broke away from the draperies and materialized as three of the children, standing shoulder to shoulder.

"What are you doing here?" Emily whispered hoarsely. "If Mrs. Winters should discover you . . ."

"But we need to speak to Mr. Lennox, miss," spoke up Will, who hardly ever offered a word in conversation.

"He is engaged just now, I am sorry to say," Emily said, feeling a good deal sorrier than they knew. "The Duchess of Glendennon is only just arrived."

"We know the lady is here, for we watched her and Mr. Havers leave their carriage. It is very grand," said Timothy.

"But she is not so pretty as you, miss," said Anne loyally.

"Thank you, dear," Emily said, feeling more pleasure than she should. "But she is a duchess and so it does not matter. Ah . . . what would you wish to discuss with Mr. Lennox?"

"Will found a letter," Anne announced solemnly. "It fell from the duchess' carriage as it drove away."

"I read it, miss," Will said, and Emily felt an uncommon rush of pride. No matter the inappropriateness of reading words intended for other people, here was something the child could never have hoped to accomplish before she came here.

"You know you must never read other people's letters," she admonished, with no effort at severity. "But would you like for me to return it to the duchess?"

"No, miss. We think it should be given to Mr. Lennox," said Anne, and the two boys nodded.

Emily's heart ached as she asked, "Is it addressed to him? From the lady?"

"No, miss. We think it is about him."

"I see," said Emily, though she did not at all. "Shall I gave it to him?"

The children nodded nervously, and Emily heard people starting to stream back onto the dance floor. Will held out his hand, in which a crumbled ball of paper sat, and Emily accepted the letter with all solemnity. She had done no more than circle the ball with her fingers when the three children dashed off.

Glancing up at the crowd, but seeing no one who might be approaching her for the next dance, Emily carefully un-folded the little scrap in her hand, and squinted to read the tiny script in the poor light of the archway.

Daniel stood at the head of the long line of men and bowed politely to his partner as the music started. He knew it his place to give this dance to Jane, but heartily wished he might have passed her off to his cousin, who instead took comfort with Catherine Milrose. He glanced around at the company, seeing Harriet Martineau with Jeremiah, Dr. Cafferty with Nell, and Peter with Mrs. Carroll.

But neither on this line nor the next did he see Emily, nor could he imagine where she had gone.

When he dropped her hand after the second dance, he had assumed she would walk at his side to Jane and Peter, but when he turned to her, she had already disappeared.

He quickly covered his mistake by leading Jane out onto the dance floor, as was his right as the host, and acting as if he would have no other.

"I believe you have made an enemy of Peter, Daniel," Jane said softly.

"There is no surprise there, Your Grace," he answered abruptly. "You know better than most the dislike between us. But why this sudden revelation?"

He assumed she would point out how he had usurped a dance already promised, but her thoughts went beyond matters of politeness.

"You seem to frustrate him at every turn, and he can scarcely conceal his anger. Your success at the mill, your ability to host the grandest party, the reverence with which all the neighborhood honors you, are all irritants to him. And your relationship with a certain lady has made him profoundly jealous."

Daniel felt his wound rub uncomfortably against his stiff bandage; just now, it felt raw and painful.

"He is hardly justified in feeling jealous, if he can be with you when I am generally prohibited from such a honor," Daniel said impatiently, assuming she was the lady in question. When, he wondered, would he ever be allowed to escape the memory of his youthful infatuation?

Jane smiled at him, but it seemed an expression of regret.

"I am not speaking of myself, Daniel. I am a married lady, as you might recall."

"How can I ever forget . . ."

"I am speaking of Miss Clarkson."

Daniel had several moments to brood over this in silence as the dance took him away from his partner.

"Miss Clarkson has nothing to do with this," he said gruffly.

"You can no sooner fool me than you can anyone else here in the party. And Peter made certain assumptions right from the start. From what I understand, you cannot dispute them," Jane said with a knowing smile. "You are in great danger, Daniel."

"I am capable of handling Miss Clarkson," he said rudely.

Jane stiffened and offered him only two fingers when he reached for her hand.

"I am sure you are. I would worry about Peter. I have reason to suspect he will soon act against you."

"I have reason to know he already has. But why this change of heart, Duchess? Have you not already aligned yourself with him, bargaining on his expectations, absurd though they may be?"

Jane looked him directly in the eyes and, for the first time, he saw the pain in hers. She had made her bed, as they say, but he knew better than most how uncomfortable it must have been.

"My alliances are no one's affair but my own. But I am speaking because I truly never had a change of heart, Daniel. I loved you then, and I love you still."

Daniel could remember when such a profession was all he desired. But now he could only feel pity for her.

"It is too late, Jane," he said gently.

"I know. But I would have you careful, lest I feel any more guilt about my circumstances than I already do."

As the violinist played the final measures, Daniel bowed to his partner, and then to his two corners. Over Miss Martineau's elaborate crown of curls, he saw the object of his desire hidden behind a marble column, her form a fitting complement to its classic lines. When the musicians took up their task, almost immediately, and the strains of a waltz echoed in the room, he knew he had every reason to pursue her.

"Are you waiting for the stroke of midnight to make good your escape, Emily?" he asked, as he came up to her. She looked as if she had been expecting him. "Or do you merely intend to disappear behind the draperies?"

She opened her mouth as if to speak, but then bit down on her lower lip. She shivered, something which would have made him pull her into his arms if they had not had an audience.

"Are you ill?" he asked, and would have carried her off, the audience be damned.

"No, Daniel," she said, just loud enough for him to hear her. Her use of his first name moved him in a way he thought he had surely outgrown years ago. "I am only worried about you."

He groaned his relief. There seemed to be more ladies concerned with his well-being than in the dances, and he began to feel a little impatient with it all.

"Here," he said, and pulled her hand to his heart. "Will

you be satisfied? I am quite healed and as fit as a chimney damper. And I believe I might be able to dance all evening if only I can find partners to keep up with me. Will you be one?"

"I wish to speak to you first."

"People will wonder if we are not dancing. Besides, you have promised me this waltz, and it should provide enough privacy for you to discuss all the things I am doing to injure myself."

He pulled her away from the column before she could argue, and brought her out to the center of the dance floor. She hurriedly thrust something—a scrap of lace, perhaps—into the bosom of her gown and he sorely wished to retrieve it for her. But he dared presume nothing more than to put his left hand upon her waist and clasp her hand with his right. She stepped closer to him, which seemed more than he should expect, and he felt the softness of her body against his sore ribs.

"Peter Havers means to do you an injury, Daniel," she said.

Really, this topic proved more than tiresome.

"Tell me something I do not already know, my love."

"Then you know? About the fire here?" Her eyes were wide in surprise.

"The place is razed . . ."

"I am talking about a fire yet to be, a future tragedy!" she cried, and he pulled her closer lest anyone hear. "The children dared to bring me a message Peter must have received from someone at the mill, confirming that he will wait until most of your guests are gone before setting Shearings ablaze!"

"How did they receive this message?" he asked, disbelieving.

"They found it in the drive, after the duchess' carriage moved on. It was written on the briefest scrap of paper."

Now he knew what tempted him from the valley between her breasts.

"How did they know what the message contained?" he asked, and was surprised to see her smile.

"They can read, Daniel. You must admit here is a very persuasive argument for their lessons, especially as it might save your life."

"It seems to be your mission, Miss Clarkson."

"Then do not allow it to be in vain! You must take this seriously, Daniel. He means to kill you." Emily's plaintive cry was nearly muffled against his chest. But, very clearly, she added, "And he means to kill me."

"It is what I feared. Do you still think you would not be safer in London, my love?" He glanced down, wondering at the effect of his endearment. Emily blushed very prettily, and her warm brown eyes heated his spirit. "But it is me he is after. He missed his target on several occasions, but only just. If I am gone, you have nothing to fear from him."

"If you are gone, Daniel, then I will have nothing to fear but a lifetime of loneliness. That would be sufficient injury."

"Hush," Daniel said, empowered by something greater than the desire for self-preservation. "Now I shall be ready for him, thanks to you and your able students. I will have men standing guard, ready to intercept him. You can sleep peacefully this night."

Emily said nothing, but Daniel knew she was not reassured. Nor was he. But she allowed him to lead her in the wide circle around the dance floor even as he suspected she also allowed him to direct a conversation with which she was not at all satisfied. He thought about her words, said hurriedly in the first moments of their reunion, and realized she might not have told him all the contents of that damned note.

"If he means to set fire to the place after all my guests are gone, surely you will escape with impunity, Emily. He will not dare also tamper with the schoolhouse."

Still, she did not speak, but he sensed her desire to do so. Slowly, subtly, he drew her into a corner of the room, where they could continue to dance in a circle of their own making.

"Will you tell me what else the letter contained?" he asked softly. He slipped his hand from her grasp to the soft flesh of her upper arm. "Come, you know he cannot hurt me more than he has already attempted, and I am not afraid of him or his thugs. I will protect myself and mine. And that, my love, includes you."

He felt the muscle in her arm tighten and, without looking, knew she clenched her fist.

"He means for us both to die in Shearings, Daniel. He . . . his informant believes I will not leave your home with the other guests. That I am accustomed to spending the night with you."

Daniel bumped into another couple and felt the jolt to his bruised arm. "Is that what he said? And in those words?"

Emily blushed even deeper and would not meet his eyes. "No, not in those words. What he said was far ruder."

Daniel could well imagine the specifics. But he was accustomed to living in the society of mill workers and ship captains, and Emily was a well-bred lady from town.

"Did the children read it?"

"They did, but I do not think they understood what it meant. To be honest, I did not understand it all myself."

"It is just as well. Was it disgusting to you?" he asked, more curious than not.

"Not as much as it should have been," she said, still unable to meet his eyes. "But the damage done to my poor reputation would be irreparable if a rumor such as this should ever be started."

"Leave your reputation to me," he said, and meant it. He wished to take care of her for the rest of his life. "To begin, I think you ought to stay in Shearings tonight, for it will be the safest place at Glenfell."

"That does not seem to be a very auspicious beginning, Mr. Lennox. You wish to disprove a theory by adding support to it?"

Though he felt ready to do murder himself, he could not help but smile. Finally, she looked up at him, and he knew he would never doubt her, nor himself. Somehow, she managed to put him at peace, to apply reason when even a hint of her perfumed water could set him to distraction.

"You are right, my love. You will retire to the schoolhouse, with Miss Martineau and the full entourage of children, and I will post a man at the door to protect all of your slumbers."

Emily smiled up at him, and he wished all of his problems might be solved so easily.

Emily danced the next several sets with Mr. Colman and Captain Milrose and promised a third to Mr. Drummond.

As contrary as it seemed, the presence of the incriminating missive scratching between her breasts gave her a confidence she had scarcely thought possible, for Daniel Lennox's words had managed to reassure her completely. They were not particularly loverlike, nor did he promise her anything but the same protection he would have afforded anyone in his care, but she knew now how very much she mattered to him. And just now, it seemed all that mattered to her.

"Thank you for your indulgence, Miss Clarkson. It has been a pleasure to dance with you, something I did not dare to imagine Daniel would allow." Captain Milrose spoke graciously as he bowed.

"Is your friend so dictatorial?" she asked.

The captain grinned, and lines etched his young, tanned face.

"Never dictatorial. But sometimes possessive. We are accustomed to sharing a good deal, but your time is something for which I dared not hope."

"You do not need Mr. Lennox's permission to dance with me, sir. I am still very much my own woman."

"I do not doubt it," he said as he began to lead her off the floor. "Nevertheless, I obtained it. I . . . ah . . . also obtained some information of a most disturbing nature."

Emily started to pull away from him.

"I see you distrust me, Miss Clarkson. I cannot say I altogether blame you, for the relationships in our small society can be very confusing. For what it is worth, you must believe I am Daniel's staunchest ally, and would do anything for him. I hope I can be your friend, as well."

"You would say that in any case, would you not?"

He laughed. "Indeed, I would! But I hope you imagine otherwise, for I am to be stationed outside the schoolhouse tonight, with only a pair of pistols for company. Now, to whom shall I deliver you for the next dance? I do not see Daniel anywhere in sight."

"It is not Mr. Lennox," she ventured. "I believe I am promised to Mr. Drummond."

"Indeed, I do not see him either. But wait . . ."

Emily felt him stiffen beside her and then suddenly hasten his step. As she began to protest, she saw what engaged him, and then wondered why it had taken her so long to perceive half the company standing at the row of windows, watching some show without.

Mr. Drummond came up hurriedly, but not to claim Emily.

"David, I think you must go to him," he said urgently.

"To Daniel? Where is he?"

"In the garden just outside. With Havers, the idiot. They are going at it like schoolboys."

"Damn!" said Captain Milrose, and added a few other choice expletives. "Forgive me, Miss Clarkson. I will leave you now."

He started away, in the direction Mr. Drummond had indicated, but Emily would not be left behind. She lifted the hem of her gown and ran after him, scarcely believing the words she had just heard, or the complete impropriety of the evening's host being engaged in some argument while his guests watched. If Peter was an idiot then so was Daniel . . .

David Milrose edged his way through the crowd, and pushed open a door so well concealed in the woodwork one would not have guessed it there. Emily, close on his heels, felt the rush of cold air as soon as they went through it, and guessed they were in a servant's hall connecting the house to the garden.

"You may be entering upon a scene not suitable for a lady's eyes, Miss Clarkson," said Captain Milrose very clearly, giving the first indication he knew Emily raced along behind him.

"If you know anything about your old friend, you must know I have stumbled upon much worse than the results of a fistfight in the garden. Mr. Lennox's life seems replete with hazards, and he has bled upon me without discretion."

Captain Milrose made a sound suspiciously like a chuckle.

"Even so, it would be a pity to ruin your splendid dress."

"Thank you for the compliment, sir. I shall ask for extra wages, if need be." Emily paused and asked, more seriously, "But do you think this situation dire?"

"Peter Havers would have it so. And Daniel seems prepared to answer him. In recent weeks, my friend's taste for revenge seems to have sharpened."

"And to what do you attribute this change in appetite?"

Emily asked, expecting to hear another version of the warehouse-fire tragedy.

"You need not be so modest, Miss Clarkson. He wishes to impress you."

Emily drew in her breath, and the air felt as cold as death in her lungs.

"He will not impress me by dying in the effort. I want more from him than that," she said angrily. "Now I have said too much."

"Nothing I would not have guessed." He reached for her hand and led her along the corridor until they reached another doorway. This stood ajar.

"Daniel!" Captain Milrose shouted, and dropped Emily's hand as he lunged forward. "Peter! Are you both mad?"

Emily would have added some similar protest, but the sight of Daniel Lennox and Peter Havers locked in a grunting, struggling embrace left her utterly speechless. This could be no random meeting in the garden, for their jackets and cravats were hung like the morning laundry on a nearby pear tree, and they were poised as if in a boxing ring.

"Get off him, man! Can you not see he is already injured?" Captain Milrose shouted and pried them apart. The two men fell backwards, into the shrubbery, and cursed with conviction.

Daniel straightened up, looking stronger than he ought with the tails of his white shirt fluttering in the cool breeze and blood beginning to ooze through the fabric. His hair was brushed with brambles, and matted with sweat and dirt. He winced as he flexed his arm, and in the flickering light he looked very pale.

The wave of pity and compassion—and love—that swept over Emily nearly knocked her to her knees. Until she saw him smile.

"Does this amuse you, sir?" she asked tartly as she moved quickly to his side. "Is this the sort of entertainment hosts customarily provide for their guests in the countryside?"

He looked at her curiously, as if she spoke at a great distance, and suddenly began to slip backward.

Emily caught him quickly and edged her shoulder under his arm, like a crutch. She swayed under the burden of his weight and brought her free arm around his stomach, the better to balance them both. The scent of his skin was heady, but she could not be distracted just now. For Daniel, despite his bravado, looked as if he had just fought his final bout, and was likely to faint dead away in front of his curious audience.

She drew him into the shadow of the trees and, for once, he did not argue.

"Captain Milrose," Emily said authoritatively, "I believe Mr. Havers wearies of our company. Will you see him to his carriage?"

David Milrose looked at her with something like glee, and then spared a glance for his friend.

"Will you be able to manage Daniel? He looks a bit weary himself."

Emily shifted her shoulder, and heard Daniel curse under his breath.

"I am sure I can handle him," she said.

"Yes, I am sure you can," he said slowly, and nodded appreciatively. "But you may wish to enlist some of the servants to deliver him to his chamber."

"Of course. Anything else would be entirely inappropriate," she answered, and looked sharply at Mr. Havers, who narrowed his eyes. Still he said nothing. "He will need to change his clothing before he returns to his guests."

David Milrose's eyes opened in alarm, and he looked ready to argue, but was stopped by a warning glance from Emily. She hoped he understood as well as she how Daniel must continue to present a show of strength and normality.

"Ah, Mr. Haines, I am glad you are here. Mr. Lennox will rejoin his guests in several minutes. Would you be so kind as to oversee the party in his absence? I recommend starting up the music again, so his guests will have something to do other than gawk out the windows. Thank you very much."

Satisfied there remained nothing left to do in the garden, and anxious to see to Daniel's wound, which seemed to be bleeding profusely, Emily turned them both away from the scene. Her hand moved under his loosened shirt.

"Accustomed to giving orders, are you?" Daniel said gently into her ear, tickling the sensitive skin at the back of her neck. "It will stand you in good stead."

"If I am going to be a schoolmistress all my life, it most certainly will."

"That is not what I had in mind, Miss Clarkson," he said.

Emily sighed and rubbed her hand over the soft dark hair over his stomach. She felt his muscles tense as she caressed him and knew with absolute certainty she did not wish to be a schoolmistress all her life. She felt too close to heaven to return to earth now.

He seemed to read her thoughts. "It appears I am needy of an angel to accompany me on life's hard journey. Do you know any who might be available?"

Emily did not trust herself to say anything for several minutes, but continued to walk carefully along the dark hallway, wondering how she managed to support him. But then they turned the corner onto the staircase and stopped abruptly. As Daniel caught his breath, she contemplated the task before them.

"If you do," he continued lightly, "she shall need a sturdy set of wings. However else shall we manage this?"

"I will be here at your side," she said simply, and his hand tightened upon hers.

Together, and with great difficulty, they ascended the first set of stairs, and then the second. Emerging from the servants' corridor into the elegant hallway of Shearings, Emily felt grateful no one stood waiting for them, and that, by blessed fortune, they happened onto the wing of Daniel's bedchamber.

"I do not think you should come in with me," he said as he leaned against the heavy oak door.

"I should think my reputation is already too far gone for it to matter much, sir," Emily said, but could not meet his eyes. "However, if you do not wish me in your bedchamber . . ."

He answered by pushing open the door and bowing low so she might enter first. This she did quickly, for he could not be comfortable in that pose.

His room was splendid, as she had known it would be. Built in the same style as the rest of Shearings, it seemed a testimony to his strength and masculinity. Dark green draperies hung at the windows and mahogany furniture lined the fabric-covered walls. In one corner he had assembled a small library, where a large cushioned chair stood facing a bookcase. Two large volumes stood open upon a table.

Several portraits hung upon the wall, and Emily had no trouble recognizing the family resemblance in a young couple who surely were his parents or in the grouping of three very sweet little girls and their scowling brother. Another, somewhat familiar, face looked down from a heavy wooden frame and Emily stood wondering why she felt she knew the gentleman. Indeed, she was certain they had met only recently.

She turned back toward Daniel, thinking that if she caught him in a moment of vulnerability she might finally get the truth from him. But she stopped short when she saw him raise himself onto the step surrounding the huge bed and brace himself on the mattress. He removed his shirt and his bare back was scratched and bloody.

Some questions could wait. Others would not.

"Will you sit? You look awful. Is the water in the basin clean? And will Mrs. Winters mind very much if I use these linens? No, I suppose not."

Emily pulled several cotton cloths from their rack near the washstand and rinsed them in the cool water of the basin. She felt even more nervous about her doctoring skills than she had on that dreadful night weeks ago, and when she turned back to the bed and Daniel, she knew the reason why. Stitching up an unconscious man was one thing, washing the blood off the body of a man fully awake and aware quite another.

He settled himself upon the mattress and reached one hand toward her. Whether it was to beckon her, or merely to take the cloth from her hand, she did not know, but, as naturally as if she had been doing it for years, she stepped up to his bed and sat down beside him.

Tentatively, carefully, she washed him. When the first cloth seemed completely stained with blood, she wordlessly handed it to him and started on another. As the scabs and grime came away, she saw the results of her handiwork and admitted to herself she had done a fair job of sewing him together. The edges of his skin had healed and pink flesh followed the tantalizing pattern she was coming to know too well. Her hand traveled along the line of his scar, and then to his shoulder. And then, because it seemed to be the thing to do, she continued to run the cloth around his neck and down his back.

He sucked in his breath, but did not move.

"Am I hurting you?" she asked, suddenly unsure.

"You cannot even begin to guess at it, beloved," he said and twisted to face her.

She looked into his clear blue eyes and knew her own power in a way she had never understood before. She raised her hand to his cheek and stroked the deliciously scratchy skin along the line of his bone and felt his jaw tighten. His arms came around her then, urging her toward him, until she practically sat upon his lap. And then, in a surprisingly deft move, he leaned backward against the cushions so she lay across his chest. Knowing it must give him pain, she slipped to his side and nestled in the protection of his shoulder. He still smelled of sweat and the sickly-sweet blood, but she rubbed her nose against the taut skin of his chest.

"You know I love you," he said simply, into her hair.

"Then do not send me away. Ever. I wish to . . ."

He stopped her effectively and wonderfully. She twisted her body higher along his and brought her hands to either side of his face. Beneath her arms she felt the strong thumping of his heart and the growing warmth of his chest.

"What do you wish?" he asked, in a voice barely recognizable.

"I wish to stay here forever, in this room, at Shearings, in Glenfell. London, for all the happiness I knew there with my dear aunt, seems like a dream to me now. This, here, is real."

"With all its blood and dirt? And the threat of others who would damage your reputation and harm those around you?" His voice rose slowly as his anger grew. "And you would suffer all of this just to remain in the society of a man both dictatorial and heedless of his social responsibilities?"

"I would suffer worse. You must know I love you too, no matter how impossible it seems."

"Because of our social positions? Are we back to that again?" he demanded.

Emily was surprised he could even imagine it. "Of course not, Daniel. I am only remembering the wretched circumstances of our meeting, and how poorly it bode for our future. Do you not recall it? You were uncommonly rude to me."

Beside her, he relaxed.

"Let it suffice to say I was speechless."

"You sometimes have that effect on me, as well."

It was not intended as an invitation, but Daniel took it as such, taking her mouth with his, and kissing her until she quite forgot about anything they had ever argued about or, indeed, anything before this very moment.

"As much as I should love to thoroughly compromise you, and accede to your wishes never to leave this dark cave, I believe we have to return to my guests," he said, finally breaking away. "They will all be speculating about us, and will be quite right."

She looked at him blankly for a moment, and realized she had quite forgotten about his great party below.

He rose up on one elbow and pulled her up with him from their nest amongst the pillows on his bed. Emily never took her eyes from him, realizing he bore no resemblance to the wounded invalid she had nearly carried to the room. His eyes sparkled in the candlelight and his skin looked flushed with good health.

"Do you not hear the music below, my love? This night is far from done. There are many people below, and Mrs. Winters' food to sustain us, and a murderer to catch. Might we manage it all?"

"At the moment, I am not even sure I can manage to pull my appearance together into any semblance of respectability." Emily frowned, glancing down at her bodice.

"I am not sure I can help you with your hair," Daniel said, as he fingered her tumbled curls, "but I do happen to have some experience with ladies' gowns."

Emily backed away and nearly tripped off the step by the bed. "I am sure you do, sir. And I am equally sure I do not wish to hear why that is so." She tugged on a little scrap of lace that had adorned her neckline, concealing a small rip that certainly had not been there when she dressed hours before. She glanced up at Daniel. "But of course, it hardly matters, as all the attention will be to you. Everyone will want to hear about your fistfight with Mr. Havers."

"Ah, yes. I quite forgot about that," he said, and ran a careless hand through his dark hair. He stepped down from the platform of the bed and walked to a huge armoire, wherein lay folded at least twenty white shirts. He ran his hand over his wardrobe with the familiarity of one who is quite capable of dressing himself, and made a selection. Shaking out the stiffly ironed garment, he turned back to Emily and shrugged his large body into it. She, watching him, thought the act of his dressing surely as fascinating as when he undressed. She rose to her feet.

"May I ask what you fought about, sir?" she asked.

Daniel's hand stopped over the row of buttons and he looked at her, surprised.

"Do you mean my argument with Havers?"

"You are polite to call it an argument. I rather thought it resembled a fistfight between schoolboys. If such a thing happened in my schoolhouse, both parties would be punished."

Daniel grinned mischievously. "I am quite prepared to be punished by you, my dear love. Whatever did you have in mind?"

Emily raised her chin. "Whatever I dole out to you must necessarily be shared by Mr. Havers."

Daniel brought himself up short, surely taking more offense at her teasing comment than it merited.

"Therein is the cause of our hatred, my dear. He and I already share too many things, and my fault may have been that I am overly generous in that regard. We have lost our hearts to the same lady, and he has come to believe he may take what he does not deserve."

Emily felt her blood grow cold. She knew Peter Havers did not show any sincere preference to herself and she could only think of one other candidate for their mutual favor.

"Are you speaking of the duchess, sir?" she said softly.

He looked surprised. "The duchess? Do you mean Jane?"

Emily made a small sound of impatience. "Is there another duchess with whom you are both associated? Of course I mean the lady. Did you fight over Jane?"

"No, my love. We fought over you. I challenged him over the insinuations against your virtue, and asked to meet him at dawn. Perhaps he thought me insincere, as I did not name my second, but, in any case, he thought to have a more immediate resolution."

"And you did not think to defer him? To a time when the neighborhood was not all assembled here at Shearings?" she asked, thinking she would never comprehend masculine logic.

"Your honor stood at risk," he said, that very logic unanswerable.

Emily sat silently, watching him across the span of his bed, and thought how the very honor he felt determined to protect already stood in great jeopardy. And if he now came at her and threw her down beneath him, it would be easily shattered.

"Emily?"

She shook off the tantalizing vision.

"But I do not understand. Your hatred towards each other is surely of greater duration than the few months since I came to Glenfell. Did a lady other than the duchess come between you in the past?"

"You might say that," he said, and returned to the business of fastening his shirt. "A very grand lady, indeed."

"Yet another?"

"Dear Emily. Whatever must I do to convince you you have nothing to fear from any other lady? In due course even Jane will be consigned to her proper place."

Emily did not feel altogether reassured. "Then who is the grand lady?"

"I am speaking of Gleneyrie, the home of the Dukes of Glendennon. The duke may, of course, will it to any of his heirs, but it has always been the Glendennon Seat."

"Gleneyrie?" Emily whispered hoarsely, and her eyes instinctively went to the portrait of the man on the wall. She recognized him now, though age and illness had done much to ravage his visage since he sat for this portrait that hung in Daniel's own bedchamber.

"Emily, there is something I must tell you, though I fear it will make you unhappy. I have attempted to say something before."

Emily waved her hand in impatience. "Is there anything worse to fear than ignorance? Or anything to make me unhappier than the thought of losing you?"

Daniel dropped his hands and started around the bed toward her. She knew she could not escape, nor did she wish to, now that all her reason practically screamed the truth to her. The forbidden knowledge, that which seemed to hold the whole town hostage, held no terror for her. She leaned against the bedpost, and waited for him.

"I also have some small claim to Gleneyrie," he said quietly, standing before her.

"Because you and Peter are cousins."

"Of course. But Peter has staked a very pervasive claim there and hopes to subvert tradition."

"Is it possible to do so?"

"Of course. But it may come to naught. The duke may have many years before him, and Jane may deliver a brood of babies for him. It would be for the best." He continued to fumble with his shirt and did not look at her. "But for now, they believe that I stand in their way."

"Because there is no son?" Emily asked, but it was not truly a question. She was hearing what she had vaguely suspected for some weeks. "What are you telling me, Daniel?"

He said nothing, but looked at her as if he still stood in great physical pain. Could he still believe her the social snob who had first come to him months ago?

"It does not matter to me who you are to the rest of the world, only what you are to me. A title could mean but little. I would not have said such a thing once, but deeds have persuaded me as a hundred of Harriet's speeches could not. Will you not be satisfied and quit this fearful battle with your cousin?"

Daniel looked very solemn and bit down on his lip. "It is not for me to conclude what I did not start nor wish to continue. But Peter will not let it end while I live to silently mock him."

"Do you mock him?"

"You know me better than that, I hope. I pity him. I have always pitied him his desperate ambition and false hopes."

"Mr. Lennox? Sir?" An open hand came through the door like a banner of truce.

"Damn!" cursed Daniel. "What will it be, Dawson?"

A young man, whom Emily recognized as Daniel's valet, slipped through the door. "Mrs. Winters sent me here to attend . . . oh! forgive me, sir. She could not have known you were with a lady."

"Like hell she did not," said Daniel under his breath. "Well, what do you want, man?"

Dawson came forward, clearly mortified. "If you please, sir. Your guests are waiting for you. Mr. Colman and Miss Martineau themselves are here, quite anxious to know you are safe."

"Damn them too!"

Emily stifled a laugh, and then stifled her lover. She put a finger to his lips.

"Hush, Daniel! They are your guests of honor, and might very well be wondering if you are alive or dead. Harriet, I know, will not be deterred from anything she sets her heart to."

"But there is more to tell."

"Let it wait. You have already answered my question, for I should have guessed there would be familial connections between those on both sides of the river. If you prevent any serious offenses tonight, nothing will change until the morning. And then we could speak in the light of day."

"So we shall. In the meantime, and if I have no more interruptions, I may yet stand up with you for the next waltz." He kissed her palm, still stained with his blood.

Chapter Fourteen

*I*t must not yet be day, for the night could scarcely have run its course; and yet rosy light seared through Emily's heavy eyelids and she felt the warmth of the sun upon her face. She stood next to Daniel on the royal barge at Gleneyrie. But how came they here, when Daniel was forbidden entry?

She glanced up into his face, and she saw not her lover, but the wizened face of the old duke. He stood straight and tall, and looked at her with Daniel's eyes. As he leaned towards her, she saw flames reflected in their depths.

"Daniel!" she gasped in horror.

"Emily!" came an answering cry. Hands grabbed her hands and started pulling her up and away, but she resisted. She would not leave Daniel.

"Let me be! Will you allow us no privacy?" she protested.

The hands released her, but only to slap her across her cheek. She opened her eyes, fully awakened now, and looked into Harriet Martineau's terrified face.

"Come quickly, Emily! The whole place is ablaze. We must get out!"

"Where is he?" Emily asked, finally realizing the source of the bright light. Outside, in the hallway, she heard the roaring flames of an inferno and heard shouts from outside her window.

Harriet yanked off the covers and threw a bedcoat from the foot of the mattress. Emily looked at it, dazed and confused, and struggled to put her arms into the appropriate openings.

"There is no time for it. Please, Emily! We have only minutes to escape."

But Emily stood her ground. "I will not leave without him, for he must be here."

"He is with the children, getting them all out safely. He knew we still had time on this side of the building and called for someone to rouse you. I came."

"Harriet! You might have been killed!"

"So might I yet be, if you will not move," she cried.

Emily felt the heat of the fire in the boards of the floor beneath and finally comprehended how her delay threatened them both. Gathering up the ruffles and lacy hem of her nightgown, she led the way to the hall and needed only a moment to know the center staircase was no longer accessible to them.

"Come quickly," she shouted, finally taking control. "We can yet reach the servants' staircase!"

And so they did, and ran directly into Noland Haines.

"Ladies! Come with me," he said calmly, but he quickly

reached for them. "Nell is at the bottom of the steps, waiting for you."

And so she was, with blankets to throw upon them, and a bucket of water to protect the stairway. Emily nearly fell onto her small body, while Harriet remained clinging to Mr. Haines. But within moments, they managed to stagger their way into the night air, strangely aglow with the flames behind them.

On the lawn, servants and townspeople stood huddled together, the stunned survivors of a disaster. Emily counted a sobbing Mrs. Bernays among their numbers, several of the maids, but only a few of the children.

Little Anne hid her face in Mrs. Bernays' apron.

"Where are the rest?" Emily asked anxiously as she crouched beside Anne and held her about the shoulders.

"They are there!" the housekeeper cried, and gestured towards the garden in the back of the house.

Emily squinted into the smoke and saw another circle of activity and the figures of several men. As she rose to her feet and started toward them, she knew what she would find.

Daniel stood in a first-floor window, though its glass hung shattered in its frame. The children who were not already in the arms of the people on the ground stood around him, amazingly calm and quiet as they awaited their turn for deliverance. This was accomplished with remarkable efficiency, like the workings of the mill itself. Beneath Daniel, on the hard ground, the men stacked a large pile of hay, and one by one the children were urged to jump down upon it, and to safety. Emily ran to them and gathered them to her body, though her eyes were all for the man in the window.

His gaze met hers, but only briefly, and she thought he nodded in recognition. It was enough. He would know she was safe, and she would wait until she could gather him into her arms along with the rest of them.

Suddenly, Timothy's sooty face blocked her line of vision.

"The letter said Shearings would burn, miss," he said indignantly.

"Most certainly it did, dear. But villains do not always stick to their plans, especially if they know their wicked plots are no longer secret. Mr. Lennox took special care at his home this night, and he posted . . ." Her voice wavered when she realized Captain Milrose had given her his assurance of protection. Surely it must be as she always feared: he remained in collusion with Daniel's enemies. "Where is Captain Milrose?"

Jeremiah Colman answered, though she had not heard him approach.

"Knocked out cold, he is, with a lump on his forehead the size of a piece of coal. They took him up to the house, and he looks to be recovering. No permanent injury, except to his pride."

"This is not a night for pride, Mr. Colman," Emily said softly. She faced Harriet's favorite and saw he wore a nightgown of red and white stripes and an absurd fur cap.

A cheer rose up near them, and they looked up to see the last of the children jump from the window. Only Daniel yet stood there, the glow of the flames behind him putting his sturdy body into silhouette. He stood up on the sill, paused to beat down a flaming curtain, and jumped with no more care than a boy into a pond on a summer's day. Emily would have run to him, but for the burden of several children clutching the cloth of her cotton nightgown. As she stood there, her tears rained down upon their heads.

Suddenly Noland Haines appeared through the haze and helped his friend to his feet. Though the man's back was to her, Emily immediately perceived he delivered a message of some urgency, for Daniel looked intent and then angry. He shouted something, and pointed in her general direction. He started toward her but then threw himself up onto a horse brought forward by one of the men.

And rode off into the night.

"Daniel!" Emily cried, little caring how she must sound like a deranged mistress.

"You need not worry, miss," came a comforting voice. "Mr. Lennox said we should bring you and the children up to Shearings and keep you safe there."

Emily brushed a sleeve against her swollen eyes and wiped her tears.

"I will not rest until I know he is safe as well," she said as she recognized Mrs. Winters. "I must know where he has gone."

"His business is at Gleneyrie. With the duke."

Emily knew the answer even before she heard it. "Then I must go to him. Please bring me a horse."

"I cannot let you follow him, miss," came the rigid answer, and the woman's hand closed over her wrist, like a shackle. "He must deal with it himself."

"You cannot . . ."

"Those are his orders," Mrs. Winters said on a note of finality, and Emily knew she was a prisoner.

But as she allowed herself to be led away, behind the children and other servants, escape came most unexpectedly. The floors of the schoolhouse suddenly collapsed in a great roar of fire and smoke and a million sparkling embers lighting the dark night. The terrible spectacle stopped all of them in their tracks as they gazed upon the destruction of the large building. Mrs. Winters forgot herself in her distraction, and her hand released Emily's wrist as she shielded her eyes from the glow of the fire.

Emily did not hesitate for a second, but gathered her gown up around her knees and dashed out into the darkness.

"Miss Clarkson!"

She heard the frantic cries behind her and knew any healthy man could outrun her within a minute. But, aside from the angry shouts of protest, she heard nothing behind her nor anyone waiting to ambush her along the path she stumbled upon.

Unfortunately, she did not choose her way wisely. Emily knew the general direction she must take, and believed she would need to go through a thick wood before she emerged on the road. Then, if she followed the stone wall in the direction of the town, she would come to the ancient bridge over the Fell and cross it directly to a servants' gate of the great estate. The hill appeared steepest at that point, but she preferred to risk it rather than appear on the main drive of Gleneyrie looking like a madwoman.

Her nightgown snagged in the thorny bushes and tore at the hem. Underfoot, pebbles and twigs attacked Emily's bare feet and impeded her desperate progress. She dared not think about whatever else awaited her on the path, for her thoughts were only for reaching Daniel before he entered the lion's lair and almost certain death. In the scattered moments of lucidity interrupting her otherwise mindless crusade, she knew he rode on horseback and undoubtedly knew the terrain infinitely better than his headstrong defender. But Emily could scarcely help herself.

She reached the road faster than she had thought possible, but then was thwarted, necessarily waiting behind the trees until the caravan of would-be rescuers and the merely curious waned. No one seemed to notice the ghostly figure of the woman in the woods.

But Emily, in her turn, noticed a good deal. High on the hill, the lights of Gleneyrie burned almost as brightly as the fire at the schoolhouse, as if a great celebration was being held there. Indeed, it might be. Below her, along the line of the Fell, a line of men and women assembled to bring water to the raging fire, shouting their orders and entreating others to join in.

The air felt quite cold. Far from the heat of the flames, and quite alone in the darkness, Emily shivered and tucked her icy hands under her arms. She must go on.

Seizing her opportunity, she dashed across the road and scampered up and over the low stone wall. Her feet were wet and most likely bloody, but she wasted no time examining herself. In any case, she could scarcely see a thing.

Using the top of the wall as her guide, she held out one hand to run along its edge and tripped along the woody terrain, certain she would arrive at the stone bridge. As her eyes scanned the landscape ahead, she unexpectedly fell over an obstruction.

Crying bitter tears of frustration, Emily straightened her elbows and rose to her knees, sparing a backward glance for whatever had contrived to add to her agony. In the dim light filtering down from the heights of the estate she caught a glimpse of hair, and the rising bulk of something like a man's chest.

Pressing her hand into her mouth to stifle her cry, she threw herself onto the body lying against the stone wall, not knowing how Daniel might have arrived in this spot and if he still lived.

But it was not Daniel. It was Alsop Parker, and when she pressed her ear against the shallow wet chest, she knew he was the latest victim of a murderous scheme. He most surely was dead.

Emily wondered what she ought to do. She could not leave him thus, to the cold night and to the animals, but she could not manage to move him on her own. She felt no affection for him, but pitied a man caught in a trap intended for another, the by-blow of a wretched affair in which he played no part.

She knelt over him and pulled the edges of his jacket close together. She undoubtedly needed the protection more than he did, but she could not bring herself to cover herself in the garments of a dead man. Following the thin lines of his arms to recover his hands, she pulled them forward and crossed them on his chest. But as she did so, something dropped from his hand.

A small packet of curled wood, bound by yarn, fell upon the ground and scattered in the breeze. Thinking it odd, Emily picked several up and realized she held spills, fire-starters.

Wiping her nose, she sniffed the air and recognized the unpleasant smell of oil.

Sick at heart, weary of spirit, she rose to her feet and looked down upon the fallen body of one of Daniel's enemies. Had Daniel suspected the man of complicity? Did he know he welcomed a traitor into his employ? All the while, Parker must have associated with the bitter duke, whose contempt for all things associated with the mill made him vengeful. Or with Peter Havers, whose ambition made him desperate.

A brief explosion fired from Gleneyrie, followed closely by two others. Emily raised her face to the hilltop, breathing out the fumes of the oil, and instead sniffing the acrid odor of smoke. And she now knew that in her headstrong pursuit of Daniel from the scene of the fire, she had sought to save the wrong man.

Daniel would not be killed in the lair of the lion. Instead, he would take revenge against the ancient beast himself, believing him the cause of all the injury done to him.

And then he would be condemned in a court of law.

Emily stepped over the body of Mr. Parker, no longer concerned about leaving the villain in the dirt. He was a murderer, and would have murdered more, and his death must only be a blessing. There seemed little enough of such things this night.

Emily reached the gravel path and wearily climbed the hill to Gleneyrie. She was light-headed from the smoke in her nostrils, and weary from the exertions of Daniel's ball. The added injury to her bloodied feet seemed like penance for her ignorance. Like an old woman, she followed the way through the woods and into the lovely gardens and up to the terraces surrounding the house. In the distance men ran and women shouted; Emily could not doubt what upset their nightly slumbers.

Finally, after an eternity, the great stairway of the house beckoned, and the smooth marble felt like a healing salve on her feet. She bloodied the white stone with every step, but knew it the least of the scars Gleneyrie would bear this evening. Not bothering to announce her presence, Emily pushed open the heavy door and stepped into the hall.

Against the wall, as limp as a rag doll, the duchess sat on the floor amidst her bedclothes. Her cheeks glistened with the dampness of tears and her hair hung loosely about her shoulders. Emily would have pitied her and offered her comfort were it not for the look of absolute hatred in her fierce gaze.

"Where are they?" Emily asked hoarsely.

The duchess did not answer. "One of us is widowed tonight, Miss Clarkson. I would have wanted it you."

Emily stepped back, as if avoiding a blow. "But I am not a married woman, my lady," she said tersely.

Daniel's first love laughed hysterically, until the bubbles of her mirth dissolved into hiccoughs.

Anxious and afraid, Emily needed to escape her. Her eyes darted about the hall, remembering when she came to this house as an invited guest. She had little dreamed to return in such a state. All she felt now was misery and despair.

Then the duchess started to rise, and Emily ran for the nearest door, through which was a narrow corridor. When she heard men's voices, she ran its length to another doorway, and pushed very gently against the heavy oak.

She was in the queen's barge, where most recently she stood in her dream, and then did not know whether she looked upon Daniel Lennox or the Duke of Glendennon.

She stood in their company once again.

The ancient duke lay on the floor, a book splayed next

to his lifeless hand. His knees were bent, as if he had been seated, and indeed, a stiff-backed chair leaned precariously against a small table. He was dead; Emily would have known it in an instant even if the duchess had not already pronounced it so.

Emily knew it, and certainly Daniel knew it even as he crouched above the old man and gently fingered the wrinkled skin of the dead man's cheek. Around him, the staff of Gleneyrie stood respectfully, in awe of the tragic scene before them.

She must have made some noise because Daniel finally averted his gaze and looked at her. In the light blue depths of his eyes, Emily saw all the misery and pain that this night brought, and the smallest expression of shock.

He rose and straightened his back until he looked very tall and large over all the others. As he came toward her, wordlessly, he began to slip his jacket from his body until it hung from his arm. And then, when he stood next to her, and the warmth of his body made her wish to cling to him for protection against the insanity around them, he draped his jacket around her shoulders and fastened the top button.

"Are you well?" he asked, his eyes never leaving her face.

"I believe so," Emily sniffed.

"Then what is this blood?" He touched her cheek very gently.

"It is Mr. Parker's," she said, and her voice cracked so badly she could hardly get the words out.

Daniel sucked in his breath and drew her into his embrace, but only briefly. He kissed her forehead, possibly the only part of her that was clean and uninjured, and then pulled her around to face a woman whom Emily recognized as the housekeeper of Gleneyrie.

"See to my lady, Mrs. Currer. I must finish affairs here."

The older woman gathered Emily into her plump arms.

"We will be in the parlor, Your Grace," she said and bowed her head.

Emily, hearing the incriminating words, first imagined them addressed to the dead man, and wondered why the old duke should care. And then the truth, the very truth that had trifled with her dreams and imagination, burst like a flame through her smoke-dulled mind. She twisted out of Mrs. Currer's arms to face Daniel.

He said nothing, but stood dignified and solemn, his features so like those of the grandfather whom he could only approach in death. Emily thought of the terrible waste of it all, and of the shame so intense it could not be put into words.

"Why would you not tell me?" she cried. "A relation, indeed!"

"Hush," he said softly and brushed her hair off her forehead. "I will join you shortly. Please take her, Mrs. Currer."

"Yes, Your Grace."

"Emily?"

"Yes," she said, and then, almost accusingly, "Your Grace."

Daniel Lennox, the fifth Duke of Glendennon, rubbed his forehead wearily before he put his hand against the door of the parlor. He was in for it now; he doubted it not. The night was already full of terror and tragedy, and he had acquitted himself bravely—and even nobly. But dealing with Miss Emily Clarkson, whom he hoped shortly to make the Duchess of Glendennon, would prove something else altogether.

He waited until she was quite alone, after she had accepted Mrs. Currer's makeshift ministrations and settled into the front parlor of the great house that now belonged to him. Though he had never before been permitted to walk the halls, his mother had spoken of her childhood here so often, he knew the way as well as if he had lived here his whole life. As was his birthright.

He opened the door and was surprised to see the sun streaming in from the open windows. Somehow it seemed a whole night had been lost; contrarily, one could scarcely measure the enormity of all the gain it had brought. For here was the morning of the next day, and Daniel Lennox knew his life would never be the same as it had been.

He did not see Emily at first, and thought she might have retreated to the mill, against his wishes. Indeed, she would no sooner obey him as a duke than she had when she believed him nothing more than a mill owner. He doubted anything would change if he were her husband; he mused on the thought even as he wondered if he should find her elsewhere, possibly in her own bed.

Then, with a start, he realized she no longer had a bed in Glenfell, nor a school in which to teach the children. Her very reason for being here was thoroughly undermined—or would have been if he had not already hoped for greater things.

He heard a rustle of movement, and squinted against the sunny window. In front of it a tall chair faced the Fell and a small slip of white fabric peeked out from under its sculpted arm. He drew a deep breath, and through the smell of smoke and blood and dirt sensed something distinctly hers. And went to her.

Emily's eyes were wide open, nothing in their brightness diminished by the lack of sleep nor the horrors she had witnessed the night before. She sat curled up upon his grandfather's—now, perhaps, his—chair, enveloped in clean sheets and blankets and revealing only one very white shoulder where her nightgown had slipped away. He meditated upon her lovely skin and would have claimed it if she had given him the slightest encouragement. But she did not.

Looking around him, he pulled up a cushioned footrest, thinking it very likely the workmanship of his own mother, the oldest daughter of the old duke. He sat down. At this unaccustomed angle, he saw a basin of soapy water positioned beneath the chair and the requisite folded napkins and towels next to it. With a rush of foolish pride, he realized that even as the stool on which he sat represented the workmanship of his mother, these cloths were the products of his own mill.

He picked one up and examined it closely, knowing full well Emily silently watched his every move. He then dipped the clean fabric into the soapy water, splashing and undoubtedly damaging the ancient rug. Well, it looked as if a thorough cleaning stood in order, in any case. He should have to speak to Mrs. Currer about it immediately.

Perhaps not immediately. He might have to clean his own house first, as they said.

Daniel reached under the white sheets and felt about for Emily's foot. More than anything else he retained of the lingering vision of his beloved standing alone in shock and horror at the scene of his grandfather's death, was the sight of her poor bare feet, just visible under the tattered hem of her nightgown. In the early hours of the morning he found a trail of blood and soil leading from the front door all the way to the queen's barge, and guessed whose foot marked the path.

Gently, wordlessly, he pulled it out from its shelter of sheets and blankets and examined the damage inflicted by a barefoot journey through wood and gravel. The scratches and cuts on her flesh were still marked by crusts of dried blood and caked dirt, and looked wretched. He considered his own wounds, which she had treated without complaint, and admired anew her fortitude.

A fine couple they were. Survivors of a battle neither had expected to fight.

Daniel wrapped the wet cloth around Emily's foot, daring to touch her ankle and caress the muscles of her lower leg. He felt her tense and then relax as he continued his ministrations, until he dared to reveal her other foot. Gently, carefully, he removed the painful souvenirs of her gallant journey and wondered how long other, more insidious, scars might linger. In spite of her veneer, Emily had already endured more than any lady might expect in a lifetime of experience.

"I am quite certain, Your Grace, that any of your minions would be honored to perform the ignoble task in which you are engaged. I include myself, of course, as I am quite capable of washing my own feet. It is not a fitting occupation for the Duke of Glendennon."

Her sarcasm gave him hope when he scarcely dared hear it.

He rubbed a finger along the underside of her arch, watching the instinctive reaction. She started to pull away, but he held her firmly by the ankle.

"Perhaps not, my lady, but then, I was not raised to be a duke," he said solemnly.

"And I am not your lady!" she gasped. She must find it very difficult to remain a stern accuser while he tickled her foot.

"It is a situation I would remedy as soon as I maintain proper mourning. I ought to show my grandfather due respect and not disown him as he would me."

"Did he disown you, Daniel?" she asked softly, and he

then understood she felt the pain of it as keenly as he did himself.

"Never in fact, and the terms of the letter patent were always quite clearly in my favor. But Peter Havers sacrificed his life in the belief it would happen."

"Sacrificed? Do you mean to tell me . . ."

"He is dead," Daniel said abruptly. "As nearly as I can piece the events of last night together, he arrived here at Gleneyrie to nurse his wounds."

"What wounds?" she asked. "What happened to him?"

"My love, please encourage your humble suppliant by recalling how he thrashed Havers soundly in the garden of Shearings."

"Oh dear, yes. It seems like the memory of another life," Emily said. "But surely you did not murder him!"

"No, indeed. My grandfather shot him, before taking his own life, and saved me the trouble of revenge. His one act of generosity towards me proved his very last."

Emily made a small noise, like a wounded animal.

Daniel Lennox, the Duke of Glendennon, rose, picked her up in her bundle of cloths, and sat down with her upon his lap. She wrapped her bare arms about his body and nestled her head against his shoulder.

"It is over, my love," he said into her tangled curls.

"It is not over," she said defiantly, and pulled away. "It is not over until you explain why I remained ignorant of what everyone else was aware of and why you did not think it might matter to me. Had I not already proved my trustworthiness?"

"That, and a good deal else."

"Do you not think who you are and what you do matters to me?"

"I dared to hope so," he said quietly. "Tell me they do."

She turned on him fiercely.

"How can it be otherwise? Why do you think I followed you to Gleneyrie this night?"

For once, he had no answer. He only knew it was her place to be here, beside him.

"I came to save your life, Daniel," she said, after some time. "I thought the duke would have you killed, or you would kill him. I could not bear the thought of losing you, either way."

The determination of his protector almost completely un-manned him. And when Emily brought up her hand to lay it upon his heart, he could scarcely bear the exquisite pain of her torture.

He shifted position, wishing there were no cotton sheets between them. "You will not lose me; have I not already promised as much? Although now it appears you may have more than you bargained for."

"Indeed. As I recall, the terms of our agreement when first I arrived in Glenfell were very vague. I believe you misrepresented yourself, Your Grace."

"When we met, I thought you already knew the truth, for you had lived in London and were acquainted with at least one of my sisters. Laura can scarcely remain quiet about a new hat, so I never imagined her reticence about the fact of her brother's somewhat vague expectations. Then when you were so fond of belittling my worth because of my merchant's sensibility, I knew you did not connect me to the owner of Gleneyrie. Inasmuch as the good people of Glenfell were instructed by the lord of the manor thirty years ago never to speak of the uncomfortable relationship between us, I presumed the secret was safe."

"And so silence hid a great injustice. I was not very long in Glenfell before I realized how very much more the peo-ple respected you over the duke. You earned their loyalty, where your grandfather did nothing to deserve it."

"Sentiments such as these were what prevented me from speaking. At first, I would not have you know the truth because you would not then see my endeavors and myself in an honest light. I never expected to inherit the cursed title, and lived my life accordingly. Your considerations of class had you set against me. But later, when I sensed your changing sensibility, I was both proud of it and somewhat threatened. After I had worked so hard to prove my worth to you, could I then undermine it by announcing I was next in line for a dukedom?"

"It certainly changes everything."

"Does it?"

She did not answer, and he felt a crushing feeling in his chest even though her hand rested very lightly upon it. It was as he feared. Now that Emily nursed republican ideals, she would deny him for the very reason other women would flock to his side and parade before him. Within weeks, his sisters would ensure that every marriageable woman in England would be brought to Glenfell for his approval, but for the only one whose good opinion he sought.

"If I believed you idle and lazy, if I imagined you scheming to seize an inheritance that might just as easily have gone to another, I would not respect you nor be induced to look upon you generously. But you have responded to deprivation with remarkable energy and resilience, proving yourself in a business in which most gentlemen would be utterly inept."

"I was not a gentleman, as you were fond of telling me. My father was a mill owner, as was his father before him."

"And your mother was the daughter of a duke. But I now believe a gentleman should be so called not by the nature of his inheritance, but by the manner of his deeds. Besides . . ."

"Yes?" Daniel asked anxiously.

"I believe I would have loved you if you were a chimney sweep."

Daniel thought of several clever responses to her declaration before deciding not a word was needed. Instead they sat in silence, and he felt more content, more at home, than he could have imagined himself in his grandfather's great pile of a castle.

Emily looked up at him and smiled.

"What would happen if someone intruded himself upon us, Your Grace? Would this not be even as scandalous as all the criminal acts of the past months?"

"Scandalous, indeed," he said and chastely kissed the top of her head. "There would be no hope for redemption unless I were to marry you before a decent mourning were observed. And to be honest, such consequences do not seem very harsh at all."

"Are you certain it is what you now desire? I believe you might now choose from among the most elegant ladies in the land. Why, even Harriet Martineau might give you a second glance."

"I have endured the knife, near-drowning, fire, fisticuffs,

last night's gunfire and, yes, even Harriet Martineau for want of you, dear Emily. My trials are surely at an end. Have I acquitted myself to your rigorous standards?"

"Perhaps not all, Your Grace. Will you kiss me, so I might offer further judgment?"

Chapter Fifteen

*E*mily stood on the broad flat rock that jutted out into the Fell like Princess Caroline's haughty chin, and looked out over the small peaceful kingdom she would soon share with Daniel Lennox, the Duke of Glendennon. From this vantage point, the windows and part of the front lawn of Gleneyrie were in full view and it appeared as if the day's business proceeded very efficiently. As large trunks were hoisted onto a wagon, a small band of people stood in the drive.

"I am sorry you did not get to know her better, my dear." The deep rich voice sounded calm and unhurried, even though Emily knew Daniel had just hiked down the steep slope separating the great house from the water's edge and come over the bridge.

She turned around just in time to see him pulling himself onto the rock, preferring to take the shortest way up rather than relying on the rough-hewn steps made generations before. As always, she worried he might injure himself, but then considered how his wounds must surely be entirely healed by now. In a few weeks' time, when they were properly married before an audience of his sisters, her aunt and her aunt's own betrothed, Mr. Tilden, and all of Glenfell, she would once again see for herself.

"The former Duchess of Glendennon? Your grandmama-in-law?" she said teasingly. "I do not think I ever wish to know her better."

"Never say you were jealous," Daniel said, standing near.

"I envied her nothing, for I could only pity a woman condemned to such a husband as hers. But once I understood how very much she hurt you, I decided she and I were not to be anything but the briefest of acquaintances."

"And now you will scarcely be that. She declined my offer of Shearings as a dowager house, preferring to live with a cousin somewhere further north. Jeremiah Colman, of all people, has offered his services to see her well settled."

Emily felt no surprise at any of Daniel's news. "The dear man. He must realize Harriet used him as she uses so many people to achieve her idealistic goals. I received a letter from her yesterday, in which she reports how delighted she is to have met Mr. Andrew Pears, the soap manufacturer."

"I suspect his clothes smell better than those of a mustard merchant," Daniel said under his breath and walked to the very edge of the rock. "Do you believe Harriet used me, as well?"

Emily followed him, no longer interested in watching the departure of the former duchess from the house for which she had sacrificed her youth, her dreams, and the man who loved her.

"Oh, most certainly. And she used my mother, too. Of course, I suspect she set her sights upon you very early on, and might have married you herself if I had not proved more convenient."

"Would I have had nothing to say in the matter?"

"My dearest love, for someone of your considerable power and charms, you seem to have been buffeted about by a relentless fate. Your grandfather had nothing to do with you, for no reason attributable to yourself. Your love jilted you, seduced by a title, and perhaps by the hope she might have another turn at you when her ill and aged husband died. Alsop Parker turned out to be the spy within your own camp and your cousin was bitterly resentful of the circumstances of your birth and his own. If these are not examples of your lack of 'say,' what would you call them?"

"The misfortunes of others, I should think."

Emily looked at him sharply and saw he seemed quite serious.

"I grew up surrounded by a warm and loving family while less than a mile away an embittered old man cut himself off from all the joy and comfort such a relationship would bestow. My mother must have anticipated her father's response before she married Francis Lennox, but never seemed to look back with any sense of deprivation. Would you not think my grandfather suffered a great deal for his pride?" But before Emily could answer, he continued. "And Jane gambled poorly. Her husband might have lived a good many years and she might have had a dozen children by him. But until she did, the only son of the duke's oldest daughter remained his legitimate heir and patience might have rewarded her with a vigorous husband as well as the title."

Emily guessed he fished for a compliment just then, but wanted him to work a little harder for it.

"And what of Peter Havers? He nursed expectations your grandfather would leave Gleneyrie to him. And if the letter patent was changed, or if you died, he would have the title as well."

Daniel sighed, though Emily did not know if it was in sadness for a man so much a victim of ambition and fate, or for her desire to hear more of what they had relentlessly discussed—what half the countryside had relentlessly discussed—for these several weeks since the tragic events of the night of the ball.

"So one would have thought. But Peter ever seemed to live in a sort of fantasy about his position and expectations. Though I scarcely knew her, I believe his mother was much to blame."

"Your mother's younger sister."

"Of course. After my mother disappointed her father by marrying Francis Lennox, who had nothing more to recommend himself than a successful business, an alliance with the duke, an elegant home, and smart looks, her sister must have thought it expedient to aim higher. She did not succeed with Campbell Havers, the younger son of an earl. The man certainly had greater pretensions than a mill owner, but after several years of drunkenness and abuse, the good man abandoned her and her son to the care of her father." For the first time, Emily heard bitterness in Daniel's voice. "They appear to have invested much energy in plotting to put Peter above me."

"They were deluded, Daniel. The duke must have felt something for you or else believed blood thicker than water."

"And tried to prove the adage by spilling as much of mine as possible? No, my love; I do not think he felt anything for me at all. In any case, the damage was done well before I was born." Daniel bent and examined a pebble before tossing it into the river. "Their hope, however, may have been entirely misguided from the first. My grandfather married three wives after my grandmother, and might have had a son by any. If Jane had not miscarried her baby, and if it had been a son, that tiniest infant would have had it all."

Emily watched the pebble sink into the water. "No, not all," she said quietly. "It would have gone so much easier for Peter if his mother had but thought to move against you while you still lay in your cradle. She might have thrown you into the river and been done with it. Indeed, the title might have become extinct."

Daniel glanced at her and raised his brows. "How quickly nobility has corrupted your virtue, my love. No, I am only teasing; you do not need to toss me in the river just yet."

"If I did, it would be because my virtue was corrupted by someone less than noble. Or someone more. I am still very confused about this, Daniel, and not sure I yet believe it."

"I am first understanding it myself. If anything, my family's story becomes more and more wretched. So much good might have been accomplished, but instead the inhabitants of Gleneyrie spent a great deal of energy scheming to remove me from contention."

Emily crossed her arms. "That is not so difficult to understand. They wished to kill you."

"Or drive me to ruin by destroying the mill. My grandfather's hand must have had a part in the smuggling of silk to Glenfell, but using my own storehouse to conceal the contraband was Alsop Parker's and Peter's idea. They tried to recruit David Milrose to do their dirty work, thinking he would hold a grudge against me because I did not court his sister."

"Daniel, I cannot imagine why I imagined life in the country to hold none of the intrigues of the city! It appears much more intricate, and infinitely more deadly."

"I hope to change your perceptions, my love. We shall surely live long and happily here, and be bothered by nothing more then leaky drains."

"I shall have to think of something to liven things a bit."

"I am sure you will," he said, and flashed her a look she was getting to know quite well.

Emily laughed softly, but held up her hand. "Why was the storehouse burned? How could the deaths of so many people further anyone's ends?"

"I do not think it was intended to go as badly as it did. At least, that is David's opinion. He was in Peter's confidences, although he would not deliver the silk, and believes the fire was intended to do no more than call attention to what was contained in the storehouse. And thereby discredit me. But Parker got careless, and burned the whole place, killing everyone in it."

"As dreadful as it sounds, I do not mourn his passing. He was a murderer, as was your cousin."

"A fine band we are, we provincials."

"I would not put you in the same class."

"Though you believed me off to murder my grandfather."

"I do not know what I thought. I hardly thought rationally."

Daniel pulled her close and rested his chin on the top of her head. Everything else seemed to fit equally well, making Emily imagine them two parts of a very satisfying whole.

"I suspect neither was Peter. We will never know what happened that night, but I can only imagine that when he realized yet another plot to destroy me had failed, his irrational rage caused him to lash out against his cohort. Alsop had botched his murderous attempt against me on the road, though he came pretty close, and had not proved himself very successful as an arsonist."

"Thrice he missed his objective, but did great damage."

"So he did. But I would not have wished for him to die

so brutally nor at the hand of the one for whom he had risked so much."

"The same must be said for your cousin. Such cruel revenge could not have been expected." Emily shivered in Daniel's embrace.

"And yet, the duke saved him the pain of a trial and inevitable imprisonment. He served his own justice."

"Your grandfather must have been very desperate to act as he did," Emily said sadly.

"I prefer to believe pain and illness moved his hand more than frustration. I am sorry he chose to take his own life. But I am even sorrier he chose to forever keep me out of it."

"I dreamt of the two of you together, Daniel. On the very night of his death. It made me believe you were someone a good deal closer than a mere relation to him, closer than you dared tell me, and I awoke ready to take you to task on it."

"That is reassuring news. I thought you awoke in a sea of flames."

"All the more reason to take you to task, my love," Emily said severely. She reflected upon how, if events had unfolded only slightly askew, she might have been dead herself. "I did not ask to be a part of your family history."

"And yet, within weeks of your arrival in Glenfell, I would have done anything to ensure you would be. Unfortunately, I must not have appeared as reserved as I hoped, for my enemies clearly gleaned your importance in my life. I am sure you were invited to Gleneyrie so my grandfather could assess the situation."

"You do not think he merely wished to appraise my ability to teach?"

"He would no sooner want laborers to read than he would . . . well, it could not matter. What matters is that he and his lady were not able to convince you to leave. And, so failing, that my cousin and Parker did not succeed in murdering both of us."

"It would have made for an excellent tragedy. We might have become the subject of local legend."

"I believe we already are."

Emily pulled herself out of his arms and confronted him. His bright eyes twinkled in the afternoon sun and his day's exercise had left him tanned and his hair slightly wind-blown.

"Why, what might people say?"

He reached for her, but she ducked out of arm's length.

"You might as well return to me, my lady duchess, for our audience surely expects it. No, you need not look around; take my word on the fact we have at least a dozen pairs of eyes watching us. We might as well give them a good show. Come here."

Emily went.

"Is this the gossip then? Do they think me improper for allowing a man not yet my husband to hold me thus?"

"I doubt it. Judging by what I hear, the people of Glenfell would run me out of town if they suspected I compromised you in any way. You seem to have a very loyal following."

"I shall endeavor to deserve it. And, as for being compromised by you, sir, rest assured I shall not discuss your improprieties with anyone. Though it might do much to raise your lordly status in the neighborhood."

"My reputation might bear no more elevation."

Emily glanced up at him, amused.

"Is this, then, the source of your legendary status? Have you already become a hero to your people?"

Daniel looked surprised.

"I have led no revolution nor fought any great battle," he said quietly. "But local gossips seem very much taken by the fact that their mill owner, a rather regular fellow by any reckoning, has inherited a dukedom. And, even more intriguing, that the beautiful schoolmistress from London shall remain here as his duchess. Do you not think this the subject of legendary romance?"

Emily thought it a very fine subject indeed.

"But I remain uncertain on one point, sir. Will the duke continue to oversee operations at the mill? And will the beautiful London lady be allowed to participate in the teaching at the school?"

"I believe it necessary for the mandatory happy ending, Miss Clarkson. To ignore the practical side of life in Glenfell would be contrary to their character, not at all the sort of thing to make them happy. Of course, their trusted assistants could manage just fine if anything distracted them. Their own children, perhaps, or a mother just returned from the American wilderness."

"I . . . see. Yes, it all makes perfect sense, Your Grace. I suspect we now lack only one thing for a happy ending."

Emily stood in Daniel Lennox's warm embrace for several minutes until her words hit their mark. Suddenly she felt his arms tighten as he laughed out loud.

Waiting, expectant, she nevertheless was perfectly surprised when he scooped her up in his arms and, for the benefit of their hidden audience, turned full circle. He stopped when they overlooked the Fell and bent his head to kiss her long and lingeringly on the lips.

"There," he said, while she gasped for breath. "Will that do?"

"Oh, yes," Emily answered, and raised her mouth to his again.